"EIGHT  WOUNDED."

Caine's upper lip tightened. "How many witnesses?"

"Ooooh," Tripp said with a head tilt, "how about all of South Beach . . . including Ken LaRussa."

"A U.S. attorney at a drive-by?" Caine asked. "Are we talking target?"

"He wasn't here—he was having dinner down the street. Came runnin' when he heard the shooting and screaming."

"Where is he now?"

"Inside. But your instincts are right, Horatio."

"How so?"

Tripp gestured toward the restaurant. "It probably was a hit. Kurt Wallace and three of his bodyguards are among the dead. Another guy at Wallace's table bought it, too, only him I don't recognize."

"Public place, lots of civilians . . . not exactly mob style."

Tripp shrugged his shoulders and threw raindrops. "Which mob? There's a lot more than one these days . . . and they've all got their own sense of 'style.'"

"Too true," Caine said hollowly. "Is it finally here, Frank?"

"Is what here, Horatio?"

"That all-out gang war we've been dreading?"

Tripp sighed. "If not, it's a damn good imitation."

Original novels in the CSI series:

by Max Allan Collins
CSI: Crime Scene Investigation
Double Dealer
Sin City
Cold Burn
Body of Evidence
Grave Matters
Binding Ties
Serial (graphic novel)

CSI: Miami
Florida Getaway
Heat Wave

by Stuart M. Kaminsky
CSI: New York
Dead of Winter

CSI: Miami™

HEAT WAVE

a novel

Max Allan Collins

Based on the hit CBS series "CSI Miami" produced by
ALLIANCE ATLANTIS and CBS PRODUCTIONS in
association with Jerry Bruckheimer Television.
Executive Producers: Jerry Bruckheimer,
Carol Mendelsohn, Ann Donahue, Anthony E. Zuiker,
Jonathan Littman, Danny Cannon
Series created by Anthony E. Zuiker, Ann Donahue, and
Carol Mendelsohn

POCKET **STAR** BOOKS
New York   London   Toronto   Sydney

This book is a work of fiction. Names, characters, places and incidents are products of the author's imagination or are used fictitiously. Any resemblance to actual events or locales or persons, living or dead, is entirely coincidental.

An Original Publication of POCKET BOOKS

A Pocket Star Book published by
POCKET BOOKS, a division of Simon & Schuster, Inc.
1230 Avenue of the Americas, New York, NY 10020

CSI: MIAMI and related marks are trademarks of CBS Broadcasting Inc.
Copyright © 2004 by CBS Broadcasting Inc. and Alliance Atlantis Productions, Inc.
All rights reserved.

All rights reserved, including the right to reproduce this book or portions thereof in any form whatsoever. For information address Pocket Books, 1230 Avenue of the Americas, New York, NY 10020

ISBN 13: 978-0-7434-8056-7
ISBN 10: 0-7434-8056-2

First Pocket Books printing June 2004

10 9 8 7 6 5 4 3

POCKET STAR BOOKS and colophon are registered trademarks of Simon & Schuster, Inc.

Cover design by Patrick Kang
Front cover photos © Getty Images

Manufactured in the United States of America

For information regarding special discounts for bulk purchases, please contact Simon & Schuster Special Sales at 1-800-456-6798 or business@simonandschuster.com

I would like to acknowledge my assistant on this work, forensics researcher/co-plotter, Matthew V. Clemens.
Further acknowledgments appear at the conclusion of this novel.

M.A.C.

For our pals,
Ed and Steph Keenan . . .
. . . gang of two

*"There are more things in heaven and earth, Horatio,
Than are dreamt of in your philosophy."*

—*Hamlet*, Act One; WILLIAM SHAKESPEARE

*"We all realized we were sitting on a keg of dynamite
with no means of determining the length of the fuse."*

—ELIOT NESS

"Be quick, but don't hurry."

—JOHN WOODEN, former UCLA basketball coach

1

Storm Warning

COBALT WAVES LASHED the beach, whipcracking as they broke, the gray sky deceptively placid, accepting of the storm gathering just beyond the horizon. This was a cool time of year for the greater Miami area, but something nasty was coming. Something hot, and not weather.

Here and there empty hotels seemed like great tombstones, as if the city were slowly turning into a cemetery, however much the remainder of the skyline greeted the Atlantic with glittering optimism. Tonight, the ocean seemed unconvinced, moving in like a dark-hooded figure with a scythe, the threat of the impending storm growing more absolute by the minute and Miami Beach's neon welcome ever more strained as the sky went from gray to charcoal to now very nearly black.

Along Ocean Drive, with only the thin emerald strip of Lummus Park between concrete and roiling water, cars passed in their usual slow parade while the

well-lighted line of Art Deco hotels studded the darkening sky with their vibrant pink-blue-yellow geome-
try. Occasional storefronts in the row of businesses
were dark now, gaps in the street's commercial smile,
the stiff competition of South Beach killing off the
weak. Still, despite the strobe flashes of lightning at
sea, a party atmosphere managed to thrive.

This was Miami Beach, after all, and there was a
reputation to uphold—not necessarily a good reputation, but a compelling one for the young of all ages.

Hundreds of pedestrians, mostly tourists, strolled up
and down the west side sidewalk, gawking at menu
boards, confronted by hard-bodied, navel-baring, pretty
hostesses who hawked their restaurants and hotels
(each "the best" along this pastel strip).

At every stop, the pedestrians were inundated with
pulsing music that poured as easily from assorted
sound systems as the liquor in every South Beach bar.
Cool jazz rolled from the Tides, reggae from the
Breakwater, classic soul from the Leslie, and so on
down the row, the only pauses coming as the rubber-
neckers passed the vacant husks of dead rival clubs.

At the Archer Hotel—a three-story, white stucco
building with mint-green-and-pink trim—both the
lobby bar and front dining terrace were jammed with
patrons apparently not put off by what the sky might
bring. Sixties rock blared from state-of-the-art speak-
ers, and a queue of potential diners stood near the
hostess stand on the front walk, seemingly oblivious
to the storm knifing toward the coast.

The distant rumble of thunder was lost in the promi-
nent bass line of the Spencer Davis Group ripping

through "Gimme Some Lovin'." Here and there, diners tapped their feet to the familiar, infectious beat, while a few others tapped silverware on the table, keeping time with the pounding drums. At a square table, at the south end of the open front porch, however, the four men seated there seemed to not notice the music at all.

With his back to the window that looked in on the lobby bar, Kurt Wallace gave not a thought to the possibility of getting shot.

The burly, well-dressed men seated to his left and right as he faced Ocean Drive were security staff who'd been with him for years. On his right, the pug-faced Cummings watched the street. On Wallace's left, Stevens eyed the restaurant, the watchdog's head seeming to swivel from side to side without the benefit of a neck.

A third bodyguard, Anthony, was out of sight inside the bar, but he, too, was a longtime employee, and Wallace trusted the wide-bodied ex-pro footballer (a lineman, of course) to cover his back. The small security contingent's custom-fitted suits—Anthony's was black, Cummings was in brown, and Stevens's a gray pinstripe—helped them fit in to the Miami Beach nightlife, even while that expensive tailoring hid the fact that they were heavily armed.

One of the best haberdasheries in the city took care of Wallace's boys; as for their employer, tonight he had chosen an Armani suit, tailored especially for him.

Tall, with curly black hair showing flecks of gray, Wallace was handsome and knew it. What might have been conventional, male-model good looks—his long straight nose sat absolutely perpendicular to the thin line of his mouth, for example—had an edge, thanks to dark brown eyes that seemed always to suggest anger or cruelty or both, depending on the light, the angle, and, of course, his mood. Thick dark slashes of eyebrow provided punctuation whenever his expression changed.

With the assassination of Peter Venici earlier this year, Wallace had solidified himself as the new padrone of organized crime in Miami. For perhaps a decade, Wallace had dreamed and schemed of this rise to the top. But right now, the all-American businessman who had finally displaced the old Sicilian Mafia leadership was wondering if killing Venici had really been worth it.

Though he now controlled the docks, the unions, prostitution, and most illegal gambling, Kurt Wallace found himself constantly battling the youthful gangs that had matured into mini-cartels in recent years, stealing away much of his drug business. The most bothersome were Las Culebras, the group of second- and third-generation Cuban–Americans once headed by Juan "El Patan" Padillo.

That Padillo, known in certain circles as Johnny the Slouch, had been "disappeared" by Venici was no great secret, and Wallace had figured the Culebras might be a new ally when he dispatched the crime boss.

It hadn't turned out that way.

Las Culebras' new leader, Antonio Mendoza, seemed to hate Wallace even more than he had Venici. That Wallace had betrayed Venici—however despised the old-school mob boss might have been—labelled Wallace a traitor to Mendoza. Didn't these young punks understand how business worked? That the occasional unfriendly takeover was to be expected?

Las Culebras weren't the only ones horning in on Wallace's drug trade, either; the list was depressingly long—the Mitus from Colombia; the Faucones, whose headquarters were in Little Haiti; the Trenches, named after the famous Kingston slum; and even those self-styled neo-Nazi meth freaks from upstate . . . all of them intent on helping themselves to slices of the Venici pizza.

If he'd known it was going to be this much trouble, Wallace wondered if he still would have made his move on Venici.

Who was he trying to kid? He already knew the answer: *of course he would*.

Kurt Wallace may have looked like a fashion-plate slickster, but at heart he was a fighter, and he wasn't about to let anyone come in and divide his territory among themselves.

Which was why he was having dinner at the Archer Hotel with Sonny Spencer tonight. The current situation was, in fact, the only imaginable reason he could conjure up that would have him even *consider* sitting down with the slimy likes of Spencer.

Spencer was a representative of what was referred to nowadays as the Dixie Mafia. In his white suit jacket over a pastel T-shirt and jeans, Spencer apparently thought *Miami Vice* was the latest thing.

What . . . a . . . rube. . . .

The blond neo-Nazi sat across the table from Wallace, his blue eyes fixed in a squint that Wallace assumed was meant to make him look tough, when the effect was of myopia. Granted, he was a lieu-tenant—and nephew—of Billy Joe Spencer, head of the outfit Wallace hoped to strike a deal with . . . but Spencer was not exactly one of the best and brightest of his outfit.

Consider that Spencer had consented to coming alone and was right now also sitting with his back to the busy street. On the other hand, Spencer's apparent lack of precaution reflected something of which he and Wallace were both well aware: The younger Spencer had nothing to fear from Kurt Wallace.

Truth was, right now Wallace needed any allies he could muster in a war that seemed to be bearing down on him just as inexorably as the approaching storm was heading for the coast.

So it was that these two competitors between whom no love was lost sat preparing for a dinner that both hoped would end in a peace accord that would allow each side not only to survive but also to prosper in this world of ever-present danger.

Picking up his menu, Spencer said, "Seriously, Kurt—we're gonna need each other when all these lowlifes come outta the woodwork after what's rightfully ours."

Kurt Wallace nodded agreement even as he pondered just how much he hated the ignorant asshole across from him.

He seriously wondered if the price of survival might not be too steep if it meant lying down with the flea-ridden dogs that Sonny Spencer represented. Still, it was only business—the first rule being, it doesn't matter who you sell your goods to; and the second being, it doesn't matter who you do business with. Let this so-called superman obsess on race all he wanted; the only color Kurt Wallace cared about was green. . . .

And Wallace had to do something before Las Culebras and the others figured out how tenuous his new position truly was.

"And I think we oughta start with these candy-ass Culebras," Spencer said.

"No, Sonny," Wallace said. "I can't agree."

Spencer frowned, as if forming a thought were painful.

"Let's start," Wallace said with his most charming smile, "with dinner."

Sonny beamed. "Frickin' A," he said, and focused his tortured attention back on the menu.

Actually, this idiot was right. Though every one of these former street-punk crime factions seemed to be lining up to take their shot at Wallace's holdings, Las Culebras were at the forefront of his thoughts.

By taking over Venici's business interests, Wallace had somehow inherited Las Culebras' animosity toward Venici.

It had been Venici who'd used that team of retired hitters from New Jersey, making "El Patan" disappear from the planet—not Wallace! The Jersey hit team was gone now, one dead, the other two in jail. With Venici dead, the matter should have been closed.

Beyond Las Culebras and the competition from gangs, both Miami-Dade P.D. and the Feds were turning up the heat on Wallace's operations across the board. Not just the drugs—hell, he expected that—but gambling, prostitution, and everything from loan-sharking to construction, all coming under ever closer scrutiny.

Two cops in particular had been making Wallace's life miserable of late. Horatio Caine, that hot-shot

Crime Scene Unit supervisor with Miami-Dade, had taken down the Jersey retiree hit team, which had opened a real investigative can of worms on local organized crime.

Even worse, DEA agent Jeremy Burnett was constantly intervening in Wallace's drug business. Aiding and abetting that Goody Two-shoes was Kenneth LaRussa, a U.S. attorney who prosecuted everyone in the city caught with anything more potent than a bottle of aspirin.

Turning to Cummings and Stevens, Wallace said, "You fellas might as well order, too."

Often the security boys ate later, but Wallace felt safe enough, here in the middle of a South Beach tourist trap. Wordlessly, the two bodyguards lifted their menus.

Picking up his own, Wallace wondered if he could talk Spencer into hitting any or all three of the law enforcement agents in question. A dangerous course of action, but if the credit and blame went to this group of malcontents from upstate, the reactive heat would be focused there.

Ideally, Wallace would have the law enforcement agents gone, and eventually the Spencers, too. With a faint smile, he read the menu, thinking that everything might work out after all.

Wallace decided on the fillet of sole and looked up, his eyes meeting Spencer's.

The blond man was saying, "Hope you don't mind if I order the porterhouse. I ain't much for fish."

"Order whatever . . ." Wallace frowned.

"You okay, Mr. Wallace?"

"Yes. Order anything you like, Sonny. My treat."

Spencer was grinning greedily now, reexamining the menu in search of other high-priced fare, but Wallace's eyes were on the street.

He had just realized that something was wrong. The music still blared in the background ("Goin' back to Miami!"), and because of that he hadn't noticed, at first, the silence gathering on the street. But, looking past Spencer, he could see that no cars were passing by in front of the hotel. Cars on Ocean Drive were as constant as the tide itself, and seeing no traffic, an absence extending all the way to the corner, sent warning bells ringing inside Wallace's head.

Cummings, sensing his boss's alarm, looked up from his menu, his eyes following the path of Wallace's concerned gaze, and saw the same disturbing thing. They both heard the squeal of tires at the same instant . . . *and then time slowed for Wallace* as he took in a silver car fishtailing around the corner to nudge a parked car, then come speeding south toward the Archer.

Some detached part of his mind drew fascination from this mini-spectacle, clearly seeing the head and shoulders of a Hispanic man protruding from the passenger side window.

He had large brown eyes, dark skin, curly black hair *(Not unlike my own*, Wallace thought, *when I was younger)*, and a mustache so thick and black that Wallace wondered if it might be fake.

The passenger's mouth was open wide, his teeth bared, very white against his skin and the background of the black sky. The man seemed to be yelling something, but Wallace could not understand the words.

To Wallace's right, Cummings shouted something;

but Kurt couldn't pick out those words either—they too seemed drawn out, in this slow-motion dreamscape—and his eyes remained riveted on the man in the car. Now he saw the brutish AK-47 in the brown hands, its barrel swinging in the direction of the Archer Hotel Cafe, the round drum of the magazine hanging down like a hornet's nest beneath the weapon, ready to sting when disturbed.

Though the assassin was being tossed about by the swerving car, the man's moves seemed steady, almost elegant to Wallace, weirdly balletic, the colors so very bright as yellow and orange flames flowed from the barrel.

The crime boss heard people screaming and his two bodyguards were on their feet now, Stevens reaching under his suitcoat for his gun while Cummings moved toward Wallace with an obvious intent to shield his boss. Sonny Spencer's eyes went wide with wonder, and he, too, rose, his mouth moving, but again Wallace couldn't make out any words. Everyone seemed to be talking at once around him, and yet Wallace perceived himself in a vacuum of silence.

Then Spencer's lips stopped moving and crimson streamers of blood ribboned out of his mouth, slashing the air as he spun around, scarlet flowers blossoming from his white sports coat as he toppled.

Cummings's massive arm passed in front of Wallace, then slipped away as the bodyguard trembled and grunted and crashed through the interior window behind him, something Wallace more sensed than saw, unable to tear himself away from the hitman in the car. The vehicle was nearly past them now, and Wallace's eyes locked with those of the killer.

Still caught up in fleeting seconds that felt like lingering minutes, Wallace heard Stevens's gun clatter to the tile floor as the bodyguard went down. The assassin smiled at Wallace, and flame leapt from the weapon's barrel, and Wallace felt like he'd been prodded in the chest, once, twice, and then a third time, as if an obnoxious know-it-all had been thumping his chest with a thick forefinger, making a point.

Suddenly he was on his back looking up at the black sky. He had no idea how he'd ended up like this, but when he went to get up, no matter how he tried, he couldn't. An invisible hand kept him pressed to the concrete of the porch.

Relieved he'd not been seriously hurt, Wallace felt no pain, though he couldn't really see anything but the inky clouds and . . . how strange! . . . the shooter's grin dangling in space above him like a crescent moon. Like *Alice in Wonderland*, when that cat disappeared and left his grin behind. . . .

The acrid smell of cordite hung heavy in the moist air and—though he tried to listen for sounds—all Wallace heard was the echo of a thousand gunshots. Turning his head, he saw Anthony on his stomach next to him, a neat red hole in the bodyguard's forehead. Anthony had died rushing out of the bar to save him.

How sad.

Goddamn Culebras. Someone would pay for this.

Antonio Mendoza, Padillo's Culebras successor, was not only smarter than his predecessor but also far more ruthless. This attempted hit had Mendoza's name signed to it. Where Padillo would have just tried to muscle in and take a piece, Mendoza was the type who'd figure that if he whacked Wallace, he could have the whole damn pie his own self.

Mendoza, Wallace knew, fancied himself the incarnation of Tony Montana, the gangster played by Al Pacino in that movie, *Scarface*. Many of the local gang members looked up to that character as a hero. Wallace, on the other hand, felt contempt for anyone who couldn't see that Montana was arrogant and stupid and, in the end, had wound up dead, riddled with bullets in a pool of blood.

That was not the ending Wallace saw for himself. He would pick himself up from this close scrape and teach Mendoza that Miami could not so easily be taken away from Kurt Wallace.

He gazed up at the sky again, unaware that his perception was still turning seconds into minutes, and the first drop of rain fell and kissed his forehead.

The sensation was a kind of wake-up call, and Wallace tried to sit up again. Funny—he still couldn't seem to move. A woman's face crossed into his field of vision. Her lips moved, but Wallace couldn't figure out what she was saying.

She was beautiful, though, an angel whose long hair was a rich black that matched the sky as dark arcs swung around, the wind coming up. Her brown eyes were wide with, what was that . . . alarm? Fear?

Wallace opened his mouth to tell this bystander—understandably spooked by the drive-by shooting—that everything was all right. Instead he coughed and rather than words coming out, scarlet spittle did.

The woman's eyes went even wider, and the crime boss felt himself choking. For the first time, he realized he'd been hit. The rain came down harder now, pelting his face, and he felt cold all over. The storm had come quickly. He thought about his wife, Christina, sitting at home waiting for him. She was going to be pissed about this.

Finally he managed to speak, looking up at the hovering beauty: "My . . . wife'll . . . *kill* me."

Her face no longer soothed Wallace, and he closed his eyes.

He was lucky to have found a wife as good as Christina, who put up with his cheating ways and the kind of business he was in. He hoped Christina understood—as finally, all at once, he understood that the blackness before him was not the sky—that he hadn't meant for it to end like this.

With one last cool exhale, Kurt Wallace was gone.

Six feet and slim, Lieutenant Horatio Caine—in black slacks and a navy blue CSI windbreaker—leaned into the weather as he moved to the back of the Hummer to collect his crime scene kit. With a stiff wind whipping his red hair, he wondered glumly how much damage Mother Nature had done to his crime scene already.

Right now the gale snarled in off the ocean, nothing to abate it, ripping across Ocean Drive, rain slanting in, stinging like needles. Preserving a crime scene was impossible under such conditions, but at least he'd have his whole team with him for damage control.

The lab's resident firearms expert, Calleigh Duquesne, met him at the back of the vehicle. The petite platinum-blonde had a cool beauty balanced by a warm nature; her Miami-Dade PD ballcap was snug on her head, her hair tied back in a long ponytail pulled through the hole in the back. When Caine opened the rear Hummer door, Calleigh withdrew her crime scene kit and headed straight for the street and any possible shell casings she might find before they were carried away by the rushing water. What Caine prized most about CSI Duquesne—kiddingly dubbed "Bullet Girl" by her peers—was her passion for collecting and interpreting evidence in her area of expertise.

Caine hoped she was carrying bricks in the pockets of her CSI windbreaker, else she might just get swept away by either the wind or the torrent racing toward the sewer.

A second Hummer rolled to a stop, and, almost before the vehicle's engine died, Tim Speedle and Eric Delko—also in CSI windbreakers—were standing next to Caine, peering at their supervisor through the driving downpour.

"What have we got, H?" Speedle asked, working his voice up over the storm.

Speedle was the one member of the team that the whipping wind seemed unable to faze. His short, dark hair hugged his head, he appeared not to have shaved yet this week, and his eyes had a look that belied both his alertness and a keen intelligence.

"Drive-by shooting," Caine said, with a sideways glance toward the crime scene—the Archer hotel. "And the weather's going to get worse before it gets better. Let's collect everything we can before the rain wipes this slate clean."

"Fatalities?" Delko asked.

Delko—the newest member of their squad, taller than Speed—had an alert wide-eyed look on his latte-colored face that one could misread for naivete.

"At least six," Caine said. "And maybe more, according to the nine-one-one call. Let's get wet, guys."

The other two CSIs turned toward the back of their Hummer. Delko's specialty was underwater recovery work, and Caine wondered wryly if the weather would grow so bad that Eric would end up in his scuba suit before this was over. The rain clawed at Caine as he lugged his crime scene kit toward the sidewalk.

Detective Frank Tripp, blinking his brown eyes against the wind and moisture, stepped forward to meet Caine. "Horatio."

Caine nodded. "Frank. How bad?"

"Eight dead, eleven wounded."

His upper lip tightened. "How many witnesses?"

"Ooooh," Tripp said, with a head tilt, "how about all of South Beach? . . . including Ken LaRussa."

"A U.S. attorney at a drive-by?" Caine asked. "Are we talking target?"

"He wasn't here—he was having dinner down the street. Came runnin' when he heard the shooting and screaming."

"Where is he now?"

"Inside. But your instincts are right, Horatio."

"How so?"

Tripp gestured toward the restaurant. "It probably *was* a hit. Kurt Wallace and three of his bodyguards are among the dead. Another guy at Wallace's table bought it, too, only him I don't recognize."

"Public place, lots of civilians . . . not exactly mob style."

Tripp shrugged and his shoulders threw raindrops. "Which mob? There's a lot more than one these days . . . and they all got their own sense of 'style.' "

"Too true," Caine said hollowly. "Is it finally here, Frank?"

"Is what here, Horatio?"

"That all-out gang war we've been dreading?"

Tripp sighed. "If not, it's a damn good imitation."

"You've been interviewing witnesses?"

Tripp nodded. "And I got more to do."

"Anything so far?"

The detective let out a bitter laugh. "Twenty wits—guess how many stories?"

"Twenty," Caine said with a shrug. "In the end, the evidence will tell its own tale."

"One thing they all agree on, though."

"Which is?"

"The vehicle that carried the killer clipped a parked car back on the corner of Twelfth. Haven't found the owner yet."

"That's what we call a happy accident—we'll check it out." Caine touched the detective's wet sleeve, briefly. "I better get started before the evidence is all washed away."

As he knew they would be, his team was already hard at it. They scurried around at their various duties, but none of them hurrying. Work fast, Caine had taught them, invoking an old coaching rule, *but don't rush*. This was no empty mantra: When you rushed, you missed things. But the weather was upon them and time was running short, Mother Nature playing accomplice to a killer.

Since the shooting had been a drive-by, Calleigh started at the corner and combed the street for shell casings. Speedle photographed the deceased victims while EMTs aided the wounded. Delko pried slugs from the hotel facade and furniture, and Caine took photos and paint scrapings from the parked car that had been hit by the perp's vehicle.

In the end, however, the storm won.

Less than an hour later, Caine found himself standing in the bullet-pocked lobby bar of the Archer, broken glass crunching under his shoes, his team around him, shaking off water.

The dead had been taken away, the wounded transferred to South Shore Hospital. All that remained now were Caine's team, Detective Tripp, and one of the witnesses . . . albeit a significant one: U.S. attorney Kenneth LaRussa.

Olive-skinned, in his late thirties or perhaps early forties, the attorney wore longish black hair over his ears and swept straight back, à la Miami Heat basketball coach Pat Riley. LaRussa wore a white button-down shirt, dark slacks, and black tassel loafers. In the middle of the white shirt was a huge red splotch: not a bullet wound but a marinara sauce stain.

The ambitious attorney had burst on the scene a few years ago with a DA's office post, then had risen to his current position through hard work and an exemplary conviction rate. Rumor had it his goal was becoming the next Democratic senator from this largely Republican state.

Caine had no real problem with LaRussa, or the attorney's ambitions; no question, LaRussa had accomplished some positive things.

What Caine did have a problem with was LaRussa tossing loser cases back to the state and plucking the prime cases on some technicality that would allow him to charge a perp in federal court. Sure, that might mean that some bad guys did longer stretches when they got federal time, which was not a bad thing; but a couple of truly evil men had walked in federal court when their cases would have been a slam dunk at the state level.

Those cases, of course, LaRussa never talked about in his frequent media interviews.

Caine motioned the attorney off to one side, in a corner of the bar untouched by the drive-by shooter. They stood near a table over which a pastel impressionistic watercolor of an ocean sunset made an ironic counterpoint to the shattered room around them.

"Lieutenant Caine," LaRussa said, extending his hand. His other one gestured toward the red stain on his shirt. "Pardon the mess—afraid I spilled my lasagna when we dove for cover."

Like any good politician, LaRussa had a ready, easy smile that put people at ease, as well as a firm handshake that was supposed to imply he was strong but not overbearing, steadfast but not stodgy, and just a plain good guy to know.

Caine thought the man might be better off practicing law and not his handshake.

"Mr. LaRussa," Caine said, waving off the attorney's apology. "I'm a little more concerned with this other . . . mess."

"Call me Ken." This he said with a smile, then studiously applied a somber expression to his face. "It's good to know that you and your celebrated staff will be working this case."

"Your confidence is appreciated," Caine said with no conviction and motioned to the table, where the two men sat. Just a small civilized conversation in a room shot to hell.

Forcing himself to use the lawyer's name, the CSI asked, "Did you see what happened, Ken?"

The attorney shook his head as a frown etched itself in place. "No, Horatio . . . it is Horatio, right?"

"Yes."

"I'm afraid I didn't. I was with my wife and some friends, having dinner at the Surfsider."

Caine knew the hotel, another Art Deco structure with front porch dining a block south.

"When I heard the shots," the attorney continued, "I dove over the table to Nance, to get her under cover." He offered a rueful chuckle; everything this guy did or said seemed forced. "That's when I got the lasagna stain."

"And Nancy . . . your wife?"

"Yes."

"Nancy wasn't hurt?"

"No. None of us were, thank God. The shooting was only at the Archer . . . but everybody dove for cover anyway. We had no idea when or where the shooting would stop."

Caine's eyes narrowed; he made himself smile, a little. "I'm surprised you could hear the shots."

"Why is that, Horatio?"

"Well, Ken—over at the Surfsider, the music's pretty loud, isn't it? You were almost two blocks away?"

LaRussa's face lost all expression; oddly, he finally seemed sincere. "Horatio . . . Lieutenant . . . I was just a nineteen-year-old grunt when we invaded Grenada. But I heard the sound of an AK-47 tonight, and let me assure you, Lieutenant, it's not a sound that you ever forget—even from a distance."

Nodding in thought, Caine said, "So, you know what weapon was used—that's helpful."

"Glad to be, but that's about all I have for you." He shrugged elaborately. "Like everyone else around us, Nancy and I and our friends were behind an upturned table . . . hoping the shooting would stop."

"You didn't see anything?"

LaRussa shook his head. "Just a bunch of scared people. Myself included."

Appreciating this surprisingly human comment, Caine gave the lawyer a short nod. "And what did you do after the shooting stopped?"

LaRussa pondered that a moment. "First, I made sure that everyone was all right. That is, my wife and friends."

"Of course. And then?"

"You understand, we were having dinner with Brad and Darcy Willis."

The attorney spoke these names with reverence, but they meant nothing to Caine.

LaRussa was saying, "I told Brad to get Nance and Darcy back to their car and get them the hell home."

"Why didn't you go with them?"

"I thought maybe I could help here."

And get some TV air time, Caine thought.

This must have registered on Caine's face, because LaRussa blustered, defensively, "Wouldn't you have done the same thing, Lieutenant? As a law enforcement professional?"

"Yes," Caine admitted.

As if on cue, the first two TV reporters and their cameramen started straining at the yellow crime scene outside.

His eyes cutting to the media, LaRussa took a deep breath and slowly let it out.

Suppressing a smile, Caine thought, *You wouldn't want to appear overanxious now . . . would you, Ken?*

"Are we through here, Horatio?"

Caine considered that momentarily. "You don't have any trips scheduled? Work or vacation?"

"Nothing. As a witness, I'll make myself available should you need me, whenever that might be."

"Appreciate it."

"Thank you, Horatio."

LaRussa rose and again stretched out his hand.

Groaning inwardly, Caine got to his feet and suffered through another LaRussa handshake. Then the attorney was disappearing through the shattered lobby doors, and Caine was not sorry to see him go.

The CSI supervisor sensed someone next to him. He turned to see an eager Delko.

"Hello, Eric—something?"

Delko grinned. Nodded. "Something."

2

Dirty Job

ERIC DELKO KNEW the idea was a good one, and yet somehow he felt a little surprised that Caine liked it.

It wasn't that his boss tended to shut him down or anything. Caine always seemed open to suggestions from his team. On the other hand, the strength of their leader's personality and his focused intensity could have an intimidating quality that had not encouraged Delko to step forward in his early months on the job.

A frown of disapproval from Caine felt like a slap to Delko, who admired this man very much. But more and more now, Delko was putting that "newbie" sensibility behind him and stepping up to the plate with his views. Risking a disapproving glance from Caine was worth it, when you might receive those two precious words from him: "Good work."

Ten minutes after receiving Caine's approval, Delko emerged from the men's room in the bar in his black neoprene dive suit, the letters MDPD stenciled in yellow on the back. A man stepping out of a hotel restroom in diving gear might look odd enough, but Delko had gone the extra mile, accessorizing not with flippers but with heavy rubber fireman's boots.

Caine, twitching a smile, strolled over and laid a hand on Delko's shoulder. Quietly he asked, "And where did you get those boots?"

"Uh, well . . . they sorta fell off a truck at a call about six months ago."

"And you just haven't got around to turning 'em back in yet."

"Right."

"Well, then," Caine said, holding up his hands, "don't tell me any more—I have no desire to be an accessory after the fact. Ready to get down and dirty?"

"Oh yeah."

Caine nodded toward the street. "There's more rain coming in, Eric . . . and you know how fast that water runs down there. It would look bad on my record, having a CSI drown in a sewer. Don't embarrass me, now."

"Would never do that, H."

Caine patted Delko twice on the shoulder—a small gesture that put a big smile on the young CSI's face, even considering the distasteful task he was about to undertake.

Delko made his way out to the Hummer, where Speedle waited for him with gloves, a flashlight, and tools.

"You're gonna run out of hands down there," Speed said, an edge in his voice. "You want some company?"

Considering how often Speed played off seniority to stick him with dirty jobs, Delko was tempted to take him up on the offer. Instead, he said, "Naw, it's a chore one guy can pull off. But I appreciate it. . . . You dig out the belt?"

Speedle handed him a nylon belt with enough pockets to impress Batman, as well as a holster for Delko's nine millimeter and a ring for his flashlight. After securing his weapon, Delko accepted the long black flash from Speed and dropped it through the designated belt loop. In a big pocket on his hip, he tucked his walkie-talkie.

Next, Speedle helped Delko run the cord up his back and clip the mike onto the collar of his diving suit. Then Delko strapped a flat, black disc to the underside of his left wrist: the Borealis Aqua Pulse, the latest in underwater metal detectors. The Borealis was equipped with red, yellow, and green lights accompanied by a low-frequency vibration, alerting divers when they were close to buried metal.

Of course, Delko had never used the device in a sewer before. . . .

Well, with any luck, the water would only be up to his boot tops. Just in case, though, he was also taking along an A.J. Greenfield 8X handheld metal detector—an apparatus about three and a half feet long with a cuff like a metal crutch for easy control, and a shaft-mounted control about the size of a cigar box, ending in a ring that was maybe a foot across.

Finally, Delko put on a black-mesh rucksack, its large strap over his right shoulder, allowing the pouch to hang against his left hip. Whatever he collected would be put into evidence bags and dropped into the rucksack.

The pair walked over to where Speedle had already

pried off a manhole cover; orange cones marked the area. Speed carried the Greenfield metal detector under one arm, a loop of rope over his shoulder, and a halogen work light in the other hand, while Delko pulled on a pair of latex gloves.

Above them the sky remained a starless black void, and Delko could feel the wind whip tauntingly across his face. Time was running out. He'd lived in Miami long enough to know that the next squall line wasn't far off . . . and you just never knew how long the rain would last, or how severe the storm would be. . . .

Easing down into the manhole, heavily booted feet finding purchase on slippery rungs, Delko looked up at his partner. "Metal detector, please, Nurse."

"Here ya go, Doc," Speedle said, passing him the device.

"You set it?"

"Don't ya trust me? It'll pick up most anything that's down there."

"Borealis set, too?"

"All-Metal mode."

Speed reached down, ran one end of the rope through the handle of the halogen light, and tied a secure knot. He then flipped the switch and lowered the light into the manhole, careful to keep the thing out of Delko's way as the diver slowly made his way down the ladder.

Slick under Delko's boots, the ladder groaned; the damn rungs felt slimy even through his work gloves. Carefully he eased down one step at a time.

"Give my regards to Norton," Speedle called down from an opening that now seemed far away to Delko.

"Who?" Delko asked, voice echoing with a metallic ring.

Speed was shaking his head, way up there. "Ever see *The Honeymooners* . . . ? What a culturally deprived life you've led, Eric . . . and keep an eye peeled for albino alligators!"

Laughter resonating within his dark world, Delko yelled up, "Speed, there are no albino alligators down here! This is Miami, not New York!"

Delko got to work, appreciating the concern from his coworker, couched in gags though it had been. The smell down here was an olfactory brew of garbage, urine, excrement, and alcohol. A CSI had to put up with a lot of odors at a crime scene, but this blend flirted with Delko's gag reflex. He swallowed hard, breathing through his mouth, as he'd learned to do in the autopsy room.

Dropping off the last rung with a splash, he landed in foul water up to his ankles. He turned on the Greenfield 8X and slipped his forearm into the cuff of the handle. The halogen light that Speedle had lowered provided some illumination, but the damned thing kept wanting to spin, wobbling back and forth, making crazy film noir shadows that danced on the sewer-pipe-infested walls.

Cursing silently, Delko pulled out the flashlight and flicked the power button. With the flash in his left and the metal detector in his right, he hoped he didn't run into any of Speedle's albino alligators or, for that matter, a hungry rat, in which case he'd have to feed it the metal detector. He touched his arm to his holster, feeling the reassuring weight of the pistol there . . . and grinned for letting Speed get inside his head like that.

Slowly, he swept the flashlight beam from side to side. The concrete sewer pipe was noisier than he would have expected, water whooshing around his feet, echoing as it dripped from the grate in the distance. Even farther away he could hear the water sloshing against something else. To this hydrokinetic symphony, Delko added the low hum of the active Greenfield 8X.

He hoped to use the metal detector to find shell casings washed down here by runoff from the storm. The problems with this theory were twofold: first, he couldn't see the bottom of the pipe, due to the running water; and second, the casings themselves were about the size of his little finger and, if any were down here, were probably still moving in the current.

Unless they'd fallen into one of the traps that he knew hid under the rushing current. The sunken metal baskets were designed to catch rocks and other detritus that found its way into the sewer, possibly plugging up filters further along. These same traps were hiding beneath the water, just waiting to break his ankle, or worse. . . .

From the radio came the crackle of Speedle's voice: "How deep is it piled down there?"

"No deeper than one of your stories about your dates. Hate to disappoint you, Speed, but there isn't an albino alligator in sight."

"Patience, buddy—let 'em get your scent, and they'll be along soon enough. You find anything yet?"

"No—just getting started."

Delko swept the detector in small, flat arcs in front of him, a current feeding the coil and sending out an electromagnetic field that would receive an answering current from the electromagnetic field of any metal under the murky water.

Moving slowly, Delko edged toward the drain at the other end of the block. He'd gone only thirty or so methodical feet when the metal detector vibrated against his hand.

Something down there . . . but what?

He made his arcs smaller and smaller, until he was sure he was over the object. Then, carefully balancing the metal detector and flashlight in his left hand, he plunged his right hand into the frigid, goopy water, and groped around the rough concrete floor of the pipe.

Through the latex glove, the bottom felt not only ice-cold but slimy.

Whose idea was this again?

He stayed at it, feeling along the bottom, touching something . . . but when he reached for whatever it was, the current carried the thing away. It was like trying to find a bar of soap in a great big bathtub. Only there wasn't a hell of a lot of soap down here. . . .

The notion that he could be down here the rest of the night, searching for God knew what, settled around him like a damp, depressing fog. He transferred the metal detector back to his right hand and started making arcs again—this time back in the direction he had come from.

It took only a couple of sweeps to relocate the object.

This time, instead of fishing around for his prize, Delko turned off the Greenfield 8X, switched on the smaller Borealis wrist detector, and transferred the flashlight to his right hand, along with the Greenfield.

Carefully he crouched, the Borealis vibrating against his wrist, telling him he was still directly over the object.

When his fingers wrapped gingerly around it, he brought the object above the surface, to be rewarded with the sight of a 7.62 mm shell casing—the very size fired by the AK-47, the gun Kenneth LaRussa claimed had been used in the drive-by.

Dropping the casing into an evidence bag, Delko sealed it, dropped the bag into the rucksack, then keyed the mike. "Shell casing," he reported.

Speedle's voice sounded eager. "Can you make it? Or do I need to send Calleigh down there?"

"Even she wouldn't want to go wading for slugs down here. It's an AK-47."

"LaRussa was right."

"Looks like it. I'll see what else I can find."

Speedle cranked the urgency in his voice up a notch. "Don't waste a lot of time, Eric—rain's coming down again. You don't want to be down there if a flood comes rushing through."

"Ten-four," Delko replied and went back to work.

He'd made it maybe three-quarters of the way down the block, collecting two more AK-47 shell casings, when he noticed the water rising around his feet . . .

. . . and when he shone the flashlight at the drain grate ahead, he saw rainwater cascading in.

Speedle's voice came over the radio again, a spike of concern under the CSI's usual casualness. "Better wrap it up, Submariner—it's gonna get pretty wet down there."

No shit, Sherlock, Delko thought, but he bit back the comment. "Soon."

He wanted to rush but he remembered his mentor's mantra: Horatio Caine had told him any number of times, "Be quick but don't hurry."

Always good advice.

Turning on the Greenfield metal detector, Delko started making arcs in the direction of Eleventh Street. A swift swing of the flashlight told him the water was pouring through the grate with greater ferocity, and another swing toward his feet showed him that he was now slogging through water to his midcalf.

It wouldn't be long before his boots started taking on water.

He pressed forward until the metal detector vibrated so hard that it almost shook out of his hand. Bending down, he felt the edge of something deeper . . . and knew he'd almost stumbled into a damn drain trap.

Crouching again, the light and metal detector both balanced in his left hand, he felt around the edge of the trap, and soon realized it was nothing more than a tray made out of heavy metal screen. Carefully tracing the edge with the metal detector, he figured the dimensions at about two by three feet.

These traps didn't need to be extraordinarily large— it wasn't like cars were falling through the sewer grate, just water bringing the inevitable detritus stowaways.

The problem was that in order to pull out the trap, he'd have to put down both the flashlight and metal detector. Speed had been right: Delko was running out of hands. He wondered if he could even get the trap out in complete darkness. Maybe he should call for Speed to come down here and give him a hand, after all.

But Delko was wearing the only diving suit they'd brought, and he would never subject Speed to this swampy concrete hell in street clothes, not with the rain threatening to flood the passage.

So he laid the Greenfield down, took one last, quick look around to get his bearings, then flipped off the flashlight and carefully replaced it in his belt loop.

The halogen light down at the far end of the tunnel was of no use now, and the pitiful amount of light filtering in at this end didn't help, either. On his knees, the cold water rushing over him, pounding off his chest, splashing up into his face, and now definitely filling his fireman's boots with that lovely sludgy water, Delko pried at the edges of the trap . . .

. . . but couldn't make the damn thing budge!

The water rushed at him even faster now. He looked up, fighting back panic. Must be one hell of a storm going up on the street.

Finding the edges of the trap, Delko pulled again and felt the metal screen basket move slightly. He yanked once more but couldn't seem to make any more progress. Hunkering down, grunting, he jerked with all his strength, the effort burning in his biceps as he strained to free the trap.

With a sudden jolt, the basket broke loose, sending Delko backward, his head nearly going under the torrent of runoff; but somehow he managed to keep the basket from spilling its contents into the water.

Finally able to steady himself, an upright Delko

braced the basket against his leg, tugged the flashlight from its loop on his belt, and hit the power button.

The basket was a heavy, rusty mess that looked like it hadn't been cleaned out since Al Capone was spending time at the Biltmore. Palm fronds, muck, a few stones, and four more shell casings covered the bottom of the basket. He wanted to take the basket up to the street to work on it, but there was no way it would fit through the manhole without spilling its contents. And the water pouring through the storm grate made that exit impossible, as well.

Working carefully, he tucked the flashlight under the arm holding the basket against his leg and with his free hand pulled the casings out one by one. With some careful juggling, he got them into an evidence bag, which he tucked into his rucksack.

Next, though it was not the most fun he'd had lately, Delko ran his hand through the muck until he touched something solid.

To his shock, he pulled out a smallish, silver-plated revolver.

"How the hell did this get in here?" he said aloud, the echo emphasizing his surprise.

Delko bagged the gun, dropped it into the rucksack, and gratefully replaced the heavy metal basket in the bottom of the pipe.

Feeling around under the ever deepening water, he finally located the Greenfield, nearly three feet down the pipe from where he'd set it to rest. Then he began the slog back toward the manhole with his sack full of evidence.

His boots were still full of water, and climbing the

slippery ladder was a greater struggle than coming down; but finally he felt Speedle tugging the Greenfield from his grasp even as he tried to help Delko up the last few rungs.

Rain pelted their faces, and Speedle looked like a scruffy hitchhiker, the kind Noah wouldn't pick up even if the ark were short one of that species.

"Where the hell have you been?" Speed asked, his relief posing as irritation.

Delko tapped the sack at his side. "Collecting evidence. That's what we do, right?"

"Well, what I've been doing is standing out here in this downpour, worrying about your ass. I think H was about to send me down there looking for you."

"Too bad, Speed. You'd have loved it. Where *is* H?"

Speedle pointed toward the Archer. "Still in the bar, working evidence."

"Calleigh in there too?"

Nodding, Speedle said, "Yeah, you can deliver your shell casing. . . . Why are you grinning? What else have you got?"

"Nothing much. Come on and see, if you like . . . Ralphie Boy."

"Pulling my chain again, huh, Delko?"

Delko beamed. "Isn't that what sewers are all about?"

Rain slanting through broken windows made the tile floor in the front part of the lobby bar slickly treacherous. Delko and Speedle moved carefully to avoid going down on their dignity.

Delko pulled a chair up next to the vacant window frame, then yanked off one boot and emptied it outside—the sound of water and things that went plop gave him a shudder.

Then he slipped the boot back on and repeated the action with the other one.

"I hope you've had your shots," Speedle said, looking on with wide eyes. "Seriously, dude, what the hell you been doing?"

"You'll see."

The pair of CSIs found Caine, Calleigh, and Detective Tripp huddled at a booth in the back, well out of the rain.

"You were starting to worry me," Caine said, tossing Delko a police-issue blanket to wrap up in. "Any finds?"

One by one, Delko laid out the bags he had brought up. The casings he'd found separately each had their own bag. The ones from the trap were together in another bag. Finally he revealed the bag with the silver pistol.

The latter Delko laid in front of Calleigh as if she were his sweetheart and the weapon an engagement ring.

She smiled dreamily as she picked up the bag. "Eric," she drawled in her faint but unmistakable Southern accent, "you do know how to turn a girl's head."

"What is it?" Caine asked.

"It's a gun," Speed said.

Caine gave him a look. "I was looking for a more specific answer."

"That's Calleigh's department," Speed said with a shrug.

Caine raised both eyebrows in an *it's-been-a-long-night* manner.

In the light of the lobby bar, Delko could see the

pistol better now: a silver-plated snubnose revolver with a white handle, the word *Valor* in black within double black circles on the left side of the grip. *Cal 32 S&W lg* had been stamped on the left side of the barrel, and *Made in Germany*—and the scraped-off place where a serial number had been—were apparent on the right side of the barrel.

Fondly, Calleigh said, "Gertsenberger and Eberwein, Gersetten-Gussenstadt."

Delko and Caine just stared at her, and Speedle said, "Gesundheit."

Cheerfully ignoring Speed, Calleigh went on: "It's a Valor—a six-shot revolver that fires, just like it says on the barrel, thirty-two caliber Smith and Wesson cartridges, long."

"That's one I've never heard of," Caine admitted.

"No reason you should have," Calleigh said with a shrug that let them all off the hook. "These were originally twenty-twos—starter pistols."

Caine frowned. "Starter pistols?"

She nodded, her ponytail swinging. "Yup—then they were modified. In the mid-sixties, these little angels were imported over here from Germany and sold as Valors . . . but they were outlawed by the 1968 Gun Control Act."

Caine seemed to be thinking about that while Calleigh took a closer look at the bagged weapon.

"Eric's find," she said, "doesn't look like it's been in the sewer since 1968 . . . so it's probably safe to say that this is one sold in Europe."

Caine's eyes were tight. "And smuggled into this country."

She nodded, sunnily. "And smuggled into this country."

Speedle scratched his head and gave her a look. "How do you even know this stuff? The thing's been illegal in the U.S.A. for thirty-five years, way before you were even born—none of us has ever even *heard* of them, let alone seen one, and you know everything about it."

She gave him a compassionate smile. "It's what I do, Tim."

Speed's eyes widened. "Well, that explains everything."

"Ask her if she knows who Ed Norton is," Delko said to Speed, with a little half-grin.

"Oh, I love *The Honeymooners*," Calleigh said.

"Before this degenerates any further," Caine said, rising, "let's get Eric's discovery back to the lab . . . I don't see how it could've been used in this crime, but the casings were and I want to find out whatever we can as soon as we can."

Everyone nodded.

As they began to move away, Caine held up a "stop" hand, and his crew froze.

"People," their supervisor said, "a drive-by on South Beach is going to get everyone's hackles up— the mayor, the media, the chief. They're all going to be breathing down our necks in the next twenty-four hours. So. Let's have something to tell them. Oh, and Eric?"

"Yes?"

"Good work."

Delko grinned and Speed patted him on the back.

Calleigh bestowed one of her lovely trademark smiles . . . and a wink.

Few had liked Kurt Wallace, and fewer still would mourn his passing; but after the death of Peter Venici, Wallace had kept the gangs from going at each other's throats.

Truth was, Horatio Caine knew well, there weren't many people in the city who gave a damn if the gangs wanted to slaughter each other—all they asked was that no civilians become casualties of war. This was a view that Caine found not only cynical but immoral.

But tonight the innocent had died along with the guilty, which meant public opinion would be behind him. Caine found this hypocritical, to say the least. And yet he would run with the mandate.

He didn't want anyone else to die, innocent or guilty.

Call him old-fashioned.

As the CSI team gathered their equipment and headed back to the Hummers, Detective Tripp hung back with Caine.

The detective wiped his face with a towel for about the twentieth time since they'd come in out of the rain, and he locked eyes with the CSI. "You think it was Antonio Mendoza and Las Culebras that hit Wallace?"

"I don't think anything yet."

"No?"

"Frank, wouldn't you rather wait to see what the evidence says before we start talking about who did it?"

Tripp snorted. "Hell, Horatio—I don't want to go to court! Just asking your opinion."

"Not sure I even have one."

"Let's pretend you do."

Caine flinched a non-smile. "Lotta people on this planet who didn't like Kurt Wallace. Mendoza for one, Chevalier of the Faucones, for another."

"How about the Haitians?"

"Among others."

"Hell, I didn't like the bastard, either."

Caine smiled. "How's your alibi, Frank?"

With another snort, Tripp mopped his brow again. "Wits said the shooter was Hispanic. That sort of lets out the Faucones."

"Unless they hired it out." Caine shrugged. "Could have been one of Manny Calisto's boys, too."

"The Mitus, yeah—those pricks didn't love Wallace either. They thought his getting product from Calisto was an insult to them and their pipeline from their hometown."

Caine shook his head slowly. "Plenty of suspects, Frank. See why we should let the evidence have its say before we decide who to chase?"

"Great. What about in the meantime?"

"You consider yourself an expert on these gangs?"

"You just heard about the extent of what I know."

"Me, too. That's why I'm going to talk to somebody who deals with this world on a more regular basis than we do."

Tripp frowned thoughtfully. "Who do you have in mind?"

"Jeremy Burnett."

"The DEA agent," Tripp said, nodding. "Yeah—I can see that."

"Last few years, he's been at the forefront of dealing with the various gangs. If anybody knows who's up to what, Burnett's the guy."

Tripp kicked at a piece of broken glass absently, moving it around with his toe. "Uh . . . wasn't Burnett part of the Narco task force? With Ray?"

Raymond, Caine's younger brother, had been gunned down in a drug heist shoot-out three years ago.

Caine understood why Tripp seemed reluctant to bring the subject up. He also knew why Tripp felt he had to do so, even if he risked touching a sore point with Caine.

A lot of cops in Miami—both local and federal—believed Ray had been a dirty cop, a "tweaker" who got more crank off the street by snorting it than he'd ever confiscated.

Caine had always believed those rumors to be lies . . . and the liar with the most to gain had been a tweaker named Chaz, who had been the source of most of the drug scuttlebutt about Ray. Caine knew his brother had sometimes lacked focus and had held onto cases a little too tightly; but that hadn't made Ray a bad cop.

Caine gave the detective a tired nod. "Yeah, they worked together, time to time."

Tripp had never said anything negative about Ray to Caine, though the detective obviously had heard the same unsubstantiated dirt that every cop in town had been privy to. John Hagen, Ray's former partner, shared a locker room with Tripp and the rest of the detectives, and Caine knew damn well that Hagen still had doubts about Ray's honesty.

For that matter, Hagen didn't trust Caine, either, apparently figuring one dirty cop in the family, whether the allegations were true or not, meant that both brothers had to be bent.

Irony was, when Ray had been alive, the balance had tilted the other way, everybody expecting the "kid" to live up to his older, highly decorated brother's reputation.

Tightly Caine said to Tripp, "You raise this why?"

"Nothing. Just . . . wondered if it would be a problem, that's all. With Burnett, I mean. He's the original straight shooter, after all."

"Well, then," Caine said with strained friendliness, "why don't I find out? If you'll excuse me."

Walking away to get some privacy, Caine withdrew his cell phone. He checked his watch, then punched in a number he still knew by heart, despite not having used it for some time.

On the same ring came a familiar baritone: "Burnett."

"Jeremy, Horatio Caine—sorry to call so late."

"Crime scenes don't keep regular hours, and neither do we. Don't sweat it—just in bed reading. What can I do for you?"

"Kurt Wallace got himself assassinated tonight."

"Do tell. I hope you're not calling to ask me to give the eulogy. I don't think the family would like what I'd have to say."

Caine let the dark joke slide. "I was just hoping—"

"That I could tell you the most likely candidate for hitting him."

"Well, yes."

"Aren't you the guy that likes evidence to lead the way?"

"I am. But it would be nice to have a context going in."

"What do you need, Horatio?"

"I was hoping you could stop by my office tomorrow, give me your thoughts on who might want Wallace dead, and just generally get me up to speed on gang activity."

"Why don't you buy me breakfast?"

"It's a plan."

"Know Lobito's? Coffee shop corner of Collins and Marti?"

"Sure," Caine said.

"Good. Eight o'clock, and don't forget—you're buying."

"Why am I not surprised?" Caine said with a smile and clicked off.

Feds—they always wanted something for free, even the honest ones.

And Jeremy Burnett had always been one of those, a hard worker with an enviable record and a formidable list of commendations.

Burnett might be the one guy in the entire state who could help Caine stave off the gang war that the CSI feared had kicked itself off this evening.

The coolness of the night was deceptive, Caine knew; things were about to get hot. Very damn hot indeed.

3

Burnett Down

LOBITO'S—A COFFEE SHOP that attracted the edgier denizens of the city, particularly after dark—had been a Miami Beach institution for as long as Caine could remember. The onetime wholesome, family-style restaurant had turned into a 24/7 joint when the original Lobito had passed away fifteen years ago and his sons had expanded their hours, unintentionally narrowing their clientele.

Typical of Miami Beach, the exterior of Lobito's was a combination of pink and aqua, with its name spelled out in twinkling lightbulbs that alternated gold and white. What once had been classy now looked every bit the dive it was; but that kept away the tourists, who never found out how good the food was, leaving it a secret shared by locals.

Inside, the tile floors, once pastel colored, were now a dingy black and gray. With its Naugahyde booths and Formica lunch counter and tables, the place would have been a nostalgia trip, if most of the

Naugahyde wasn't torn and the tables weren't all cigarette scarred, scratched, and stained.

Horatio Caine sat in a back booth waiting for DEA agent Jeremy Burnett, nursing a second cup of coffee, wondering why he didn't eat here more often—the food was good, in its greasy spoon way, and the coffee gave a guy a real jump start on the day.

Idly, he watched a miniskirted, mesh-stockinged trio of transvestites at the next table trying to look nonchalant as one of them passed a tiny folded piece of paper to another across the table.

Oh yeah, he thought, smiling wryly to himself. *Now I remember why I don't eat here more often.*

"By the way," he said over the rim of his cup, not looking at them. "I'm the heat."

One of them turned to him and said, "Yeah, and I'm Britney fuh—"

The epithet caught in the transvestite's throat as Caine held his badge up, still without looking at them.

Turning toward the counter across the room, the nearest one raised a hand and said, "Check please!"

Caine couldn't help but chuckle.

A minute past 8 A.M., Jeremy Burnett strolled through the door with a loose-limbed confidence that Caine admired. Tall and thin but packed with sinewy muscle, Burnett wore his black hair short, tiny Caesar bangs just touching his forehead. Sideburns came to the middle of his ears, but otherwise he was clean shaven.

Like the late Kurt Wallace, the DEA agent had a conventionally handsome appearance, with his strong, square chin, straight nose, and a thin, nearly lipless smile that often made him look pained even when happy.

Today, Burnett wore a white linen suit (which had been in style for a century or so in Miami), white shirt, and gray tie, with black oxfords. He spotted Caine and moved over quickly, sliding into the booth across from the CSI supervisor.

"You look bright-eyed, Horatio, considering how late you must've been up."

"I find sleep overrated."

"In our line of work it is. Yours wasn't the last call to wake me up last night."

"Oh?"

"My boss—Matthers?"

A good man, Caine knew, hard-nosed, but reputedly a micro-manager.

"Yeah?"

"He rang me maybe an hour after you. Says we're on a Code Orange."

Caine smiled lazily. "Afraid I don't keep up with the federal color chart."

"Well, it varies agency to agency. But Matthers reads this as the starting gun of a gang war, and since I've kind of been on the front line in that arena, my people and I are on alert."

"Which means?"

Burnett grunted a laugh. "Which means Kevlar underwear until further notice."

A waitress came, freshened Caine's coffee, provided Burnett with a cup of the stalwart stuff, then took their breakfast order.

Caine had not sat down with Burnett for several

months; before they dove into business, some catching up was needed. "How's Joanna?" he asked.

Burnett's wife—a striking brunette—had been as much a friend to Caine after his brother's death as Burnett himself. Not everyone in law enforcement had been supportive in the cloudy wake of Ray's demise. Caine would always value the Burnetts for their friendship in a dark time.

"She's beautiful," Burnett said with a grin, "but then you know that." He shrugged elaborately; he was one of those guys with a really lovely wife who seemed vaguely embarrassed about it, as if unworthy of such luck.

"You know Joanie," Burnett was saying, "jumping from lost cause to lost cause. Always staying busy."

"Beats the hell out of boredom."

"Does indeed, Horatio. Does indeed."

Less cynical than her husband, over the years Joanna had been involved saving whales, manatees, libraries, and some Everglades plant that Horatio had never heard of; currently she was working with Habitat for Humanity, a charity in which Caine had been involved.

As they waited for their food, Burnett got to business. "And so, Kurt Wallace went and got himself whacked. Will Western civilization survive, do you suppose?"

"Have you seen the papers this morning or watched the news?"

Burnett said, "No—all I know is what Matthers told me, which was pretty skeletal. Flesh it in, would you, Horatio?"

"Eight dead altogether. Eleven wounded, two of them seriously."

Frowning, Burnett said, "That can't be strictly Wallace's people, unless he was travelling with a small army."

"He wasn't—just three bodyguards and a small-timer from upstate he was having dinner with. All of whom currently reside in the morgue."

Burnett's expression was grave. "The rest civilians?"

With a grim nod, Caine pulled out a photo of the central crime scene—Wallace and his dinner companions—and pushed it across the table to Burnett, who looked down at it.

"These are the obvious targets," Caine said. "But you know how indiscriminating a drive-by is. With an AK-47, no less."

With an "ouch" squint, the DEA agent said, "The wounded?"

"Strictly civilians, seems—though we're of course running checks on all of them."

Burnett tapped the photo. "The blond boy? That's Sonny Spencer—Billy Joe Spencer's nephew."

"What's that—Dixie Mafia?"

Burnett nodded. "Makes sense, Wallace tying in with those neo-Nazi boneheads."

"Why?"

"Well, there's surprisingly little racial tension between these ethnic gangs—it's strictly business with them."

"Assimilation into the capitalist system?"

"Oh yeah. But Spencer's yo-yos? Wallace could have manipulated them not only on business grounds, but good old-fashioned bigotry. See, the other gangs have been plotting against Wallace, ever since he took down Venici."

"Plotting *together?*"

Burnett shook his head. "I don't think so. With their business rivalries, I doubt they could get along with each other long enough to take out Wallace . . . but individually, each gang makes a prime suspect."

"Not exactly a shortage of those."

"No. Each faction wants a piece of that Venici pie sittin' on Wallace's windowsill."

Caine squinted in thought. "So—Sonny and Wallace would have been meeting to work out an alliance?"

"I'd say more a preliminary meeting. Sonny was a dim bulb, so he must've been an emissary. After all, this went down at a public place."

"Which suggests what?"

Burnett smiled slyly. "You already figure it for a rat, don't you, Horatio?"

Nodding slowly and sipping his coffee as he decided how much he wanted to share, Caine finally said, "Somebody who knew where Wallace and his boys would be . . ."

". . . told the hitters. And if not someone in his own organization, then who?"

"The Dixie boys?"

"Possible—but of all the factions, they had the least reason to hit Wallace. Why hit a guy who was going to share a piece of the pie with you?"

"I don't know, Jeremy—maybe a greedy bastard who wants the whole pan?"

"Good point."

The waitress brought their food, and they lapsed into silence as they ate.

Minutes later, pushing his plate away, Caine asked, "Do you have a favorite among these factions—an informed hunch about who's the most likely to be behind something like this?"

Burnett chewed a corner of dark toast and shrugged. "Well, Mendoza and Las Culebras are probably the only ones who could cap Wallace and then actually *hold* the territory they took."

"So you like Mendoza for this."

Burnett rubbed his chin. "Not necessarily. Mendoza's a madman, that's a given; but he's a smart madman, and well aware he's the most likely suspect if Wallace gets hit."

"Smart enough not to do it?"

"Well, let's put it this way—smart enough not to hit Wallace in a place like the Archer Hotel and take out civilians and get himself on the radar of the legendary Horatio Caine and his CSI crew."

Caine laughed, once. "I appreciate the vote of confidence, Jeremy. So—who does that leave?"

A slash of thought-furrow appeared between Burnett's dark eyes. "Probably not the meth freaks— they don't have the power or the money or, for that matter, the drive."

Caine half-smiled. "Meth freaks are busy being meth freaks."

"Yeah, it's a full-time gig. You can probably rule them out. Chevalier and the Faucones? I don't think they have the wherewithal to pull off anything of this magnitude, either. Witnesses say the shooter was Hispanic, right?"

"Right."

"Well, Chevalier wouldn't have shit to do with any Hispanics if he could help it."

"Racial?"

"Naw. Again, it's business rivalry—he doesn't trust 'em."

Frowning in thought, Caine asked, "What about Peter Shakespeare and the Trenches?"

Burnett began to nod. "Ruthless enough, no doubt. I just don't know if Shakespeare wants the hassle he knows hitting Wallace will cause whoever did it."

Caine shifted in the booth; he sighed. "Okay, Jeremy. You keep telling me who might *not* have done it."

"We're left with Manny Calisto and the Mitus. Calisto never liked Venici . . . and he liked Wallace even less."

Eyes narrowed, Caine asked, "Why Calisto?"

Burnett's gaze was steady. "Wallace thought of himself as the top dog. But Calisto's self-image is as a middleman—after all, it's Calisto's people back home in Colombia who were manufacturing the coke. With Wallace gone, and Calisto moving in on other rackets, suddenly Calisto's self-image improves."

"New top dog," Caine said.

"That would be my guess. Informed guess."

The waitress stopped by to refresh their coffee cups.

Caine had a thoughtful sip and asked, parceling out the words, "No one knows more about these gangs than you do, Jeremy."

"Arguably so."

"Tell me, then. Does hitting Wallace lead to a gang war?"

"Worthy of Code Orange?" Burnett asked wryly, then he shrugged. "I suppose it will depend on who hit Wallace and what the other gangs think they can, and should, do about it. In a weird way, Horatio, this is politics—banana republic–style, and I'm not talking about apparel."

"Who gains from a gang war?"

Burnett grunted a hollow laugh. "Hell—Wallace's own people might start it, figuring they've got nothing else to lose."

Caine considered that briefly. Then, locking eyes with his old friend, he said, "Thanks, Jeremy. Let's hope the evidence points us toward one faction. Then maybe we can cut this off before it gets out of hand."

"I sure as hell hope so. And if there's anything I can do to help, you let me know."

"Thanks, Jeremy. You know I will."

The DEA agent's eyes tightened and he leaned forward. "Listen—something else you should know."

"Always willing to learn, Jeremy."

"Last night, Matthers was already talking task force. Us throwing in with Miami-Dade."

Caine winced.

Burnett held up a hand. "I know . . . I know. Every time there's a task force formed on a case like this, the feds take over. I have no interest in that happening."

"Well, that's nice to hear, Jeremy . . . but why?"

Burnett's smile was sly. "I happen to know how good you and your people are, Horatio. I relish having you turned loose on this. Which is why I'm going to recommend *against* the task force."

Nodding, Caine said, "I think that's wise. I think we can accomplish more, working this from our own ends . . . but sharing."

Burnett nodded. "Keeping each other in the loop."

"I'll show you mine," Caine said, arching an eyebrow, "if you show me yours."

Burnett grinned, and the two men shook hands over the remains of their Lobito's breakfast.

Caine left the meeting with the Damocles sword of an impending gang war still hanging over him, but he felt better knowing that Burnett would help him if he needed it. With Burnett as a resource—and no one in south Florida knew more about the gangs and their activities than the DEA agent—Caine might get a leg up on this investigation.

Maybe a full-scale war was still avoidable. . . .

But the Lobito's breakfast, grinding in his stomach, seemed to disagree.

If the mauve walls of the crime lab were meant to be soothing, they weren't having that effect on Calleigh Duquesne.

Truth be told, she was unaware of her surroundings, lost in her work, neither angry nor stressed, though her frown of concentration might make the casual observer think otherwise.

Perched on a chair in front of her computer, her white lab coat as spotless as when she'd put it on, her long blond hair tied back in a loose ponytail, Calleigh was trying to match the shell casings from the Wallace murder scene to AK-47 casings in NIBIN, the National Integrated Ballistics Information Network.

Created in 1997 and overseen by the ATF, NIBIN had numerous success stories to its credit, including one due to Calleigh herself. The CSI Unit's firearms expert had tied a gun in the murder of hotel executive Thomas Lessor in Miami to a fifteen-year-old unsolved New Jersey homicide. That discovery had been the first step in bringing down the retired hit team that (the late) Peter Venici had imported from up north.

Now, here she was again, hoping to hit pay dirt with the ATF database. . . .

She had plenty of shell casings to enter—over fifty gathered from the block of the shooting, plus the handful Eric Delko had brought up from the sewer. After that she would start working on the bullets recovered from the bodies of the dead and wounded, and other slugs caught in the walls of the Archer Hotel, as well as a few strays gathered from the next hotel south, and finally, one from the purse of a woman dining at the Archer whose bag had been on the floor next to her chair.

All of that had to be done before she could even begin to address the thirty-two caliber Valor revolver that Eric had liberated from its hiding place in the sewer. That gun was now with Eric for fingerprinting.

She hadn't heard the door open, but she sensed something and looked up to see Caine standing there.

"How're you doing?" he asked with a small, patient smile that managed to convey so much: an apology for interrupting; pride in her work; and innate curiosity.

Favoring him with a small, less complex smile, she said, "Let's just say it's going to be a *looong* shift."

His eyebrows rose. "But we're making progress, right?"

"Slowly."

"Keep at it."

And he smiled again.

Her, too.

Leaving Calleigh to her work, Horatio Caine moved on to the autopsy lab, domain of Alexx Woods, a slender, African-American coroner with high cheekbones, dark eyes, full lips, and a depth of compassion matched only by her IQ.

The mother of two, Alexx had an affinity for working with the dead that fascinated Caine. Somehow, she seemed to almost commune with them. Right now she was bent over the corpse of crime boss Kurt Wallace, who lay on his back nude except for the flimsy white sheet covering him modestly.

"What a horrible thing they did to you," she whispered to the body on the cold metal slab before her. "But you won't have to hurt anymore. Those days are behind you now. Just need your help to find the bad people who did this. . . ."

Caine marveled at how gently she spoke to the dead, even a ruthless sociopath like Wallace.

Here Caine and his CSIs were, investigating the murder of a man no doubt responsible for dozens of deaths himself, from knocking off rival mobsters to making it possible for drug addicts to die of overdoses when they weren't out stealing and killing for drug money.

But Caine made no judgments about the dead; now, the living . . . that was a whole different deal.

"Don't hide in the shadows, Horatio," Alexx said

musically, glancing back at him with a smile. "You can come and go as you please . . . unlike my charges."

The walls here were white, the lighting fluorescent and harsh, with another large, round work light over the stainless steel autopsy table. To the right was the long row of cupboards and cabinets where Alexx kept the tools and supplies of her trade.

Along the left wall, stainless steel vaults, two doors high and six wide, held the bodies of the recently deceased; after the massacre at the Archer, there were few vacancies at Alexx's hotel. Above the vaults was a glass-enclosed viewing area complete with computer access, files, and a plasma screen monitor that allowed onlookers to watch an autopsy in detail.

Caine settled in next to Alexx. "I just didn't want to interrupt your conversation."

A smile tickled Alexx's lips. "It's not nice to eavesdrop."

"What does Mr. Wallace have to say?"

"Well," she said, glancing down at the pale corpse, "unless I miss my guess, Mr. Wallace has learned his lesson."

Caine's eyebrows went up and down. "Yes, I would say he finally got a dose of what he's been handing out to his competitors the last few years. But just for the record, Alexx—cause of death?"

Alexx lifted the sheet so Caine could see the trio of dark holes in Wallace's upper torso—a jagged line of unconnected dots.

To the corpse she said, "You got hit by three bullets, didn't you, sweetie?"

Caine asked, "Do we know in what order?"

Pointing to a wound near the dead man's left shoulder, she said, "First entered the left shoulder, nicked the subclavian vein and went on through." Rolling the body slightly, she exposed the back. "Exiting through his left trapezius muscle."

"I see it," Caine said.

"The second—the one that killed him—entered through the chest, lacerated the left pulmonary artery, ending up lodged against his spine."

Caine nodded. "What about the last one?"

She turned Wallace the other way so they could see both entry and exit wounds on the right side. "Entered through the right pectoral, blew through the middle lobe of the right lung, then exited through the Teres major."

The coroner eased the body back to its resting position.

Hands on hips, Caine asked, "Any of the other victims done?"

She shook her head. "I knew Wallace was your priority, so I started on him first."

"I appreciate that."

Her smile had a pixie tinge, though melancholy was in there, too. "Doesn't freak you out, does it, Horatio? My little conversations with my clients?"

"Not," Caine said, "as long as I don't hear them answer you."

She laughed silently, and Caine gave her a supportive nod; they both knew she had a long line of autopsies ahead of her.

Speedle was next on the supervisor's list, and Caine found the young CSI in the lab working on identifying the paint that Caine himself had lifted from the parked car.

As usual, rock music by some band Caine didn't recognize played from Speed's boom box. The music was loud but not too loud; personally, Caine liked to work in silence, but Speed didn't like things too quiet.

Whatever worked.

"Anything yet?" Caine asked.

Out of habit, Speedle turned down the music before he answered his boss. "Going through mass spec and the GC right now. I'll know precisely what it is soon; then I'll be able to match it."

The gas chromatograph, or GC, was used to break down samples into the various compounds that made them up; the mass spectrometer then bombarded the compounds with electrons that divided the compounds into ions. Next in line, the mass analyzer sorted the samples on a mass-to-charge ratio, producing the mass spectra that could be used to identify the nature of the sample when compared to the library of knowns.

"Soon as I know, you'll know, H."

"All I ask, Speed."

Caine found Delko in the fingerprint lab. A large double room with mauve walls matching Calleigh's firearms lab, the tables and counters were covered with various kinds of equipment, chemicals, and computer gear. Delko was at the far end, hovering over a large Plexiglas cube—the Super Glue fuming tank.

"Any luck with the pistol you found?"

Delko's shrug was noncommittal. "It was down there for a while. Pretty dirty. Not much chance of a fingerprint lasting, but we gotta try."

"Good job finding that weapon."

"Thanks, H."

Caine stepped in closer and looked at the gun within the Plexiglas cube. First introduced in Japan in 1977, the Super Glue technique was a lucky development courtesy of Fuseo Matsumur, a trace evidence examiner with the National Police Agency, who was using the adhesive to mount hairs on a microscope slide when he noticed that the glue made his latent prints on the slide stand out.

The concept was actually fairly simple. The object to be tested—in this case, the Valor revolver—was placed inside the cube; then Super Glue fumes were pumped into the cube, where they would bond with perspiration residue on the latent prints. What Fuseo Matsumur had discovered by accident nearly thirty years ago was now an integral part of crime scene investigation internationally.

"I look forward to what you come up with," Caine said.

"Me, too," Delko said.

Caine headed back to his office, thinking that Eric was really starting to fit in—at first, the young man had seemed insecure. While Caine was not stingy with kudos, he did not believe in overdoing it—praise should mean something. What he tried to do was be "hands on" without getting in his people's way, which was why he checked in on them frequently—enough so that they weren't nervous when they didn't have results for him.

Lab work took time; he knew that. Patience was one of the qualities that helped Caine excel at his job. On the other hand, the mayor, the chief, and the public would not be so patient, not when innocent lives had been lost.

Caine knew they needed to get a handle on this case as soon as possible. Miami was a tourist town, and tourists didn't relish travelling to war zones. To Caine such matters were secondary at best, but he knew his superiors would not agree; pressure from upstairs would be coming soon.

He would do his best to keep the heat off his people.

Joanna Burnett studied her reflection in her dressing table mirror.

The inventory did not displease her: dark hair to her shoulders, accented by a few blond highlights; full, nicely shaped eyebrows over large wide-set brown eyes free of noticeable crow's-feet (thank you very much); a narrow, rather patrician nose that her husband Jeremy called (to this day) "cute"; a wide mouth with lips that thickened just fine with the right application of lipstick; high cheekbones a model might envy; and a youthful, pink complexion (even in Miami, she stayed away from too much sun).

She was worried about her weight, but everyone said she carried it well; at one-hundred forty pounds on her five-eight frame she had curves that might not have been in fashion but seemed to please the other sex.

All in all, not bad for thirty-two.

She looked healthy, she told herself, and happy—or at least she soon would be happy, when she got this terrible thing off her conscience.

The problems all dated back to her thirtieth birthday, which had caused her so much anxiety that she'd thought Jeremy might actually leave her. She'd driven him crazy—driven him away—with her thirty-is-the-end-of-the-world nonsense that he'd had a fling with one of her best friends (who was thirty-five!). The usual recriminations and screaming matches had ensued, but they'd weathered that rough patch, like everything else.

That had been his fault, or mostly his. This time, the fault was all hers—resenting his long hours at work, and ultimately trying to get even with him. Well, now they were even—she'd had her fling, stupidly, so goddamn ill-advisedly, but she had broken it off, finally, this afternoon.

And she had determined she would tell Jeremy. Tonight. And she prayed he would forgive her as she had once forgiven him.

It had taken a while to come to this conclusion—at first, she had herself convinced that she needn't tell him. That she could live with it. That what he didn't know wouldn't hurt him. But what if he found out? He was a detective, after all!

And then night after night of tossing and turning, being unable to sleep; well, last night she'd slept soundly, having come to the decision. She couldn't live with the lie. She would end it. And she would tell Jeremy. He would understand.

She hoped they could be together forever. Grow old together, like both their parents had. Finally have that family they'd always talked about . . .

She gave the mirror a brave smile. They would work everything out—they always had before. She still loved him. He was the only man she'd ever truly loved, and she believed things could be set right.

Already he'd sensed the change in her. Hadn't he asked her to get all dressed up to go out tonight? When was the last time that had happened? The dress she'd chosen for the evening was a special favorite of Jeremy's. White chiffon with pink, orange, blue, and green pastel swirls, the midcalf dress had a flouncy skirt and a halter top that showed off her bustline . . . another particular favorite of her husband's.

She lifted a spray bottle of perfume from the dressing table, spritzed her neck, her wrists, and, finally, just a hint at the bottom of the V of the low-cut dress. His call today asking her to be ready so he could take her out when he got home sounded like the old Jeremy, the man she'd fallen for back at Duke University, the man who had been ready to save not just her but the whole damn world as well.

She hadn't even minded getting the second call to tell her he was going to be late because things were heating up at work—that drive-by shooting in Miami Beach that was all over the TV.

Yes, she should still get dolled up (his phrase), and yes, they were still going out to dinner. After that, she could decide whether they would go on to a late movie or simply come straight back home to be together.

Should she tell him over dinner? In public? Or at home? Doubt whispered in her mind: *Why tell him at all? He loves you. You love him. Why borrow trouble?*

But they'd built the marriage on honesty. She would tell him. She would find a way. Tonight . . .

She heard his car pull in, the car door slam, the

front door open, then close, followed by Jeremy's voice at the bottom of the stairs. "Jo, hon—you ready?"

Smiling at the mirror one last time—*yes, she was holding up pretty well for thirty-two*—Joanna grabbed her purse and bounced down the stairs to meet her husband.

"Hey, you," she said.

Their familiar greeting.

"Hey, you," he said fondly.

"How was your day?"

"Brutal and long," he said, then he got a good gander at her as she fell into his arms. "Whoa! Look at you. . . ."

"You should do more than just look," she said and gave him a nice warm kiss.

He returned it with some urgency, and things began to heat up fast. His hands started to roam over her and she let him have his fun for half a minute, then pulled back. "Don't we have dinner reservations?"

He grinned lopsidedly at her. "Do more than just look, she says—then the ol' bait and switch. . . . Should I take time to change my suit?"

"No, I love you in that white linen suit."

"Been in it all day."

"You're fine. You can take a nice shower later."

His look turned playfully lascivious. "Maybe we can take it together."

"Oh, Jeremy . . ."

And she clutched him, desperately.

He hugged her a while, then pushed her away a little to look at her. "Jo—is something wrong?"

"No. . . . It's just . . . we need to talk about something."

He shook his head. "After dinner. Nothing's going to spoil our night out. You need a jacket or anything?"

"No, I think I'll be fine." She looped her arm in his. "If I get cold, I've got you."

"Always," he said, and gave her that familiar, wide smile again—the one that had melted her back on the Duke campus.

He opened the front door for her, and she went out onto the small stoop. It wasn't an exceptionally large house, but they liked their Pinecrest neighborhood— not far from Biscayne Bay, low crime rate, nice neighbors. The two-story house at 130 Terrace was just right for the Burnetts.

As they crossed the lawn toward the car, she heard tires squealing behind her, an unfamiliar sound around here. Joanna turned to look, feeling Jeremy turn next to her as well, his eyes apprehensive. *Must be some kid. . . .*

She'd taken a few steps down the walk when the silver car came speeding up the street. Her mouth dropped as she saw the Hispanic man hanging out the car window, big gun in his hands.

Jeremy stepped in front of her, arms spread protectively, and the night thundered as her husband took several bullets in the chest and dropped, half on the sidewalk, half on the lawn.

Exposed now, screaming over the rapid gunfire, she raised her hands as if she could ward off what was coming. When the first bullet hit her, she was surprised at how much it hurt, ripping through her left hand to punch her in the shoulder.

Joanna's scream cut off as she staggered backward.

Next to her, Jeremy had crawled to his knees and was reaching for his own gun. Then something like a bee sting clipped her forehead and she wobbled, her head suddenly going light, tiny sparklers of color shooting off behind her eyelids. Still shaky, she looked up as something pounded into her stomach, driving her back, dropping her on her rump in a very unladylike fashion, and she worried that she was going to get grass stains on her dress.

Something was going terribly wrong with her body. Her arms and head felt hot, but her legs were cold and didn't seem to be working.

Next to her, she heard Jeremy's gun thunk onto the lawn, and she looked over to see him flop next to her, blood spilling across the front of his suit. His eyes were closed, his color drained, and she had the sinking feeling that he was already dead. She looked down at her own white dress, the pastel swirls turning dark as blood streamed out of her abdomen.

The silver car had long since disappeared, and the roar of the shots was just a faint echo in her ears now. Something warm trailed down the right side of her face, and the stain on her dress was growing; she knew she needed to do something fast. Why weren't the neighbors coming out to help?

They're scared, a voice said inside her head. It sounded small and distant, yet distinct. She pressed her hand to the wound, hoping to keep pressure on it even as she used her other hand to dig the cell phone out of her purse.

She had to get help. . . .

Now!

She touched the little white lights on the phone: 9-1-1.

The call was answered on the second ring, the dispatcher's voice female but steady and calm. "Nine-one-one emergency—how can I help?"

The light-headedness was coming back, and Joanna felt herself growing weaker, feeling about to faint. "Help us."

"Where are you, ma'am? What kind of help do you need?"

"Shot," Joanna said, her voice a harsh, dry whisper. She wished she had a bottle of water, just the tiniest drink would be nice, not even Evian, tap water'd be just fine. . . .

"Who's been shot?"

"My . . . husband! . . . And I."

The dispatcher asked, "Where are you?"

I know our address, Joanna told herself. *It's . . . it's . . .* She just couldn't quite put the pieces together—letters into words, numbers in the right order. There was a one in it . . . or was there?

Finally, she mumbled, "Help us . . . ," then the phone tumbled from her grasp, and Joanna Burnett slumped next to her lifeless husband, her blood flowing out into the lawn.

Living with her infidelity no longer a problem.

4

Gun Control

LIKE MOST SEASONED CSIs, Horatio Caine had hardened himself to the tragedies that could await at a crime scene. A CSI had to detach from feelings of anger or sadness over what had happened to some poor innocent soul; getting emotional was actually a disservice to a victim.

But as he hurtled in the Hummer, siren wailing, lights flashing, toward the double 420—radio code for homicide, in this instance *two* homicides—Caine could feel the pounding of his heart, his hands clenching the steering wheel until they were a bloodless white.

He knew the address he was being dispatched to: It belonged to Jeremy and Joanna Burnett.

"Dial Delko," Caine said, using the Hummer's hands-free cell phone.

In three rings Delko answered, and Caine said, "Horatio. Talk to me, Eric."

"I'm at the Burnetts'. With Speed."

"Status?"

"One fatality—Mrs. Burnett. Sorry, H. I know they're—"

"And Jeremy?"

"He's alive, but bleeding. Not sure exactly. He's getting the attention he needs. H, it's another drive-by."

Caine's eyes tightened. "I'm close. Get back to it."

By rights he should have recused himself, but his team was on call, and that was all the justification he needed. His friends needed him—including Joanna. He would help them just as he would a stranger . . . and he hoped with the same professionalism.

He made a left on Montgomery Drive, also known as SW 120th Street, then took a right on Sixty-seventh Avenue, and finally another right onto the Burnetts' street. As he rounded the corner, Caine took in a landscape that screamed tragedy.

About halfway down the block, in front of Jeremy and Joanna's house, the flashing lights of three squad cars streaked the night with red and blue. Delko's Hummer, an ambulance, and at least three unmarked Crown Vics told Caine that not only MDPD detectives but the Feds as well were on the scene.

With the anonymous cover of darkness, and the re-assuring presence of the police, neighbors had crept out on their porches to gawk. A few had made it out far enough to huddle in small groups on the sidewalk, chatting quietly in that combined concern and excitement that so often dwelled on the fringes of crime scenes.

Caine cut his speed and allowed his vehicle to roll slowly down the street; because of all the emergency responders he was forced to park three houses east of the Burnetts'. He climbed down and—a rarity for him—did not take time to collect his crime scene kit.

First, he wanted to check on Jeremy. Then he would see how his detail was doing; but even from this distance, Caine could make out the flash of Delko's strobe as he took pictures on the lawn. As he drew closer, Caine caught sight of Speedle combing the blacktop street with his flashlight, obviously searching for shell casings.

Another damn drive-by!

Whoever was behind this was bold: Declaring war on both sides of the law was unheard of. But Caine knew that foolhardy as cutting down a DEA agent might seem, eliminating the most knowledgeable expert on gangs in the city made a sick kind of sense.

Not until he was in front of the house next door could Caine make out, between blinding flashes of Delko's camera, the white sheet covering a body on the Burnetts' gently sloping lawn. All the way around, the edges of the yard had been cordoned off with yellow crime scene tape, and Caine had to flash his ID to get past the uniform at the sidewalk. Once he was inside the perimeter, Caine saw the cluster of officialdom—men in suits near Jeremy's car in the driveway at the far end of the house.

When you died violently, the world got formal all of a sudden—men in uniforms or suits would take care of you now, from ambulance attendants in white and police in blue to the suits and ties of detectives and undertakers.

Detective Frank Tripp stood with his back to Caine, facing a semicircle of four or five men. In the dark, Caine couldn't tell for sure how many lapdogs were huddled beyond the two front men, FBI Special Agent Robert Sackheim and DEA agent Leonard Matthers, Jeremy's somewhat uptight boss.

What Caine could tell immediately was that he was walking into an argument in full sway.

Each suit made a statement about the man wearing it. Sackheim's charcoal number fit perfectly and said that he was in charge and not a man to be trifled with; Matthers's brown pinstripe—a nod to style, the gold pocket hanky a wink at class—implied the same thing, albeit in a more subtle manner. Tripp's suit shouted indignantly that it had all but jumped off the rack onto its wearer, and that it hadn't been dry-cleaned since the weather had finally cooled off, and what the hell was it to you?

Tall, broad-shouldered, all-American-type Sackheim had come to the FBI right out of law school after being a second team all-conference quarterback at Bowling Green. He was used to being the guy who got listened to in a huddle.

"The shooting of a federal officer," Sackheim was saying, "demands a federal investigation. End of discussion."

"Couldn't agree more, Bob." DEA honcho Matthers—an African-American every bit as tall and broad-shouldered as his FBI counterpart—had a shaved head, tan-framed glasses, and a well-trimmed black mustache that somehow seemed to always etch a frown even if the mouth beneath it smiled. "But the thing is, he's my guy—that makes it *my* federal investigation."

Tripp's mouth formed a tight round hole from which he shot words like bullets. "This is an MDPD matter, and I won't have you people commandeering it. Burnett and his wife are citizens of Miami, the crime took place here, at their home, and—"

"And he's a federal officer," Sackheim interrupted.

"With the DEA," Matthers added.

Caine eased up next to them all. "Well I guess I shouldn't be surprised."

All faces turned toward him, eyes wide.

Caine smiled like an angel. "Why not have a pissing contest? You're behaving like pricks."

Sackheim's eyes blazed, and the FBI man got right in Caine's face. "Screw you, Horatio! Do your job, and we'll do ours."

Caine smiled tightly. "Bob—you don't need to be this close."

Sackheim swallowed, his eyes embarrassed now; he backed away.

"But you make a good point, Bob," Caine said, his voice calm, with a cold edge. "I have a job to do and so do my people, as the CSIs first on the scene. And you have jobs to do as well—and the longer you argue over territorial rights, the colder this case gets, and the less work gets done."

Now it was Matthers's turn. "Horatio, you were friends with Joanna, and you're friendly with Jeremy. Is it even appropriate that you handle this?"

"My people are handling it. I'm strictly supervising. But I do have one request for all of you."

Sackheim frowned. "Which is?"

"Stop trampling my crime scene."

The trio, and the two federal spear carriers nearby, all looked around them, as if realizing for the first time that the priority was preservation of evidence.

Caine raised a hand, half stop, half benediction. "Here's the deal, fellas—Bob, Len, neither of you has the equipment or expertise to process this crime scene correctly—my people do. Let us do our job and Frank here will keep you in the loop . . . right, Frank?"

Like a kid assuring the principal he'd behave, Tripp said, "Sure."

Caine rested his hands on his hips and said, "I'm sure there are aspects of this case that are better handled on the federal end. But with a local homicide, we need to take the lead, here—for the sake of the victims."

Sackheim began to say something but thought better of it.

"When we catch the guy who did this," Caine continued, "you can all get together and decide who gets the credit, and who gets to prosecute. All I care about is finding the ones responsible."

"You self-righteous—," Sackheim began.

"I resent your tone, too, Horatio," Matthers said. "Jeremy's like a brother to—"

"To all of us," Caine said, cutting him off. He looked toward the MDPD detective. "I gather Joanna is gone."

"Yes," Tripp said and shook his head solemnly. "Gut shot—bled out before anybody got here."

"Jeremy?"

"One in the arm, but he took two in the chest. If he hadn't had his vest on, he'd be dead, too."

Caine glanced at Matthers. "Looks like you were right to call that Code Orange."

Choking back sorrow, Matthers said, "Didn't . . . didn't do Joanna any good, did it."

"That's the thing about wars," Caine said. "So many of the casualties aren't soldiers."

The CSI looked over at the ghostly white sheet on the lawn. Joanna Burnett had been a good soul, a caring person who'd been socially concerned as long as he'd known her. She'd never done anything but try to help people, and now she was dead because she'd been standing at her husband's side.

Turning back to Matthers and Sackheim, Caine said, "Tempers are always short when something like this goes down. We'll work together, gentlemen, and get whoever did this."

Matthers and Sackheim traded looks, then both turned to Caine.

"Miami-Dade takes the lead," Matthers said.

"But we're constantly kept apprised," Sackheim put in.

"More than fair," Caine said.

Slowly—watching where they were stepping—the group dispersed, except for Tripp.

In the not too distant past, Tripp had jumped on Caine a few times for overstepping the detective on investigations; perhaps that was why some embarrassment seemed to tinge a nonetheless sincere, "Thanks, Horatio."

Caine waved it off. "No problem. Just keep my

word, Frank, and keep them posted—and don't be afraid to use them as resources."

"You got it."

"Now . . . what do we have?"

After getting a big sigh and an elaborate shrug out of his system, Tripp said, "Drive-by, MO is the same as the Wallace hit—silver car, Hispanic guy doing the shooting . . . some kind of automatic weapon."

"Was Jeremy conscious?"

"Yeah, but not a hell of a lot of help. He was pretty torn up about Joanna. EMTs that got here first said they found Jeremy in the yard, holding her in his arms. They said he was practically hysterical."

"Who wouldn't be?"

"There was blood, so the Kevlar didn't block every shot. And from how he was breathing, I'd bet he broke at least one rib."

"Not uncommon. Kevlar stops the slug, but not the impact."

Turning back toward the yard to watch his two CSIs, Caine caught Delko's eye and the younger CSI came over to them. Delko wore black slacks and a black silk T-shirt, the collar of which now peeked out from inside his CSI windbreaker.

"I'm so sorry, H," he said.

"At least we have a survivor."

Delko raised his eyebrows. "Who's also a witness."

"Always a plus. What have you got?"

Delko shook his head glumly. "I wish I had more. Just pictures of the scene . . . but Burnett himself messed that up some, when he held his wife."

"I wonder," Caine said, "if we'd do any better?"

"What do you mean, H?"

"If we'd react at a crime scene involving a loved one appreciably better than a civilian. What would you do, Eric? Preserve the evidence, or cradle your dying wife in your arms?"

"I'm afraid I'd hold onto my wife. You know . . . if I had one."

With a quick smile, Caine patted the young man on the shoulder. "Good answer."

Delko pointed toward the house. "I pried a dozen or so rounds out of the siding, and I'll go over the ground around the bodies with a metal detector to look for shots that might have ended up in the grass."

"Excellent idea. Should tell us if we're looking at the same weapon as the Wallace scene."

Delko nodded, pointing toward the street. "Speed's already got pictures of tire tracks up the block . . . and he's been searching for shell casings since before you got here."

Caine looked sideways toward Tripp. "Canvass?"

Tripp made a sweeping gesture. "We're hitting a six-block radius."

"Good."

"Hey, you know how it is when a brother officer goes down. We've got guys volunteering from every law enforcement agency in south Florida."

"Then if anybody saw anything, any time, we ought to hear about it."

"Oh yeah."

Glancing toward Delko, Caine asked, "What about the house?"

"I did it, H."

"And?"

Delko shrugged. "No sign of entry after the shooting. I don't think Jeremy went back inside."

Tripp grunted. "He wouldn'ta been able to."

Delko went on: "Nine-one-one call came from Joanna's cell phone—then eventually, three or four of the neighbors called in."

"The good neighbors were a little slow on the draw."

Tripp said, "Neighborhood like this doesn't get hit by an AK-47 drive-by that often."

"They were scared," Delko said, with another shrug.

"And the Burnetts," Caine said, "were bleeding. . . . How was our response time?"

"Not great, H. Mrs. Burnett never gave dispatch the address, and it was a cell phone. It took a while to figure out where they were."

He smiled grimly. "Until the neighbors finally got concerned."

No one said anything.

Speedle came up the sloping lawn to them. He wore an untucked dark button-down shirt that had probably been ironed once, just not lately; his jeans were faded and baggy, his tennis shoes in fair to decent shape, though the days they could be called white were a distant memory.

Caine's occasional suggestions that a more professional appearance might be in order had thus far fallen on deaf ears; on the other hand, every other aspect of the CSI's performance was professionalism personified. So even the tightly wound Horatio Caine had to say to himself, *What the hell . . .*

Right now, for example, Speed held in his hand two good-size plastic bags full of 7.62 mm shell casings.

"How many?" Caine asked.

"Seventy-one—he was using a drum magazine just like he did on Ocean Drive."

"All right. Let's get those, and the bullets, to Calleigh, get our photos developed, and see if there's anything there."

"Sounds good to me, H," Speedle said.

Delko said, "Speed, if you take care of the photos, I'll sweep the metal detector across the yard. Then I can take all the ammo we've found to Calleigh."

Caine said, "Sounds like you've got it in hand."

Speed frowned. "You goin' someplace?"

"To the hospital, with Tripp—to talk to our victim."

But Caine stayed long enough to oversee the loading of Joanna Burnett's body into the ambulance. Just before he and Tripp headed out in their respective vehicles, Caine watched solemnly as the ambulance pulled away with its charge, its siren ominously silent, its flashers turned off.

No hurry. No hurry at all.

Half an hour later, a compact, blond nurse ushered Horatio Caine and Frank Tripp into a waiting room where the only other guest was Jeremy Burnett's boss, Leonard Matthers, who'd beaten them there from the crime scene.

Styrofoam coffee cup in hand, Matthers sat in the corner, a TV tuned to CNN nearby, though he wasn't watching it.

Matthers looked up when the two of them settled into the chairs across from him.

"Anything turn up at the scene, Horatio?"

"Not much."

"That's not very specific. What about keeping us in the loop?"

"Let me get the evidence processed first, Len. Don't look over my shoulder, and I won't look over yours."

Matthers's eyes bore into him; then suddenly the man smiled. "That's why I like you, Horatio—you don't take crap from anybody."

Caine said nothing. He respected Matthers but had heard enough from Jeremy about the man's micromanaging to know that establishing an arm's-length distance right now would be wise.

The silence was just getting awkward when Tripp put in, "Nurse said they're still stitching him up."

"He's lucky," Matthers said, tossing the empty cup into a wastebasket. "Damn lucky."

"He lost his wife," Caine said. "That doesn't sound lucky to me."

Matthers rolled his eyes. "He should by all rights be as dead as she is. Either of the two hits he took in the vest could have killed him . . . and he busted a rib as it is. A few inches higher, his head would've been blown off."

"I'm told he was bleeding," Caine said.

"He caught one in the right arm." Matthers pulled off his glasses and rubbed a hand over his face before he answered. "Little more than a scratch . . . but we both know Joanna meant the world to him. I don't know what the hell he's going to do without her."

"Time'll heal that wound, too," Tripp said.

Caine said nothing. How long had Ray been gone? No sign of healing yet. . . .

The nurse ducked her head in again. "You can see him now, Officers . . . but only for a few minutes."

The trio of lawmen followed her back out to the emergency room and down a short corridor to the far end, where she pulled a curtain back and they saw Jeremy Burnett lying on a bed bare-chested, a wide white bandage tinged with pink around his right arm.

His chest was bandaged, too, where one of the slugs that had hit him in the vest had broken a rib, no doubt; but an ugly purple bruise from another round was still exposed. His eyes were red from crying, and he had a look of helpless despair.

The confident Jeremy Burnett was suddenly a man who no longer cared what life held for him.

Matthers went around the bed to Burnett's left side. "Are they treating you right, Jeremy?" he asked awkwardly, patting his agent on the good arm.

Burnett said nothing at first. He swallowed thickly and mumbled, "Thanks for being here" to his boss; then his bloodshot eyes travelled to Caine.

Finally, he said, "Bullet just missed the brachial artery."

"Lucky," Caine said.

An awful smile came to the wounded man's thin lips. "You think?"

"Jeremy," Matthers said. "You're still alive. Losing Joanna . . . there's nothing we can say to help. But you are still alive. That's a place to start."

Eventually, Burnett nodded, but there was no enthusiasm in his movement, no real sign of agreement in his eyes.

Caine asked, "I wish I could just tell you we're with you, and leave you to your grief. But you know I can't."

Burnett sighed, a catch of pain midway. "I'm your witness. We need to talk."

"Yes. Are you up to telling us what happened?"

"No . . . but I know I have to. While it's still fresh."

"Yes."

"Agent Burnett," Tripp said, "With your permission, I'll take notes."

"Please."

Tripp withdrew a small notebook and a ballpoint from his sportjacket pocket.

The three visitors stood expectantly around the DEA agent's bed. Burnett's eyes slowly closed, and he seemed to drift off. Caine wondered if the man had passed out or gone to drug-aided sleep. . . .

Caine exchanged glances with Matthers—it showed in their eyes that they were wondering if they'd already overstayed their welcome, and if this interview just simply could not happen right now.

But then, his eyes still closed, the DEA agent began to speak, as if in a trance.

"I got home late from work tonight . . . the concern over the Wallace shooting, gangs and so on, dragged the day out . . . and we were supposed to go out to dinner." His words came out slow and measured. "I was so late, we had reservations, I didn't even take time to change. . . . We no sooner got out the front door than it started."

"The shooting?" Caine prompted.

"The shooting . . ."

"What did you see, Jeremy?"

Burnett never opened his eyes; he seemed to be replaying the event on the movie screen of his mind. "First we heard the squeal of tires."

"From nearby?" Tripp asked.

"Yes—east of the house. Sounded like the car was coming our way. We both looked up. It's a quiet neighborhood; we don't get a lot of that."

"You saw the car," Caine said.

"Yes. Silver Lexus. Could have been Manny Calisto's. Anyway, just like it."

"Catch the plate?"

"No. No, goddamnit." The anger was aimed at himself. "Not even a partial. It was just a blur."

Caine leaned in and spoke in a measured manner. "That means, Jeremy . . . you looked at the plate. *Think.* Any numbers at all?"

Burnett's eyes, already closed, squeezed tighter as he thought about it. Finally, still not opening his eyes, he said, "Dolphins plate. L . . . D . . . sorry. That's all I can remember. LD."

"That's good," Tripp said as he scribbled the letters in his notebook. "That's a start."

"Notice anything about the car?" Caine asked.

"Like what?"

"Anything off or abnormal. A dent. Something custom."

Burnett shook his head.

Tripp said, "Okay. What happened next?"

"I saw a Hispanic man leaning out the car window. He's maybe twenty-three, twenty-four. He's got curly black hair, dark face, dark eyes, heavy mustache. He was wearing a white shirt."

Caine asked, "Had you seen him before? Did you recognize him as a gang member?"

"I wish I could say yes, Horatio. No. I've gone through the mental file, running through Calisto's crew . . . just can't make the guy."

"A lot of turnover in that bunch," Tripp pointed out.

"You're doing good, Jeremy," Matthers said, leaning closer to his friend. "You're doing fine."

Suddenly Burnett's eyes popped open, as if he'd been jarred awake. "Then I saw the gun—automatic rifle, AK-47 or one of the clones. Drum magazine. Then he started shooting."

"I know this is hard," Caine said, "but you need to tell it."

"I got in front of Joanna and took the first hits. Got knocked off my feet. That . . . that put Joanna in the line of fire. One went through her hand, into her shoulder."

"You were down."

"Yes. I tried to get up, but the bullets were faster than I was. Second slug hit her body, I don't know where . . . stomach, I think. I had my gun out by then, and was going to grab her to throw her down, but I . . . I guess I blacked out. When I woke up, she was gone. I . . . I don't think she suffered long. I sure as hell hope . . ."

He covered his face with his left hand.

"Isn't that enough for now?" Matthers asked.

Caine nodded, and Tripp put up no fight.

Burnett lowered his hand and tears streaked his

face, moisture matting down his eyelids. "Horatio—don't let them take you off this case."

"I won't, Jeremy."

"I hope . . . I hope I'm not asking too much. But Joanna deserves the best, and . . . you're it."

Matthers said, "We're not fighting jurisdiction on this one, Jeremy. Horatio and his people, and Detective Tripp, are on the front line."

"Good," Burnett said. Then he managed perhaps the weakest smile Caine had ever seen. "Just be careful, Horatio . . . I found out the hard way . . . how dangerous the front line can be."

When he got back to HQ, Caine resisted the urge to go check on Delko and Speedle.

He knew they'd be hard at it, and mother-henning would not improve matters any. The brother-officer aspect nagged at him, though. None of them ever gave less than one-hundred percent on a case, but when the case involved the shooting of another officer, the urge to give two-hundred percent was overwhelming. This could lead to poor judgment and hasty conclusions. The best thing Caine could do right now was set an example by his own patience.

His office, like most of the building, was dark. Midnight wasn't far away as Caine found himself standing in the doorway, looking at the ugly sofa along the wall to his left. More than one night had been spent there, but he decided against that, flipping on the light switch. He moved behind his desk, took off his jacket, draped it over the chair, and sat down.

The chair wasn't particularly comfortable. He liked

it that way; the less time he spent in the office, the better. But tonight, after tense, long hours, the chair felt pretty good. Caine settled in, ready to dig through some of the paperwork he needed to catch up on.

He wasn't very far into the pile when he heard a tiny knock at the door. Looking up, he saw a weary-looking Calleigh standing there.

"Little late for paperwork, isn't it?" she asked.

"I'm tired, but it's that wide-awake tired. Come in. Please." He waved toward the chair opposite his desk. "What's your excuse for still being here?"

Calleigh sat down, perching on the edge of the chair. "I wanted to work the casings that Eric brought back from the Burnett attack. By the way . . . how is your friend?"

Caine twitched a non-smile. "Physically, he's going to be fine. In no time."

"But emotionally . . . another story, right?"

"He watched his wife die, right in front of him. Who knows how someone will react to that sort of thing?"

Neither of them said anything for a few seconds.

Then, delicately, Calleigh said, "She was your friend, too."

"Yes, she was."

"Different, isn't it? When you know the people."

"Hard to maintain your objectivity, yes."

"But we have to, anyway."

"Right." He looked at her—carefully. "Calleigh . . . are you all right?"

"Sure."

She sat drumming her fingers on her knees, wearing a look of dazed exhaustion mixed with jumpy energy.

"How much caffeine have you had, anyway?"

She grinned. "Maybe I'm excited 'cause I found something."

"What did you find?"

The grin disappeared. "But maybe what I found doesn't make sense. Maybe it's . . . troubling."

When she didn't elaborate, Caine met her eyes. "Calleigh. What . . . did . . . you . . . find?"

She flashed a nervous smile. "For one thing, I got a match on the shell casings from the Burnett hit and the ones from the Archer Hotel."

Caine gave her an approving nod. "Good. We sort of figured they were the same doer, but it's good to know we've got proof. Nothing 'troubling' about that."

"And, uh . . . I got a hit on NIBIN, too."

He put down his pen and studied her. "Really? That doesn't happen every day."

She raised an eyebrow. "Tell me about it. It's really kind of weird."

Caine grunted a laugh. "Weirder than when you got a hit on a fifteen-year-old murder in New Jersey?"

She considered the question as if it had been a serious one, then said, "You know, I think it is."

He sat forward. "Tell me."

Her eyes narrowed, she withdrew a printout from her lab coat pocket, and crisply said, "NIBIN found the AK-47 in question had been used in a murder, a gang shoot-out actually . . . about thirteen months ago."

"Local?"

"Local—Little Haiti, Eightieth Terrace."

They both knew she was referring to an area of northeast Miami that had become one of the fastest-growing parts of the city. Loaded with hardworking families and people who had come to a new country for a new start, Little Haiti was also the home of the Faucones and some of the bloodiest drug wars the city had ever seen.

Caine was thinking back. Slowly he said, "The apartment house shoot-out . . . the one with the fire."

"That's right," she said. "Burned an apartment house to the ground—four dead, fifteen to the hospital . . . and that doesn't include the gunfight. Eight more dead, there, on the two sides."

Squinting in disbelief, Caine said, "And *our* gun was in that shoot-out?"

She nodded.

Shaking his head, trying to make sense of this, he said, "Calleigh, I thought we caught most of those guys . . . *and* confiscated the weapons."

"We did indeed. The owner of this particular gun was a drug dealer named Julian Pelitier."

Caine didn't like the sick feeling that was growing in his stomach. "And Pelitier's gun was one of the weapons we confiscated?"

She handed him her printout.

As he slowly scanned it, she said, "Right now this gun . . . the gun used at the Wallace hit and in the drive-by at the Burnett household . . . is theoretically locked up securely in the evidence building. Pelitier is up on murder one in the state and a carload of federal drug charges."

"But the gun's obviously not there," Caine said.

"I don't see how it could be."

Caine's first inclination was to call the head of the evidence division, roust him out of bed, and tell him to get down here, fifteen minutes ago; but this, he reminded himself, was a time for patience, and care.

He said, "Let's go look at the evidence log and see if we can find out what happened."

Calleigh yawned. "Good idea."

Caine had to admire the way this bone-tired young woman attempted to put on a chipper look.

"On second thought, Calleigh . . . this is nothing I can't handle. You go home and get some sleep."

She made her eyes pop open in an unsuccessful effort to seem alert. "I'm fine, Horatio—really!"

"No. Home to bed. I need you here first thing in the morning, and I need you fresh and bright and sharp. Now, go."

"I'm fresh. I'm bright. I'm—"

"Going home. We'll talk tomorrow, and I'll tell you everything that happened."

"Okay." She got to her feet. "But I don't like it."

"You don't have to," he said cheerfully.

From the doorway, she said, "I'll be a good soldier, if you get some sleep, too. Okay?"

"Deal."

Half an hour later, Caine found himself waiting outside the new evidence building in the Doral complex on Northwest Twenty-fifth Street. He had already hit the buzzer and announced himself through the intercom to the officer on duty.

In a way, Horatio Caine and his team were partly responsible for the existence of this concrete building, which had been erected to hold the evidence that was piling up at an alarming rate, commensurate with the improved arrest rate of recent years.

Caine's successes weren't the only reason for the new building. The drug wars had always given them plenty of contraband to house, but with the new popularity of meth labs, the city had been forced to come up with some creative ways to store all the various chemicals—hence the new concrete evidence building known rather unaffectionately around police circles as "The Bunker."

Built with separate floors for drugs, guns, and other evidence, the structure probably should have been under heavier guard than several video cameras and one lone sentry. But Caine knew as well as any of the department heads that money was tight.

No one seemed to be coming to the door, and Caine wondered if he'd been forgotten. He looked up at the video camera over the gray steel door, and the camera looked back at him.

He was just wondering if he shouldn't give himself the order he'd handed Calleigh—namely, to get a decent night's sleep and let the whole thing wait until morning—when the door swung open.

The blond uniformed cop of about fifty, five foot eight, had a thinning mustache and a name tag proclaiming his name as RICHARDS.

"Afraid I'll have to ask for your ID, Lieutenant Caine," Officer Richards said.

Caine complied, saying, "I'm looking to track a gun."

Richards frowned; he obviously rarely dealt with this kind of thing on graveyard shift. "This time of night?"

"It's important."

"We prefer you do that during regular hours."

"Time and crime wait for no man."

"Who said that?"

"I did."

Richards thought about that for a moment, then said, "Well, then, I guess you better come on in."

"I guess I better."

The guard looked around, making sure Caine was alone. Convinced, Richards held the door open for him.

They went through a locked mesh door into a vestibule, and through another locked mesh door into an anteroom with a table, two chairs and an overhead light. A three-ring binder lay open on the table next to a paper bag that Caine assumed held Officer Richards's lunch and a thermos of coffee with the lid off, the plastic cup half full next to the bottle.

"Gonna need you to sign in."

Caine signed the man's book.

"Now—what can I do for you, Lieutenant?"

From his jacket pocket, Caine took Calleigh's print-out, which contained the evidence number of the gun in question. He handed the sheet to Richards, and the guard studied it for a moment.

"We'll have to refer to the computer on this one. Come with me, Lieutenant Caine."

Richards led him out a door at the far end of the anteroom and into a hallway. They turned into the first door on the right, and Caine found himself in an office lined with file cabinets and several computer stations.

Richards sat`at a monitor and keyed the numbers in. The screen displayed a table with various numbers, names, and locations. The guard used the card as a marker against the screen until he found the line he wanted.

He nodded his head slowly. "This is from the Little Haiti lot, isn't it? An AK-47 that came in the night of the big one . . . one with the fire, right?"

"Right. Where is it?"

"Well, here, of course."

"But it isn't," Caine said. "It was used in a homicide tonight . . . and another one last night."

"That's impossible," Richards said. "If it's in the record, it's here. Unless—" He read further. "Unless it *isn't* here . . ."

Curiouser and curiouser.

"I'm going to need you to clarify that, Officer."

"It was checked out, Lieutenant."

"Checked out?"

Richards said, "Yeah, that case went federal. That gun's outta here. Signed out to a U.S. attorney. It should be in his evidence locker in the Federal Building."

"Which U.S. attorney?"

Still using Caine's piece of paper as a marker, Richards read down the monitor screen. "Kenneth LaRussa."

The U.S. attorney who'd shown up at the Wallace crime scene with spaghetti sauce on his shirt. . . .

"Let me get this straight," Caine said. "This particular gun isn't here now because it's supposed to be in the evidence locker of Kenneth LaRussa?"

"Why do you say, 'Supposed to be'?"

"I have my reasons."

Richards shrugged. "However you slice it, Lieutenant—you're gonna need to contact Mr. LaRussa."

"Yes, Officer Richards . . . I am."

5

Gang War

THE SUN ROSE HIGH and fast the next morning, banishing the coolness of the last few days, turning south Florida into a sauna.

A clear day was a rarity this time of year—the city averaged only about two completely clear days for the whole month of September, typically one of the wettest months, and here they were entering their second straight day of no rain, practically a drought in south Florida.

Horatio Caine—driving around downtown, looking for a place to park (a challenge even for a detective of his skills)—couldn't get over the recent dramatic changes in this part of the city.

The feds were building a brand-new courthouse west of Miami Avenue, and the area surrounding the old David W. Dyer Federal Courthouse, the Federal Detention Center, and the James Lawrence King Federal Office Building had become, post-9/11, a veritable fortress. Large orange barriers, each about three feet high, four feet across, filled with water, stood end to end in a huge plastic necklace around the throat of the block.

Caine headed for the U.S. attorney's office in the King Building. Tripp was supposed to meet him outside, and the pair of them would go in to question Kenneth LaRussa about the mysteriously missing gun. When he'd laid out his plan for the crew earlier this morning, they hadn't been very confident that it would work.

In truth, neither was he.

The detail had converged in the layout room first thing to go over their meager evidence. Alexx had been absent, still performing autopsies on the various victims of the two shootings; but Calleigh, Speed, and Delko had been there, alert and ready to go.

With the aroma of Delko's Cuban coffee pleasantly permeating the room, Caine leaned over the large central table while the others had fanned out around him. Calleigh leaned against a counter on which Delko sat, further down; Speed perched on a chair turned around so he could use the back as a rest for his folded arms.

"What have we got so far?" Caine asked.

"You've got everything I have," Calleigh said, "from matching the slugs to both drive-bys and, of course, NIBIN making our murder weapon."

"In a most enigmatic way," Caine said.

The other CSIs looked blankly wide-eyed, from Caine to Calleigh and back again. Their supervisor prompted his firearms expert to share her knowledge with her coworkers, which she did.

When she was finished, the two were still wide-eyed, if hardly blank, but while both Speed and Delko were capable of sarcastic remarks in almost any situation, from bizarre to grotesque, neither could offer a quip about the notion of a weapon used in multiple murders turning out to be a stray from an evidence lockup.

"I'm going to LaRussa's office as soon as we wrap up here," Caine had announced.

With a humorless smirk, Speed said, "Yeah, *he's* gonna be a big help."

"He will be," Caine said with a shrug, "if he's a smart man."

"I never made him for stupid," Speed admitted.

Caine shrugged again. "The Pelitier case isn't due in federal court for a while—he'll let us have the gun to move the state case forward."

"H," Speed said, "you don't think that AK-47 is still *there*, do you?"

"If somebody put it back it is," Delko said.

"*I* don't think it's there now," Calleigh said, "but if he's innocent, Mr. LaRussa won't know that."

Delko frowned. "Guys, this dude wants to be a U.S. senator. He's not going to relish anybody knowing a major piece of evidence disappeared on his watch, much less was used as a weapon in two new murders."

"Eric's got a point," Speed said. "I said the guy was smart. Smart guys don't like to look dumb. Especially smart guys with political ambitions."

Calleigh's eyes widened. "Don't forget that he was at the first crime scene . . . and doesn't that make him a suspect?"

Caine nodded his general agreement; everything that had been said by his crew had merit.

"Think about it," Speed had continued. "LaRussa's

not going to help if he's guilty . . . and if he's *not* guilty, he won't help because he's a U.S. attorney, which in my book makes him full of—"

"Let's save our contempt for the bad guys," Caine said.

"Maybe he *is* a bad guy," Speed pointed out.

Caine smiled. "Maybe he isn't. . . . Anyway, I'm going to talk to him and give him a chance to help. When he finds out the gun's gone, he'll have the opportunity to lead the way, in tracking down how it got out of his evidence locker."

Speed, frowning in thought, asked, "How you goin' in, H?"

Hands on hips, Caine moved his head side to side, saying, "Like we think the gun's still there." He gave his team a sly smile. "When Mr. LaRussa can't produce it . . . we'll see what shakes down."

Delko and Speedle exchanged raised-eyebrow looks and short nods.

"It's the kind of crazy plan," Calleigh said, a touch of archness in her drawl, "that just might work."

The remark made everybody smile.

Which they could all use about now. . . .

Moving on, Caine asked, "What else have we got?"

Speedle said, "The paint chip from the Archer hit is silver. Definitely came from a silver Lexus."

"Any luck with the partial license number Jeremy Burnett gave us?"

"There are several silver Lexuses with Dolphin plates. Mendoza's got one." Delko said. "But the only one with LD in the number is registered to our old friend Manny Calisto."

"Leader," Caine said softly, "of the Mitus gang."

"Local arm," Speed said, "of the Colombian drug dealers."

"Which brings the question," Caine said, "where is Calisto now?"

Shaking his head, Delko said, "We've had blue and whites looking for him everywhere, starting with his fancy crib to all his favorite haunts."

"Manny's either in the wind," Speed said, "or gone underground."

"Either way," Delko picked up, "we're not finding him or the car . . . and no one around him is talking."

"Well, none of us are knocked over with surprise," Caine said dryly, "now are we?"

The CSIs shared a few more details with their supervisor, none terribly illuminating, and Caine had finally called a halt to the proceedings, sending them back to their respective tasks.

Now, as he finally squeezed into a parking space on Fifth Street, Caine had to hope LaRussa would be more cooperative than anyone expected. While LaRussa was not his favorite law enforcement official, Caine had no desire to discover that the man was in any way dirty, or, for that matter, was Caine eager to embarrass or disgrace the U.S. attorney.

The thought of the cases that could go down the porcelain vortex, because of the doubt cast over the provenance of evidence in LaRussa's care, chilled Caine. An army of criminals walking on technicalities was not something Caine relished putting in motion. . . .

With no break in the barricades on this side of the block, Caine would have to walk around. As he did, he gazed up at the rear of the Federal Detention Building. Two large concrete columns, each at least fifteen stories high, marched north toward Fifth Street, a smoked glass section between them, silver bars running the length of the glass, separating them into panes, looking like a giant fretless guitar neck. Two other wings spread east and west, each pockmarked with windows barely a foot square.

Terrorists with an eye toward making a political statement by blowing up a federal building were not the only motivation for the water-filled barricades. Inside the detention center were housed some of the most ruthless and notorious cartel members in the world, with several Al-Qaeda terrorists thrown in for good measure.

All those incarcerated in the DC had friends who would like nothing better than to spring them right from under the government's nose. Julian Pelitier was still cooling his heels in jail, but if he rolled over on his suppliers, his lawyers would no doubt be hoping to get him transferred to the cushier DC.

Heading south on Miami Avenue, barricades blocking the sidewalk, Caine was forced to watch traffic and walk in the street. At Fourth the street had been cut off on each end of the block and replaced with heavy gates and guard shacks. A uniformed guard stepped out of one shack as Caine approached.

Tall and buff and thirtyish, the brown-haired guard didn't look like the typical rent-a-cop. His name tag read Mulligan.

"Help you, sir?" The voice was deep and slightly scratchy, the tone no-nonsense; the eyes, too.

Caine showed the guard his credentials.

"Destination, Lieutenant?" Mulligan asked.

"Kenneth LaRussa's office."

"Is he expecting you?"

"If you mean do I have an appointment, no."

"I'll have to phone Mr. LaRussa's office, sir."

"Please."

The new security was time consuming, but Caine understood the need for it and couldn't argue. The guard retreated into the shack, made the call, and came back less than two minutes later, though the time had seemed longer to Caine. He didn't mind tedium when work was being accomplished, but simply waiting—time wasted in reception areas, for example—was an irritation he had to work at controlling.

Mulligan handed Caine a Visitor laminate on a neckchain.

"You know the drill, I'm sure, Lieutenant. You have to wear this while you're in the compound; when you come out, return it to one of us."

The guard showed him past the heavy gate and into the area that used to be Fourth Street. Some cars still drove here occasionally—delivery trucks and vehicles dropping off or taking away prisoners—but most of the time it served as a pedestrian walkway between the four buildings: the DC on the northwest, the James Lawrence King Federal Office Building on the northeast, the Dyer Federal Courthouse on the southeast, with the court annex on the southwest.

Imposingly tall—looking more like a bank than a federal building—the King stood ten stories, housing any number of different government agencies and their respective offices, including FBI, IRS, DEA, and ATF. The U.S. attorney's office was on the fifth floor. As Caine approached the building, he found Tripp sitting on the front steps of the building.

By way of greeting, Caine asked, "Any luck with Manny Calisto?"

Tripp shook his head. "He's a ghost."

"Who ya gonna call?" Caine said wryly, and they entered the building, skipping the metal detector by showing their badges.

When they exited the elevator onto the fifth floor, they were in the lobby of the U.S. attorney's office, which occupied the entire floor.

U.S. attorney's office was something of a misnomer, though one everyone in local law enforcement freely used. Actually, more than sixty government legal eagles occupied the space, most in the criminal division . . . and all under the supervision of Ken LaRussa.

But there were also United States attorneys who dealt with civil matters—like right-of ways, eminent domain, federal parks, and other less than glamorous activities.

The lobby was typically institutional, a few chairs in a reception area, a painting of waves crashing on a beach (*Why so many ocean paintings in this town,* Caine had to wonder, *when seeing the real thing was no problem?*), with a desk behind which sat an attractive plump brunette with black glasses, a crisp white blouse and an oval face. She seemed busy, but when she looked up and saw them, she gave them a smile that somehow acknowledged she had read them as law enforcement officers.

"May I help you, gentlemen?" she asked.

"Miami-Dade police to see Mr. LaRussa," Tripp said.

They displayed their credentials, which she read, jotting down the names on a pad. "I'll tell him."

She picked up the phone, spoke into it using the names she'd copied from the credentials, listened for a moment, then hung up the phone and smiled at the two officers again. "He'll be right out."

Three minutes later, LaRussa—in a light blue dress shirt with the sleeves rolled up to the elbows, geometrically patterned tie, and black suit trousers—came into the lobby, his hand extended, his politician's smile glued on.

"Frank, Horatio—good to see you."

They went through the ritual of shaking hands.

Then the U.S. attorney's smile transformed into something grave. "Listen, we're all broken up about the Burnetts. I knew Joanna—she was a living doll."

"Not now," Caine said.

With a sigh, LaRussa shook his head and said, "I understand Jeremy should have a full recovery. His staff was on Orange Alert . . . ?"

"Yes," Caine said. "Vest saved him."

"These gang wars—these cowboys usually target each other. Don't they know the kind of trouble they bought, shooting at our team?"

Tripp said, "Can we talk somewhere more private?"

"Certainly. Right this way, fellas—we'll chat in my office."

As LaRussa led them into the warren of offices and cubicles, he asked, "Is this visit related to the Wallace shooting? Frank, do you need a formal statement?"

"No," Tripp said. "Another matter."

They strolled down an aisle between cubicles to the far end of the floor, where LaRussa had a good-size office. His secretary, a pretty redhead whose dark glasses and white blouse mirrored the receptionist's, sat at a desk just outside.

"Hold all calls, Tina," LaRussa told her as he opened his office door and gestured for the two cops to enter.

"Have a seat, guys," LaRussa said. They did, and he closed the door.

The office was a spacious dark-panelled affair with large windows on the city (the blinds half-drawn, at an angle, to keep the light out but the skyscape revealed) behind a mahogany desk smaller than a tennis court. The file cabinets along the left wall were also mahogany, and the wall at right was arrayed with diplomas and awards and especially photos of LaRussa with celebrities, particularly political ones. Caine's favorite touch was the paired photos of a beaming LaRussa shaking hands with President Clinton next to a seemingly identical shot of the smiling attorney clasping hands with President Bush.

Covering all the bases.

On the lawyer's desk was a framed photo that Caine knew was of LaRussa's wife, a beautiful Hispanic woman, and their two grade-school-age kids. The attorney flopped into the huge leather desk chair and leaned back, his hands clasped behind his head.

He seemed to be overdoing the casualness, trying too hard to show that he and the two MDPD officers were players on the same team.

Pals.

"What can I do ya for?" LaRussa asked chummily.

All business, Caine sat forward. "We need a piece of evidence from one of our cases that you're using in a federal one."

The tight smile that flashed in response betrayed the first crack in the friendly manner. "Do tell."

Caine read him the property number.

Shrugging, letting out a sigh, LaRussa unclasped his hands and sat up. "Horatio, I never said I was a genius. If you think property numbers'll ring a bell . . . how about you refresh my memory?"

"Julian Pelitier—Faucone drug dealer."

"Ah. But why is he your business?"

Tripp said, "He's our business because we're moving forward on his arrest for murder."

LaRussa sat forward and rubbed a hand over his face. "Horatio, Frank, you know, normally, I'd jump at the chance to help you. *Mi casa, su casa*—"

"Normally," Caine said.

"But this Pelitier thing . . ." He grinned, made an embarrassed, open-handed gesture. "The negotiations are at a critical point. Perp's about to roll over on half a dozen other dealers and his suppliers. If he and his lawyer found out that the state charges were going forward, Pelitier might clam up."

Tripp's face tightened. "Ken, do I have to remind you that this asshole did a spray-and-pray in a neighborhood full of kids?"

"I understand that very well, Frank," the attorney said, "but if we roll this guy, we can keep drugs off the streets and out of the hands of those kids . . . and thousands more."

Tripp looked at Caine; they had, of course, anticipated this, but they'd devised a strategy, and this was part of it.

Caine said, "Putting one gang leader away does not stem the flow of drugs. But convicting a murderer stops him from murdering again."

"Horatio's right, Ken, and you know it," Tripp said. "And you know as well as we do that some other asshole's going to step into Pelitier's shoes, soon as he's gone . . . if they already haven't done it!"

LaRussa shrugged again. "What can I tell you, fellas, the greater good, as I see it, is served by sending Mr. Pelitier through the federal system."

Caine wondered if the attorney actually believed what he was saying, or if—as Speed and Delko seemed to think—LaRussa might have a reason to cover up the gun's disappearance.

Tripp had that look he got when he couldn't think of the next move; the big detective was clearly out of mental ammunition.

Caine gave the attorney his brightest smile. "All right, Ken, there's three ways we can play this." He held up a finger. "One, you help us voluntarily."

"Not going to happen. Sorry."

The CSI held up a second finger. "Two, I get a search warrant . . . and you try to explain to a judge why you won't honor it. Of course you may have to talk fast, because some of these state judges have an attitude and would like nothing better than to throw a U.S. attorney into jail for contempt."

LaRussa shrugged, seemingly unimpressed.

A third finger went up. "Three—I call Pelitier's attorney and tell him that my opinion, as a forensics specialist, is that he should get a court order for an independent firearms examiner."

Now LaRussa held up a finger of his own—not so friendly now.

Ignoring that, Caine continued: "And Pelitier's attorney comes to you with that court order and, again, you're in front of a state judge, trying to avoid going to jail for contempt."

LaRussa grunted a laugh. "Horatio," he said, his voice as sweet as sugar but as synthetic as saccharin, "are you threatening me?"

"You know"—Caine beamed at LaRussa, much as LaRussa beamed at the two presidents in those framed pictures—"I believe I am."

LaRussa made a scolding click in his cheek. "You know that won't work with me. I'm a trial lawyer, Horatio, you think I intimidate this easily?"

The guy had a point. . . .

Leaning forward behind the desk, fingers tented, eyes shrewd, all false friendliness gone, LaRussa said, "You have a reputation as a straight shooter, Horatio . . . well-earned. Why don't you shoot straight with me?"

Caine said nothing. Tripp gave the CSI a sideways glance.

The attorney continued. "Why don't you just tell me why you're in such a rush to get your hands on this particular gun . . . at this particular moment?"

Caine thought about it, but just for a few seconds; then he decided to tell LaRussa the truth and gauge his reaction—the honesty appealed to his nature as a "straight shooter," the experiment of it to his scientist's nature.

"I don't think you *have* the gun, Ken."

"What . . . ?"

Caine cast another of his patented smiles at the attorney. "My firearms expert matched it to both the Wallace hit *and* the attack on Jeremy and Joanna Burnett."

LaRussa's mouth dropped like a trapdoor. "No goddamn way. . . ."

"Way, Ken," Caine said easily. "You know Calleigh Duquesne? Or certainly know of her?"

The attorney nodded, eyes narrowed. "She's the best in the state . . . everybody says so. Your much-vaunted 'Bullet Girl,' right?"

"I don't call her that," Caine said. "But there's plenty of reason why others do."

"Well, nobody's infallible," LaRussa said with a dismissive shrug, "and I'm afraid she just got this one wrong, Horatio. It happens. Gun's been here for months, locked up tight in the gun safe of our evidence room."

LaRussa, skilled courtroom orator that he was, had delivered this speech convincingly; but toward the end his voice had gotten a little louder, as if he was trying to fill his words with a bravado he suddenly didn't feel.

"Well then," Caine said, with artificial casualness, "let's just go have a look."

LaRussa's gaze was hard; then it melted into the familiar politician's grin. "You're good, Horatio . . . damn good. You almost had me there . . . but I don't think so."

"Maybe you could do me a small courtesy, then."

"Try to. Of course."

Caine got out his cell phone. "Would you happen to have handy the number for Pelitier's attorney?"

They sat staring at each other with two of the coldest smiles imaginable for perhaps thirty seconds; Tripp shifted several times in his seat during the stare-down.

Finally LaRussa caved, throwing his hands in the air. "Fine . . . fine!" Then he waggled a finger at Caine, as if scolding a gifted student who insisted on disrupting the class. "We'll go look. But if the gun's here, you leave me alone."

Caine shook his head. "Sorry. If the gun's here . . . and I doubt very much that it is . . . I take it with me, Calleigh tests it. *Then* we bring it back."

"You can't be serious."

"I'll tell you how serious I am, Ken. I'm as serious as if a federal law enforcement agent and his wife had been shot with this very weapon."

LaRussa absorbed the telling words, then said, almost feebly, "What about Pelitier's attorney? The gun will have to be signed out . . . he could find out."

Caine lifted one shoulder, set it back down. "Yes, he could."

LaRussa lapsed into silence, considering his options. None of which, Caine knew, were terribly appealing.

After a long moment, the attorney said, "You really think this gun was used in the attack on Jeremy and Joanna?"

"The casings match ones picked up at both homicides. You wouldn't have to be a 'bullet girl' to make that analysis."

"All right, then, for Joanna Burnett, and for Jeremy,"

LaRussa said after a very long sigh. "He's a good agent and he deserves to have us watching his back."

"Yes, he does," Caine said.

"For him, Horatio—we'll go have a look." The waggling finger again. "But when I give you that gun, you fill out a form one-ten and have it back here in twenty-four!"

Not sure whether he was dealing with a clever politician, a clever suspect, or an honest, if self-interested, law enforcement professional, Caine nodded his agreement.

The evidence room was, typically, in the basement. During business hours, a guard held sway at the sealed door with FBI, DEA, and ATF agents coming and going intermittently. After hours, though, no guard was posted in the room. Two cameras covered the area as armed guards patrolled the halls of the building, as well as the perimeter of the entire federal complex.

LaRussa searched the log to find out where the gun should be, and less than ten minutes later they faced the gun safe—actually, one of seven gun safes lining a wall. The safes were locked, and the guard, while on duty, held the keys; the rest of the time the keys were locked in a desk near the front of the evidence room. It wasn't Fort Knox, but it was secure, particularly in the context of the general post-9/11 measures controlling the building itself.

Using the key he'd received from the guard, LaRussa unlocked and opened the oblong safe. Inside, nearly a dozen long guns stood on end, bracketed in place: two shotguns, four rifles, three semiautomatic rifles, and an old Thompson submachine gun in a neat row.

And at the far end, almost off by itself, an AK-47 with a drum magazine leaned against the back of the safe.

Caine's stomach tightened. *What the hell was going on?*

"Right where it's supposed to be," LaRussa said, making no effort to conceal his smugness.

Then the attorney, rather impulsively it would seem, reached toward the gun. Caine put a hand on the attorney's elbow and stopped him.

LaRussa looked at him with wide, irritated eyes. "What are you—"

"Ken, do you really want your fingerprints on that weapon?"

The attorney looked at his open palms as if they belonged to a stranger. "Hell . . . I'm sorry. I never even thought—"

"Mind?"

Caine withdrew a pair of latex gloves from his sportcoat jacket and slipped them on. As he did, the attorney backed out of Caine's way and stood next to Detective Tripp, letting the CSI supervisor carefully pull the gun out.

Then, together, they compared the tag tied to the trigger guard to the number on the 110 form.

All three of them could see that the numbers matched.

"I'm afraid," LaRussa said, "even Bullet Girl can make a mistake."

Caine's mouth smiled but his eyes did not as he signed the form and took the gun. "We'll see, Ken— we'll see."

The guard found them an empty duffel bag to load the weapon into, and with another round of hand-shaking and some conversational attempts to agree that all three of them were on the same team after all, Caine and Tripp took their leave.

Back at the lab, Caine delivered the gun straight-away to Calleigh. "One AK-47 with drum magazine."

Her eyes were saucers. "It was *there?*"

"Right where it was supposed to be—locked up tight in the gun safe."

She paled. "Horatio, there's no way . . . I mean, I checked and double-checked that match. There's just . . . *no . . . way.*"

He shrugged. "And yet here it is."

"I . . . I don't know what to say."

"Don't say anything. Assumptions and emotions aren't helpful right now. Just test it, and find out if this is the right gun."

Her eyes were tight. "You don't think I screwed up?"

"No assumptions, Calleigh. Only one way to find out—try to get a match."

"All right, let's say it's a match . . . if you give me just that one assumption, for a second. *Then* what?"

"Then," he said in his measured manner, "we figure out how a gun locked up in a safe . . . in the most heavily protected federal building in the city . . . managed to get out and about to kill nine people."

The unseasonably warm, clear weather of that evening served only to exacerbate an already volatile situation, and, as the night wore on—just as Caine had feared—the lid on the powder keg blew off.

First, not long after sunset, a carload of Mitus wandered into the Lemon City section of Little Haiti, where they opened fire on three Faucones standing on a street corner. Two were killed instantly, but the third managed to make a call for reinforcements, and three carloads of Faucones turned up in short order to assist him.

The four-car chase and running gun battle went on for the better part of half an hour, until the Mitus made it from Lemon City onto I-95 South. Along the way, one Faucone car—raked with automatic weapons fire—exploded in a flameball of gasoline, melted metal, and sizzling flesh. With the chase reduced to three cars, the vehicles veered west onto the Dolphin Expressway, where all three cars shot up a tollbooth as they blazed through.

The Mitus made the exit at Twenty-seventh Avenue, but before they could get off the ramp, the Faucones rammed them off the road, rolling the Mitus' car down an embankment. Then the Faucones stopped long enough to gun down any Mitus who had survived the crash.

Later in the evening, with most of the second-shift CSIs still working the gun battle scenes, a second gunfight erupted when Trenchs drove by a Little Havana dance hall frequented by members of Las Culebras. Nearly two dozen dancers who had come outside to smoke or make out or just get some air had little chance.

Two carloads of Trenchs drove by, firing automatic weapons. Nine of the revelers were killed and thirteen wounded, three so seriously they wouldn't survive the night.

Only one had been an actual Culebra member.

Not to be left out, the late Kurt Wallace's own people—thinking Las Culebras and Antonio Mendoza were behind the hit of their boss—broke into Mendoza's Indian Creek mansion and killed a dozen Culebras, two of whom were Mendoza's cousins. Then, incensed that they hadn't found Mendoza home, they burned his house to the ground. They even shot his four dogs.

The firefights went on all night. Every time the police got to one location and managed to regain control, another battle would start up somewhere else.

By the time Caine and his CSI detail were called back in to work around three in the morning, nearly fifty souls had joined the nine of the first two nights' killings, and the governor was talking about bringing in the National Guard and declaring martial law.

Caine knew that other places had survived ordeals like this—Watts, Newark, Detroit, the Tet Offensive in South Vietnam; and the city itself had survived its various hurricanes, so disaster was nothing new to Miami . . . though a full-scale gang war was.

This needed to be dealt with as quickly as possible, and Horatio Caine knew that the fastest way to deal with it was to find out who had killed Kurt Wallace and Joanna Burnett. The Wallace hit had started this bloodbath, after all: Maybe finding the killer would put a stop to it.

As the sun came up, Caine stepped outside the building for some fresh air. This morning's *Miami Messenger*, a normally staid paper, screamed at him from the coin-op machine. The headline was large, bold, and only two words long: **"GANG WAR!"**

Rubbing his face with his hands, as if that might wipe away the exhaustion, Caine returned inside to get back at it. He was short-handed now. Alexx was doing autopsies in such record speed that she wasn't even getting to know her "charges." Speedle and Delko, siphoned off to help the graveyard shift get caught up with what had happened overnight, were still in the field, and no doubt dead on their feet.

Which meant that, for now, only he and Calleigh were left to concentrate on the Wallace and Burnett killings.

He found her in her lab sitting over a worktable, a round neon work light pulled down so she could see through the magnifying glass in its center. She was doing something with a marker, but from the door, he couldn't tell what.

Looking over her shoulder, he realized she was marking both shells and casings with the felt-tip—something on the tip of the bullet, something on the bottom of the cartridge.

"What's up?" he asked.

She looked up, smiled, then put the bullet in a box and picked up the slug next to it. "I'm numbering bullets," she said with her usual sunny professionalism.

"Really."

"Yes. I'll load them into the drum in order, so that number one comes out first—"

"And seventy-five comes out last."

"Right! Then we can match casings and bullets to find out which ones did what at our two crime scenes."

She didn't need to explain any more. Caine knew that as Calleigh—or, originally, the killer—fired off an entire mag of ammo, the gun would heat up. The barrel markings on the bullets and the firing pin and ejector markings on the casings would change subtly during the process as the gun got hotter and hotter.

If she knew what number sixty looked like because she'd marked it, she'd have an easier time picking out number sixty from each of the crime scenes. That was, of course, if the gun was the right one and the bullets matched at all.

"May I point out," Caine said, "that in the face of overwork and bodies stacked up around us like cordwood . . . your disposition is a bright light in a dark world."

She beamed. "Well, thank you, Horatio! Isn't that nice of you to say."

"What are you going to do after you get done marking the bullets?"

She smiled up at him again as if the answer were the most natural thing in the world. "I'll be going to Cabrerra University—to use their swimming pool."

6

Pool Party

CABRERRA UNIVERSITY, NESTLED in upper-middle-class Coral Gables, had a respected academic reputation, but to most people, CU had made its strongest impression as a football power.

For Calleigh Duquesne, however, the school's swimming program was, on this warm fall morning, the major point of interest, even though the swimmers weren't rated as high nationally as the CU gridiron crew.

And she was not here for exercise, at least not of the physical variety; the only exercise she planned to perform had to do with test-firing the AK-47 her supervisor had acquired from U.S. attorney Ken LaRussa.

Looking crisply professional in navy slacks, a white blouse, and her CSI windbreaker, she sat in the cramped office of swimming coach Phil Cunnick, in his second year of heading the program. The odor of chlorine from the nearby pool permeated the cubbyhole—the coach probably no longer noticed it, but a guest like Calleigh found her eyes burning. Resting on the floor next to her was the duffel bag holding the AK-47, which she'd already tested for prints.

Tall and leanly muscular, Cunnick—in his team T-shirt and gym trunks—seemed young for a college coach, probably still in his late twenties. He wore his blond hair long, unusually so for a swimmer; but at this point in his career, he probably only competed in Olympic-caliber events.

She had never met Phil Cunnick before this morning, but she had seen him swimming on TV in the last Olympics. He had an easygoing charisma, not hurt by a vague resemblance to Brad Pitt. His green eyes were warm and friendly, and his grin was as wide and white as it was easy.

"Uh, is this some kind of joke?" Cunnick asked. "What am I, being punk'd?"

"Uh, no. You saw my credentials. Your department chair did call and pave the way?"

"Yeah, but . . . you really can't expect me to let you shoot up my state-of-the-art, Olympic-quality swimming pool . . . ?"

She smiled reassuringly and kept her tone light, while her words weren't. "Miami-Dade has a good relationship with the university—we would never compromise that."

"I'm gonna have to say no."

Her smile never dimmed. "Honestly, I won't hurt it at all."

"You can't be serious."

She handed him the paperwork.

Cunnick scanned the succinct note from his department head over and over. Then he looked at her firmly.

"Listen—department head or no department head, this pool, this entire building, is my responsibility."

"I understand. I feel that way about my lab."

"And you have a nice smile, Ms. Duquesne, and a commendable professional manner. But I'm not going to okay this."

She sat forward. "I promise you, Mr. Cunnick—it won't hurt your pool."

He sighed. *Riiight.* Firing an AK-47 into it won't hurt my pool."

"The water will dissipate the energy of the bullets—they'll be harmless by the time they get to the bottom."

With a frown, he said, "On TV, you ballistics people are always firing guns into trash barrels and like that."

Her smile still in place, Calleigh replied, "First, we're not 'ballistics people'—that's a television term. We're firearms and toolmark examiners, and secondly, though we do have a tank we use for firing off rounds, that procedure works best with one or two shots. I'm going to let go a seventy-five-round magazine. You do that in the tank, and the water will get so churned up, it'll distort the test."

He looked at her as if she'd fallen right out of the sky, through the ceiling, and into the chair across from him. "Well . . . I can see how you sold my department head. . . . Can you promise me the MDPD will pay for any damages if you're wrong?"

"I don't have the authority to do that."

"Oh, but you—"

"That doesn't mean you wouldn't have any recourse if there were an accident. I'm not asking you to sign off on anything. And, remember, I've cleared it with the university."

"You're *positive* I'm not bein' punk'd?"

"Quite positive."

"And you can't tell me what this is about?"

"Sorry, no—it's part of an ongoing investigation."

"Well . . . this kind of assault weapon . . . I've seen the papers and the news on the tube. It's this gang war, right?"

Obviously unable to answer that, Calleigh decided to take a different tack. "Mr. Cunnick—"

"Phil."

"Phil. And I like Calleigh better than Ms. Duquesne. Let me ask you, Phil—who on this campus knows more about swimming than you?"

He gave her a cocky grin, his self-confidence stronger than the misgivings he'd been caught up in. "Not a soul, Calleigh."

She gave him her sweetest smile. "Now . . . who do you suppose knows more about firearms than me?"

The words seemed to cold-cock Cunnick for a few moments; then he began to chuckle. "All right, we'll try it. But so much as *one* tile is chipped—I'm suing the city."

"That would be your right," she said cheerfully.

When they came out of Cunnick's office, several swimmers and divers were clustered around the pool, their bodies pearled with water, hair matted down and dripping.

She walked along beside the coach, lugging the duffel at her side. The catcalls and wolf whistles started almost immediately. She took no offense—they were just kids, and it was hardly the first time Calleigh Duquesne had been whistled at.

Anyway, she figured most of them had her pegged for the coach's girlfriend and just wanted to give him a hard time.

"Pipe down," Cunnick said as they approached the team. "You'd think you nincompoops never saw a lady before."

"Not like her," one of them in the back said, rather breathlessly.

Smiling inwardly—she had liked the coach's choice of words, *nincompoop* being a term her father used to use, such a wonderful, evocative, oldtimey insult—Calleigh unzipped her windbreaker. As she did a couple of whoops rang out . . .

. . . only to catch in young throats when the swimmers saw the gun and badge.

Now a gentle lapping of water was the only sound in the chamber.

She smiled at them politely. "I need you boys," she said, emphasizing the B word, "to give me a hand."

Grins blossomed, and clumsily suggestive offers of help tumbled out, echoing off dreamily reflective walls.

"Quiet, idiots," their coach said. "Listen to CSI Duquesne."

Murmurs among them—"She's a CSI." "Jeez, a real-life crime scene cop!"—indicated the young men were suddenly impressed with Calleigh in a whole new way.

"First," Calleigh said, raising a finger, "I need you to step outside for a few minutes while I do my work.

While you're out there, the coach will explain what you'll be doing when you come back in."

"All right, guys," Cunnick said. "In one minute, I want you into your sweats and out the door!"

They responded quickly, trained to obey their coach, though as they pulled on their sweats, they threw questions both at him and their guest, but neither the coach nor Calleigh was telling them anything. Soon the group of guys was about to go out the door, glancing back at this unusual visitor.

Their timing was excellent, because they got to see Calleigh unzipping the duffel bag and pulling out the AK-47. Wonderstruck murmurs—"Awesome!" "Cool!"—preceded the coach's herding the wide-eyed, drop-jawed bunch out with a final slam of the door.

Then—blessed silence, and she was alone.

Outside, Cunnick was being inundated with questions from his swimmers.

"Coach, who's the dish?" Rick Britton, the backstroker, asked.

"Hey!" the coach said, glaring at the kid. "Respect."

Ben Jackson, butterfly swimmer, asked, "What's she doing here? A CSI!"

"You dating her?" Ron Murray, one of the divers, wanted to know.

"He wishes!" Yoshi Tamura said.

Embarrassed, and overwhelmed by his boys' joshing him, Cunnick had his hands up, just ready to get tough, when Calleigh inadvertently helped him out . . .

. . . because when the shooting started, all his big,

brave jocks dove for cover, even though she was inside and they were out here.

Calleigh had attached the magazine filled with her numbered bullets, slipped on safety glasses and her protective earmuffs, then walked to the end of the low diving board. She had selected this over a high dive—a three-meter board just to her right—as there was no need to go up so far merely to fire off some rounds.

Besides, from that height, the arc of ejected casings would be longer, and she wanted this to be as easy for the swim team as possible, despite their good-natured, immature harassment.

Perched on the end of the low board, she looked down into the deep blue of the pool, AK-47 at the ready. Due to the high-ceilinged mercury-vapor lighting, she couldn't see her reflection in the water, but if she looked carefully through the gently rolling waves left behind by the swim team's recent exercises, she could see a dark spot at the bottom of the deep end, which she figured for the drain.

Standing carefully, feet planted about shoulder-width apart so the recoil of the gun wouldn't knock her off the board and into the water, Calleigh made sure she was at an angle as perpendicular to the surface as possible. That way the casings would eject into the pool.

Then she took aim at the underwater drain, released the safety, breathed in deeply through her nose, let the breath out through her mouth, and squeezed the trigger.

The water hissed and spat as the hot bullets plunged in; even with the muffs, she could hear their thunder resonating in the big tiled room. The recoil was considerable, but she was used to the effect and easily kept her balance.

As she'd assured the coach, the speed of the slugs dissipated rapidly, and they dropped harmlessly to the bottom of the pool. The water above, however, churned over white as Calleigh continued to spray the surface with bullets.

Had she used the tank at work, she would have found, due to the weight and the clumsy flight path of the 7.62 mm projectiles, the bullets not at the far end (as most non-gun people might suppose), but at the near—since AK rounds had a tendency to nose-dive when they hit the water.

Amateurs, on the other hand, figured the bigger the gun, the farther the shell would fly. Not always, Calleigh knew, not always.

Firing off the weapon, Calleigh Duquesne was in her element. She had loved guns since childhood, and she made no apologies for her interest, nor did she suffer any fools who made stupid sexual assumptions about her passion for pistols. The only way sex figured in was that she'd always been pretty and petite, and firearms were a great leveler.

But she also savored their power, the simple poetry of their mechanics, and the skills one needed to develop to use them safely, accurately, and responsibly.

As she squeezed off the last of the rounds, she figured that outside the swim team had run for the hills by now, and the thought of these big bad boys cowering gave her a tiny grin. With the seventy-five-round magazine exhausted, the acrid smell of cordite hung in the air. The gun felt hot and heavy in her hands, even though it was seventy-five rounds lighter; and as the water finally started to calm, she stepped back off the diving board, basking in the inner glow that came with ripping off a mag that big.

Taking off her earmuffs, she could still hear the reverberation of the shots in the chamber. AK-47 in hand, its snout down, she walked over to the door, opened it, and waved at Coach Cunnick to bring his team back in. The swimmers stared at the gun as they walked past her toward the pool.

"Do they know what to do?" Calleigh asked.

Cunnick grinned. "I was just about to tell them when you opened fire. Some of these guys moved faster out there than they ever have in the pool. Had to round half of 'em up out of the shower stall."

The team appeared embarrassed; with their wet, matted-down hair, they were like damp puppies somebody had unsuccessfully tried to drown.

"So, Calleigh," the coach said. "Did you hurt my pool?"

With a madonna's smile, Calleigh said, "Judge for yourself, Phil."

As Cunnick peered over the edge into the water, she could tell that everything looked fine to him from up here; but she knew that the bottom was what mattered to the coach. Well, if he went in with the team, he'd find out soon enough.

"Okay, guys," Calleigh said to the team. "There's seventy-five bullets and their casings at the bottom of the pool . . . and I need them. Who wants to go treasure diving?"

None of them said anything, but the sudden rash of splashes and the fact that in three seconds only she and Cunnick remained standing at the pool's edge spoke volumes about their willingness to help the little lady with the big gun.

Peeling off his team T-shirt and slipping off his gym trunks to reveal a Speedo, Cunnick told her, "While my fellas fetch your bullets, I'm gonna check on the condition of my pool, if you don't mind."

"Be my guest." She was quietly admiring his sinewy frame; she was human. "When you come up, you do plan to apologize for doubting me, right?"

His only response was to flash her a grin; she flashed one back, and he dove into the pool, swimming underwater to stroke along its sloping floor.

Shortly, swimmers started coming up to the edge of the pool and depositing bullets in a small plastic bucket Calleigh provided; another such bucket was for casings. And in less than ten minutes she had all seventy-five slugs and shells.

Cunnick would periodically appear at the surface to grab some air, then disappear beneath the water again. Once he even dropped a casing in the container before going down again, but not on any of his short breaks did he say a word to Calleigh.

When all the other swimmers were out of the pool and she was packing her stuff up, the coach finally dragged himself up and out, grabbed a towel, and started drying off.

"Thank you, Coach Cunnick," Calleigh said as she slung her duffel bag back over her shoulder.

"Oh—it's 'Coach Cunnick' now," he teased, "after you've had your way with my pool."

She laughed once and said, "Well—does the pool pass inspection?"

"Not a scratch," he said with the hint of a smile at the corners of his mouth. "I didn't think it was possible. I guess I do owe you an apology."

She shook her head. "No need. You and your team were a big help."

"Sorry they misbehaved a little."

"Boys will be boys. Actually, they were very sweet after we all got to know each other a little."

He frowned in thought. "But you still can't say what this is about?"

"Sorry—not while the investigation is still ongoing."

"It's the gang thing, isn't it?"

"Sorry."

"How about later? When the investigation *isn't* ongoing?"

She shrugged. "Maybe."

"I'd love to hear what this was about. Over . . . dinner sometime? If I'm not out of line."

"You have my card. You can call me at work. We can talk about it."

He stood with hands on hips, grinning half a grin. "You know, Calleigh—I hope I *do* know as much about swimming as you do ballistics."

"Firearms," she said, and winked.

Then, duffel bag over her shoulder, she walked briskly out.

* * *

The last two days represented everything Andrew Chevalier had been working to avoid.

A heavyset man of ample appetites, Chevalier had skin the color of burnished mahogany, black dreadlocks swept back and tied with a black silk ribbon, and a concrete block of a head, with a face showing scars from knife fights dating back to young days on the island.

Right now, business was good for his Faucones, and the last thing Chevalier and his crew needed was a gang war. But after Mendoza's hit on Wallace, followed by the ill-advised attack on that DEA prick Burnett, all hell had broken loose.

Like most of the gangs, though, Chevalier's Faucones had a mouse in the cop house . . . and that tiny voice had whispered that the investigation's focus was shifting from Mendoza to that Mitus pig, Manny Calisto.

So far, of the local gang honchos, only Trench leader Peter Shakespeare and Chevalier himself had avoided being blamed for the murders. His own gut told him that Mendoza, and not Calisto, was behind the drive-bys; but who the hell knew?

Mendoza had certainly been hit by Burnett often enough to want to see the fed dead; and the hotheaded Culebras leader was capable of doing something as crazy as hitting a DEA agent.

With his own people dying now and his lieutenants screaming for revenge, Chevalier knew what the other gang leaders were going through. That damn Florida governor had already talked about doing to Miami what his brother had done to Iraq. Chevalier knew that if the National Guard came rolling in, they'd all be screwed.

No telling how long the guard would stay in south Florida, and the longer they stayed, the more money it would cost all the gangs—business would be damn near frozen.

On one hand, what Chevalier planned to do today was designed to save his own gang and their high-stakes enterprise; but on the other hand, his plan would save his competitors, too. Even though they hated each other and were trying to drive each other out of business, truth was, if the factions could keep their mouths shut and their hands off each other's throats, they might all survive to enjoy a local pie that had plenty of slices to go 'round.

The first call Chevalier made was to Calisto.

The cell phone number he had for the Colombian drug dealer was, of course, no good, having been changed due to the crisis; but Chevalier was successful in reaching one of Calisto's lieutenants, who passed along the message to another lieutenant and probably another one after that.

Finally, an hour and a half later, sitting in the back of his chauffeured maroon Hummer, Chevalier answered his cell phone.

The voice that came out of the phone was deep and speaking heavily accented English. "Is it you, Chevalier?"

"*Oui.*"

"What the goddamn hell you doing calling me for? You think you can taunt me at will? I will see your skull hung from a spike!"

Definitely Manny Calisto.

This response might have been the gang leader's

answering machine message. The "head on a spike" line was a threat he made to all his enemies, but it was a pretty hollow one—Chevalier had only heard of Calisto actually accomplishing the feat once, and that had been a traitor within his own organization.

Still, Chevalier felt his anger rising as Calisto's diatribe continued. Instead of firing back about how Calisto's troops had been the ones to first open fire on Chevalier's, the Faucones leader forced himself to keep his voice calm as he interrupted the Colombian drug dealer. "Manny, you've made your point. Now listen to me."

"What the fuck!" Calisto shouted. "You dare to order me?"

Then the Mitus leader was off on another rant, and Chevalier just held the phone away from his ear while he waited till Calisto stopped for breath.

When that time came, Chevalier said, "Now, do you want to shout some more, my friend, or do you want to find a way to stop the killing? Before the president's brother sends in the National Guard and puts us all out of business?"

To his surprise, a brief silence followed, and then finally Calisto said, "I'm listening."

"Good," Chevalier said. "We need to sit down and talk. We must find a way to stop this before it stops us. This war will bring us *all* down."

"You think that by the two of us sitting down, we can stop Las Culebras or the Trenches from shooting at each other? And us?"

Sometimes Chevalier wondered how Calisto had ever become head of the Mitus; it was obvious the man was dumber than the chickens on the Chevalier family farm outside Belle Anse, back in Haiti.

"We *all* need to meet," Chevalier told the phone. "You, me, Mendoza, Shakespeare—I would even invite someone from Wallace's camp, if I knew who was going to end up on top."

A long pause indicated Calisto was probably thinking about how Chevalier was dumber than the chickens back in Mitu.

Then Calisto exploded with a burst of obscenities, followed by, "You're out of your damn mind, they'll never go for it! I don't think *I* even go for it!"

For a moment Chevalier wondered if he should just say to hell with it and set out to kill the other leaders. Unlike Calisto, however, the Faucones chieftain knew that killing Mendoza would only give the snake a new head, one that might be even more violent, more ruthless than Mendoza himself.

Patiently, Chevalier said, "Do you think it's a setup?"

"Wouldn't you, in my place?"

"I *am* in your place."

"No—you're the one proposing a sitdown. So how do I know, how do any of us know, it won't be a goddamn trap?"

Chevalier couldn't really argue with that thinking. "Manny, we have to do this. We have to sit down."

"How are you going to convince us it's peace, not war, you're after?"

"We divide the arrangements—you should pick the place, Shakespeare can pick the terms, Mendoza the time . . . that way I make none of the decisions."

Another long pause was followed by Calisto saying, slowly, "That could work."

Good, Chevalier thought. *Progress . . .*

"But," Calisto was saying, "then the problem is Shakespeare and Mendoza will want to know why I get to pick the place instead of one of them . . . and that doesn't allow for Wallace's man to pick anything. Not to mention, that if I was Wallace's man, the only condition I'd wanna set is to get to shoot Mendoza in the face."

"For this meet, we leave Wallace's people out. They're chickens with their heads cut off without their top man, anyway."

"What about my other concern?"

"Split up the arrangements any way that people can agree on—I don't care who picks the damn place, as long as it's somewhere neutral and safe."

Calisto said, "Three days ago I would have said anywhere public. After the Archer . . . I don't know."

Chevalier sighed to himself; this was going to take a while. But it had to be done.

Otherwise, the killings would go on until the National Guard put a stop to it or they were all dead. To survive, the gangs had to have a summit and they had to find a way to make it work. He laid all this out for the Colombian, and when Chevalier was finally finished, Calisto agreed with him.

Then they struggled with the idea for another hour and a half before they had a plan that Chevalier felt comfortable proposing to the others.

If nothing else, he thought he could at least work out a temporary peace pact with Calisto. And if the gang leaders could all come to a consensus, business and life as they knew it could go on.

Chevalier thought, too, that something bigger could grow out of this. In the old days, the days of Venici and Capone, rival gangs had moved away from killing each other into agreements that had given rise to a national crime syndicate.

Who knew? Maybe something positive could come from this, after all. . . .

A brooding Horatio Caine was at his desk running scenarios on how to end the gang war when Calleigh Duquesne came in, the large duffel bag slung over her shoulder.

"All done?" he asked.

"Shooting, yes. Testing? Haven't even started yet." She sat the bag on one of two chairs opposite Caine's desk, then took the other herself. "I just figured you'd want to get this piece of evidence back to LaRussa on time."

"Good thinking."

"I'll start checking the bullets and shell casings right away." She gave him a chipper smile. "Might even be able to give you some kind of report by the end of the day."

"Wish I had a hundred like you," Caine said.

"Sorry. One of a kind."

He smiled, the first time in a while. "Yes you are. . . . Anyway, it probably won't hurt to keep a U.S. attorney at least a little happy. If he turns out not to be implicated in any of this, we'll want him on our side."

Standing, Calleigh said, "Oh, and I printed the

AK-47 before I tested it, but I haven't had time to run the prints through AFIS yet."

Rising himself, Caine slipped on his suitcoat and came around the desk. "Don't be shy about letting me know what you come up with."

"I won't be."

Tripp didn't go with him this time and, when a weary-looking LaRussa came out to the lobby to meet him, Caine held out the duffel bag.

"Twenty-three hours, thirty-one minutes," Caine said pleasantly.

LaRussa tried to smile, but he couldn't quite pull it off.

"What's the matter?"

LaRussa walked Caine off to one side, away from the receptionist. "Pelitier's lawyer just called—our boy's clamming up."

Surprised, Caine asked, "Why?"

LaRussa shrugged. "Hey—we both work in big buildings with lots of ears. These guys have friends in the system. Maybe they got wind that you're retesting the gun, and now they think they can weather this storm without rolling over on any of their confederates."

"But we're *not* reopening his case."

"I know. What you said yesterday was just you . . . playing me."

"Ken, listen—"

"I'm a big boy, Horatio. Anyway, if Pelitier's lawyer heard somehow that you checked that gun out, they're just extrapolating that you're reopening the case."

Thinking out loud, Caine said, "Well . . . if the guy's lawyer knows the gun's being tested—"

"He also knows there's no way that's a bad thing for his client—who has a real good alibi for both Wallace and the Burnett killings, namely having his ass behind bars."

"Us testing his gun doesn't in any way erase what he did in Little Haiti."

Another shrug. "His attorney doesn't see it that way."

Shaking his head, Caine said, "Then Pelitier's lawyer is going to get his client a lethal injection."

"That doesn't help my end game of getting drug dealers off the street, Horatio."

Caine said nothing.

"What about your tests?" LaRussa asked. "You find anything?"

"Too early to tell. When I know more, you'll know more."

LaRussa stuck out his hand. "No hard feelings. We really are on the same team, you know."

This time, Caine didn't mind shaking the man's hand at all.

Andrew Chevalier was surprised.

Which wasn't something that happened to him very often. After spending the whole day on the phone, he'd managed to arrange a summit meeting between himself, Calisto, Peter Shakespeare of the Trenchs, and even the reclusive Antonio Mendoza of Las Culebras.

After Wallace's men had attacked and burned his house, Mendoza had gone underground; the only way the Culebras honcho had agreed to the meet was if everyone brought a lieutenant . . . *and* he got to pick the time and place.

The other gang leaders seemed even more nervous now, and Chevalier himself felt a shiver of fear running through his stomach; but, still, he'd done it—they'd all agreed to sit down and talk.

It might all come to nothing, but at least they were making the effort. Of course the other possibility was that he'd just helped Mendoza set them all up, and by morning they'd all be dead and that crazy Culebra would be the only one left.

After all, a man with the balls to hit a DEA agent was capable of anything.

Chevalier had a plan of his own, in that case.

While most of Chevalier's troops were untrained gang kids with little more going for them than blind devotion to the Faucones' cause, a few handpicked others had been trained to be far more lethal.

If anything happened to Chevalier tonight, Mendoza would pay for it with his life.

In the bedroom of his crib in Little Haiti, Chevalier slipped on his Kevlar vest under an oversized black shirt. He put on a black suit coat and then pulled on a large gold cross. He genuflected and kissed the cross, once, twice, three times. Chevalier, a staunch Roman Catholic, felt sure that Jesus would protect him from harm, just as He always had.

The meeting was set for 3 A.M. in, of all places, the bar of the Archer Hotel.

Boarded up now, the windows had been shattered during the shooting of Kurt Wallace, both the bar and the hotel itself were still closed for repairs. As the scene of the first killing, the Archer bar would seem the least likely place for such a summit.

Which made it the perfect meeting place for four men who wanted no one in the city to see them together.

Half an hour before the appointed time, Chevalier and his most trusted aide, Jean-Claude, pulled into the parking ramp on the corner of Twelfth and Collins. Jean-Claude slid the maroon Hummer into a place, the vehicle's roof a scant few inches from the concrete roof of the parking level.

They climbed down, and Jean-Claude clicked the remote lock. The horn honked in answer, the lights blinked once, and the pair walked out into the cool night air.

As they walked toward Ocean Drive, Chevalier said, "Is Caje ready?"

Jean-Claude—tall, skinny, pockmarked, with a fade haircut—replied, "He's ready. Anything happens to us, Mendoza dies."

"I may have to kiss Calisto's ass to keep the peace— do you have a problem with that?"

"Calisto is a pig."

"The question stands, Jean-Claude."

Jean-Claude's shrug was barely perceptible. "Tell the mother whatever you want, and when the time comes, Calisto will end up in the swamp, the gators feeding on his balls."

Up ahead, the yellow-and-black police tape was in tatters now.

"When the time comes," Chevalier said.

7

Gang of Four

THE PHONE WOKE Horatio Caine, who was sleeping restlessly, anyway, on the first ring. The bedstand clock registered just before four in the morning.

The CSI supervisor threw on a white shirt and dark slacks and a crime scene windbreaker; then, as he strode to his car, he had a thought. He flipped open his cell phone and punched in a number.

"Burnett," the familiar voice said, thick with sleep, possibly drugged sleep.

"It's Horatio. I heard they sent you home. Sorry about the hour."

"No rest for the wicked."

"Or the good guys, either, it would seem." Caine leaned against his car. "And how's the arm?"

"I'm out of the pitching lineup . . . otherwise, it's a glorified scratch. They just kept me the one night, for observation. What's up? You didn't call at four A.M. for a medical update."

"Kind of, I did—to see if you were ready to get back in the game."

"Like I said, long as I don't have to pitch."

"Listen, I know this is too soon . . . after Joanna."

Hell, they hadn't had the funeral yet. . . .

"That's why it's not too soon, Horatio. You got something?"

"I need your help. Somebody wanted you and your gang expertise eliminated from the equation. I could use that expertise right now. Can you meet me?"

"Where?" Burnett said, no nonsense.

Caine told him.

"Whoa," Burnett said. "Back to *that* address?"

"Back to that address."

The sound of Burnett sitting up in bed was followed by, "Listen, I got Nickerson babysitting me . . . staying a few days while I, you know . . . sort things out."

Burnett was talking about another DEA agent, his former partner, the retired Gabe Nickerson.

"Good to have friends," Caine said.

"Mind I ask him to tag along? He's been on the bench a while, but he still knows his stuff."

"Gabe's help would be appreciated."

A half hour later, Caine once again found himself standing on the sidewalk outside the Archer Hotel. No rain fell tonight, but a cool breeze swept in off the ocean, like the ghost of that fateful first night's nasty weather, giving the air a decided chill.

A block north, the tourists had retired for the evening, leaving the Versace mansion a silent tribute to the deceased designer. Caine recalled all too well the day he'd been called to the house and had found the blood on the front stairs where Gianni Versace had been gunned down on the steps of his home.

The famed designer, going out for the mail or morning paper, had been literally blown out of his slippers, shot in the head. They'd found two .40-caliber shell casings and a dead mourning dove at the scene. The search that had followed had led to Andrew Cunanan, Versace's murderer, inside a houseboat bedroom, lying on a bed, where he'd eaten his gun.

The MDPD had worked its tail off on that case, but when the story had made the national news, the FBI had shouldered forward, front and center, to take the credit for bringing down the "mad dog" killer. That was why a case like this one, with its blurring territorial lines, raised so many hackles and hard feelings.

Caine appreciated that Jeremy Burnett had never been the attention-seeking, headline-hogging kind of fed. Burnett took credit for what he did, and the blame for any screwups, and always made sure that if someone from the MDPD helped him on a case, that individual got the due credit. Among the personnel of MDPD, Burnett was referred to as a "damn good cop"—lofty praise for a fed.

"I thought it was the killer who returned to the scene of the crime," a voice behind Caine said.

He turned to see Burnett, just a hint of a smile on the man's otherwise haunted face.

"Well, all kinds of rules are getting broken tonight," Caine said.

The DEA agent looked gaunt, and the healthy growth of beard told Caine the man hadn't shaved since the attack on his house. Oh, Burnett's hair was neatly combed, and his eyes were sharp, and he wore a gray suit and nicely knotted tie. But he was still more than a little shell-shocked—no surprise, as his wife had been killed and he'd been shot barely sixty hours ago.

Caine hoped his judgment hadn't been poor, calling the man in on this.

Accompanying Burnett was a tall, rangy African-American with close-cropped black hair flecked with gray and bright, all-seeing brown eyes. Gabe Nickerson was a healthy, fit fifty, with only an extra ten pounds or so to indicate retirement was having any effect.

Caine was pleased that Nickerson was staying with his ex-partner. Remembering how hard Ray's death had hit him those first few days, Caine knew Burnett could use some support and company about now.

"Guys, I'm gonna apologize for the reaming you're both gonna get," Caine said, "from Matthers."

Nickerson's roughly winning voice said, "What, they gonna fire me?"

"It's just that you both . . . particularly you, Jeremy . . . have a conflict of interest. Let's establish that you're just consulting with me, at my request."

Burnett put a hand on the CSI's shoulder. "And you haven't been squeezed yet for looking into a friend's murder? Violation of department policy, right?"

"With all the bodies piling up right now," Caine said, "and the National Guard breathing down our necks, I don't think my bosses are going to argue with me working *any* case."

"I take it we're not at the Archer," Burnett said, "out of nostalgia . . . or to re-enact a crime."

"Good call," Caine said. "Something went down here tonight."

Both Burnett and Nickerson were frowning, and the former said, "You mean—the killer really did return to the scene of the crime?"

"We should see for ourselves, don't you think?"

Nickerson asked, "Haven't you been inside yet, Horatio?"

"No. Just got the call saying we had another gang hit with four unidentified victims. That's why you're here—to tell us who the dead guys are . . . and then fill me in on the gang politics of what went down."

"Lead the way," Burnett said.

New crime scene tape had replaced the frayed old strips. The front of the hotel was still boarded up, multiple holes in the plywood letting light through from the inside, where halogens were already up. The trio had to go around back, via the alley, to get in.

The rear door led them into a narrow hallway, after which they found themselves passing through the kitchen. Back here, even though the lights were off and those halogens (running off power generators) supplied the only illumination, nothing seemed to be terribly wrong.

"Electricity in the building still off, huh?" Nickerson asked as they moved past the stainless steel counters and cupboards.

Caine nodded. "Bullets did a lot of damage. The owners are talking a complete remodel job."

"Where were *they* the night of the shooting?" Nickerson joked.

Burnett asked, "What about the hotel itself?"

"It should reopen soon—though this kind of thing isn't the best publicity."

Caine passed the back staircase, at right, and pushed open the swinging door that led them out of the kitchen and into the lobby bar, where the halogen work lights were set up. With the plywood-covered windows, a war zone atmosphere held sway, even beyond the broken glass.

But a brand-new mess had been made in the closed bar.

Two card tables were overturned in the middle of the room, each riddled with bullet holes. Eight shot-up folding chairs, metal ones with puckered holes and nasty dents, lay at crazy angles around the room, and near the tables, sprawled on the floor, were four bodies.

Caine had his guests hang back as he stepped deeper into the crime scene.

Speedle, Calleigh, and Delko had come in early to work the scene and they were all hard at it now—Calleigh collecting shell casings near the bar, Delko photographing the bodies, Speed scanning the area for trace evidence.

They all looked barely more alive than the corpses; even Calleigh was sporting dark circles under the eyes. These gang-war-inspired double shifts were taking a toll.

The foursome on the floor consisted of two Hispanics and two black men, all shot to death, each hit multiple times. Immediately Caine knew two of them.

Unfortunately, one of the dead Caine recognized as Manny Calisto, and the CSI supervisor suddenly realized he'd made a major mistake asking Burnett to come here tonight.

Going back to where he'd left the duo, stepping between the DEA agents and the bodies, Caine raised his hands, palms out, as if surrendering, saying, "I'm going to have to ask you and Gabe to step back outside, Jeremy."

Burnett looked surprised and confused. "Why in hell . . ."

Caine thought about it, then decided to just lay it all out. "We ran the partial license plate you gave us on the car in the drive-by at your house."

"What did you find?"

"The plate is a partial match to a Lexus owned by Manny Calisto."

"Yeah, hell, I told you myself it looked like Calisto's ride." Then, slowly, the truth began to register with Burnett. "Oh, shit . . . Calisto must be one of the dead vics in there. You saw him, Horatio?"

"I saw him."

"Which makes me a directly interested party."

"More than that, I'm afraid."

Nickerson clutched Burnett's sleeve. "He's saying you're a suspect."

Burnett's eyes met Caine's and locked.

"Unless," Caine said in his measured way, "you can give me an airtight alibi for the time of the murder, you are indeed a suspect now."

"You know that's bullshit," Nickerson frowned.

"But you saw it, too, Gabe," Caine said. "You're a cop."

The big man was getting ready to launch into rant mode, but before he could, Burnett held up a hand.

"Horatio's right," Burnett said. He looked at his former partner. "And your instincts were right, too, Gabe." Turning back to Caine, he said, "Let's deal with it now. Right now."

"Fine," Caine said. "But not here."

Caine walked the pair carefully back outside and across the street, where the conversation reconvened in the shadow of the Versace mansion.

A businesslike Burnett asked, "What are you figuring for time of death? Did they tell you that on the phone?"

"They did. And unless the ME suddenly changes his mind, an hour or so ago—just after three."

"Well, hell," Nickerson said. "That's easy—he was with me! We were asleep then."

Burnett nodded. "Gabe's been right with me since he picked me up at the hospital."

Caine looked long and hard at Nickerson. He'd known the man for years and knew him to be as honest as Burnett. The problem was, some might say friends like this would cover for each other—cops who worked together for years were like soldiers. Which could be a bond transcending family.

Still, he would be damned if he would punish the pair for being cops.

"All right," Caine said. "I'm going to trust you, but I can't let you back in. Did you touch anything while you were in there?"

Both men shook their heads.

Hands on hips, Caine looked sideways into nothing, thinking it through.

Then he said, "You were far enough from the bodies that there won't be a lot of trace evidence—"

Nickerson was pacing. "I can't believe this shit . . ."

Burnett, however, remained cool. He said to his partner, "You know the drill, Gabe—when Horatio catches the killers, he doesn't want anything from us to've contaminated the scene."

"We're cops!" Nickerson blurted.

"You aren't anymore," Burnett reminded him. "You're a *friend* of a cop whose wife was presumably murdered by one of the vics. Settle down, buddy."

"Good advice," Caine said.

Burnett continued, "Gabe, a defense attorney would make hay outta this—my presence here could create reasonable doubt."

"Listen to the man," Caine said. "Jeremy, I appreciate your understanding here—particularly since I called you in."

"No problem, Horatio. I know where your heart is."

"Good. But my head's gotta go back inside—and you gentlemen can't."

Calmed down but still owly, Nickerson said, "What? We're dismissed?"

"I'd appreciate it if you hung here a while," Caine said. "I'll be back with Polaroids of the dead in five minutes."

"Oh, you still want our help on IDs," Nickerson said, vaguely pouty.

"Yes I do."

"No problem," Burnett said again. "We'll wait."

But glancing over at Nickerson, who was pacing the sidewalk again, Caine wasn't so sure.

Back inside the hotel, Speedle gave Caine a Polaroid camera, and the CSI supervisor snapped off face shots of the four dead men. Then he went back outside to show them to Burnett and Nickerson.

"Calisto, of course," Burnett said redundantly, looking at the first photo, then passing it on to Nickerson.

"Never prettier," the big man agreed.

Caine handed Burnett the second photo—the other face the CSI supervisor had already recognized.

" 'There are more things in heaven and earth, Horatio,' " Burnett began, looking at the photo.

Caine's eyes narrowed. "Peter Shakespeare?"

"The same. Leader of the Trenches."

Nickerson was frowning. "The Trenches and the Mitus were getting together? Isn't that like the Hatfields sitting down with the McCoys?"

"Exactly like it," Caine said. "And maybe sitting down with someone else—we got four more chairs than there are bodies, in there. They might have been waiting for somebody else."

"A supplier, maybe," Burnett offered. "Maybe they were consolidating their business to try to take on Mendoza, in the wake of Calisto hitting Wallace."

"Maybe somebody invited the gang leaders to smoke the peace pipe," Caine said, "and then that somebody smoked the guests instead."

Burnett and Nickerson exchanged meaningful glances and nods.

"This looks like a Faucone," Caine said and held up the third photo to Burnett: a light-skinned black man with long, unruly dreadlocks and a bullet hole over his right eye.

But both Nickerson and Burnett shook their heads.

Burnett said, "That's Shakespeare's second-in-command—they called him Yellow Boy, but his real name was . . ." He looked to Nickerson for help.

"Kingsbury," Nickerson said. "Robert Kingsbury."

"Shakespeare's second-in-command?" Caine asked. "I don't know every gangbanger in town, but the ones at the top usually register. How come I've never heard of him?"

"Just got a promotion," Burnett said with a shrug. "When Marcus Harriot got sent up."

"Now he's been promoted again," Nickerson said. "To dead."

Caine did know the name Marcus Harriot—Shakespeare's former top lieutenant, who'd just been sent to the federal prison in Atlanta on a life sentence.

"And number four?" Caine asked, displaying another Polaroid.

Burnett didn't miss a beat. "Jose Valdez—one of Calisto's bodyguards. Spent most of his time back in Colombia, and he wasn't related to the little guy with the burro and the coffee, either."

"He'd been seen around the Miami area more and more lately," Nickerson added. "He's a trigger-happy little prick."

"Used to be," Burnett said, with an eyebrow lift.

Caine's eyes narrowed again. "Either of you have any ideas about why these two factions would be together, other than consolidation?"

"Besides your summit notion," Nickerson said, "not a thing."

Burnett took a long moment. "What if they already *were* consolidated. . . ."

"I'm listening," Caine said.

"Maybe they both were in on the Wallace hit . . . and the attempt on me. And now they were getting together, in a neutral place that had fallen off everybody's radar. . . ."

"To plan their next move," Nickerson said, picking up the thread, nodding. "Maybe to hit Chevalier and the Faucones—maybe Las Culebras."

Caine nodded. "Any ideas on who hit the final four?"

Nickerson gave Caine a sarcastic smile. "You mean other than my partner, here?"

Burnett, gently scolding, said, "Gabe. . . ." Then the DEA agent turned to Caine. "Chevalier or Mendoza might've found out what Calisto and Shakespeare were up to, and popped them . . . but my money would be on Wallace's people."

"Really," Caine said.

"If they figured out Calisto was behind the hit on their boss, it wouldn't surprise me at all, if they were just watching and waiting for an opportunity to cap his ass."

Nodding, Caine said, "Thanks. Jeremy, I know this is hard, but I really do appreciate the help."

Burnett suddenly had tears in his eyes. "Horatio . . . this is the most alive I've felt since . . ."

Caine squeezed his friend's shoulder.

Nickerson offered his hand to Caine, by way of "no hard feelings," and the two men shook and took their leave.

Caine went back inside the most popular murder

site in Miami, to help his people process the crime scene.

By noon, results from the Archer were starting to filter in.

Caine called the team together in the layout room. Alexx leaned against the table opposite him; Delko and Speedle were, as usual, sitting on the counter, and Calleigh leaned against the doorjamb. The faces of Caine's CSIs showed tiredness, but their eyes were alert.

"Four more to add to the body count," Alexx said. "All shot to death—although I think a different gun is indicated here than in the Wallace and Burnett attacks."

Calleigh nodded. "We know the same AK-47 was used in the Wallace and Burnett hits. This time, more than one gunman, each with a different weapon. One looks to be an HK53, which takes a 5.56 mm 45 round."

"Heckler and Koch," Caine said and made a disapproving click in his cheek.

The noted German gun manufacturers had developed the HK53 for law enforcement and antiterrorist squads; now the other side was using them against the police.

"Guns are real democratic," Calleigh said. "They'll let anybody play with them."

Alexx asked if Caine minded if she got back to her work, and he released her. He didn't envy what she was up against. Then he returned his attention to Calleigh.

"What about the other weapon?" Caine asked her.

"Probably an Ingram, which is a .45 cal . . . unless our killer went old school and pulled out a Thompson."

The Ingram, too, had been designed as a police

weapon, this one manufactured in Peru. Which meant the drug cartels had a much easier time getting them on the black market.

"So," Caine said, "we don't see these as the same hitters as the others."

"Based on the guns," Calleigh said, "no. This would seem to be part of the escalating gang war." She smiled, eyes flashing. "I *did* find out some interesting things about the gun we got from Ken LaRussa, though."

"Which is?" Caine asked.

"It's definitely the gun that was used to kill Kurt Wallace and Joanna Burnett."

Caine's sigh was like the rush of breath from a punch in the solar plexus. "And how did it get back into the evidence locker?"

She bestowed her biggest, brightest smile on him. "I hope that's a rhetorical question, Horatio, because I don't have a clue. But I'm sure you'll find a way to explain it."

"Thanks."

"Is our pal LaRussa behind all this?" Speedle asked.

"Too soon to tell," Caine said. "The U.S. attorney has been cooperative, even if it took pushing him. But I'll be having a talk with Ken, soon as we're done here."

"While you're doing that," Speedle said, "maybe some of us should have a little chat with Andrew Chevalier."

"The Faucone gang leader," Caine said. "Because?"

"His prints showed up at the Archer on a chair and a table. One of his henchmen, a guy named Jean-Claude Navarre, was there too, or at least his fingerprints were."

"Starting to sound like a summit-meeting-turned-trap," Caine said. "Speed, when we're done here, get ahold of Tripp, and see if he'll accompany you for a visit to Chevalier . . . if you can track him down."

Delko raised his eyebrows. "The surviving gang leaders gotta be keeping a low profile right now."

"A sound if obvious observation, Eric," Caine said. "Anything else to share?"

Delko nodded. "Calleigh tested that Valor pistol I found in the sewer. Nothing to do with the gang shooting, but we tied it to a month-old murder in Bayfront Park."

"Interesting," Caine said.

Calleigh put in, "A woman was shot there during an apparent purse snatching."

"Any other evidence?"

Delko picked it back up. "Not much. No purse or wallet."

"The ever-popular Jane Doe?" Caine said.

"Jane Doe the day we found her—and we never have identified her."

Caine considered for a moment, then said, "Work that when you have time, Eric, but for now, I want you to concentrate on the gang case."

"Will do," Delko said. "Oh, and we found Calisto's car in a parking garage on Collins Ave."

"Tell us."

"Silver Lexus, Dolphin license plates LDX145—matches the description you got from Jeremy Burnett."

"Any body damage?"

Delko shook his head. "None—looks like it rolled out of the showroom."

"And we know the Archer murder vehicle swiped a parked car."

Speed smirked. "H, he's had time to get it fixed."

"Right," Caine said. "Let's get on the Lexus dealers, then, approved body repair shops."

Delko said, "And junkyards?"

"Yes. See if Calisto got a new fender somewhere. Anything else?"

Delko had one more. "We found Shakespeare's car parked at a meter on Ocean Drive. We processed it. Nothing of interest."

"Good work, everybody," Caine said. "That's all I have—anyone?"

Heads shook as Delko and Speed climbed off their counter perch.

"Then," Caine said, "let's go see if we can stop a war."

Ken LaRussa, seated behind his massive desk, hands folded prayerfully, leaned forward and asked, "You've got something?"

Horatio Caine, seated opposite, said, "I told you when I knew more, I'd share it with you, Ken."

"Good. I do appreciate you keeping me in the loop."

"Calleigh matched the bullets and the casings. The AK-47 you gave me, the one Julian Pelitier used to kill those people in Little Haiti, is in fact the same gun that killed Kurt Wallace and Joanna Burnett."

LaRussa turned pale. "No . . . that's impossible. Your 'Bullet Girl' finally *did* make a mistake!"

"Judge for yourself, Ken." Onto the desk Caine flipped a photo showing two bullets, side by side. The distinctive markings the bullets received exiting a hot barrel were clearly visible. And identical.

Frowning, LaRussa studied the photo. "Both . . . both of these came from the AK?"

"Yes."

"How the hell is that possible?"

"Well, now, Ken, I don't know," Caine said honestly. "But you better help me find a way to explain it, before you become the most likely suspect in these multiple homicides."

LaRussa's eyes were as dismayed as they were wide. "Suspect?"

Caine nodded.

Sitting up, LaRussa said, "You want to be very careful about how you throw around a word like that, Horatio."

"I can understand your reaction, Ken. Let's walk it through. You're in charge of the evidence room."

"Well . . . technically, yes."

"And you don't like drug dealers."

"True," LaRussa said tersely, his eyes flicking occasionally to the photo of the bullets, still clenched in one hand. "But who does?"

Calmly Caine continued: "You have access. You have motive."

LaRussa's eyes closed. "All right. All right, I can see your point."

"Unless, of course, you can explain what Calleigh came up with in that photo you're holding."

The attorney looked at the photo one more time, then tossed it wearily on the desk. He leaned on an elbow and touched two fingers to his eyes.

"I . . . you . . . you know I can't," LaRussa said. Then the U.S. attorney sat up, placing his hands palm down on the desk. "This is my *career* we're talking about."

"Actually, Ken, it's the lives of nine people, including Joanna Burnett. *That's* what we're talking about."

"I . . . I didn't mean to downplay the importance of the . . . victims."

"I want you to answer one question, Ken. And look right at me."

LaRussa's eyes met Caine's.

"Are you guilty, Ken?"

The question hit him like a slap, but then he straightened and said, "Hell, no!"

Caine held the man's gaze. "If you are, Ken . . . we'll catch you. You know how good my team is."

Slowly, LaRussa nodded. "That only benefits me, Horatio . . . because I'm innocent."

"You know . . . I believe you."

Hope flared in the attorney's eyes.

Caine raised a forefinger. "And if you're telling the truth, *and* my instincts are right . . . then I just know you're going to want to cooperate fully with me and my people."

LaRussa thought about that. "Listen, Horatio . . . I'm also an attorney. And I know I have my rights—"

"Sure you do." Caine shrugged. "I just kinda thought you'd want to help us clear your name . . . you know, before this gets to the media."

"Are you threatening to leak—"

"No. We don't play that game. But as you said yourself, we work in big buildings in a big city. We need to move discreetly . . . and quickly."

Swallowing, La Russa sat forward again. "I'm ready to cooperate, Horatio. What do you need?"

"To start with, a list of all the guards from the evidence room . . . and all the videotapes, for those periods when guards aren't on duty."

LaRussa sighed. "What else?"

"I need to have the perimeter guards from those off times interviewed. They might have seen something without even realizing it."

LaRussa's eyes again widened. "Going to take some time to get all that together."

"I suggest making that happen within the next twenty-four hours," Caine said. "Oh yes—we'll also need a complete inventory of the weapons in the evidence room."

"That's against policy, about six ways—"

Caine smiled placidly. "Do we really care, Ken? Consider this—someone not only smuggled a gun out of here, they smuggled it back in, too. What better place to find a weapon than in among a thousand others—and what better place to hide it?"

"You have a point," LaRussa said. He looked about ten years older than when Caine had entered the office. "Horatio, just how screwed am I?"

"Well, if you're lying to me, and you're behind this thing—you're lethal-injection screwed."

"Please. . . ."

"If you didn't do this . . . and I don't think you did . . . you've just been incompetent in one phase of your job, meaning you'll likely get a slap on the wrist from your boss."

"What about the media?"

"Out of my control. But nobody hears anything about this from us."

LaRussa laughed suddenly—a hollow laugh. "You know, that AK-47 is downstairs right now. How do you know, Horatio, that I won't destroy that evidence? Throw that damn thing in the ocean?"

"I think we have enough, even if you did. But I really don't think you're guilty, Ken."

The lawyer seemed slightly heartened by that. "Why not, Horatio?"

"You're not Dirty Harry; you wouldn't go around shooting up the bad guys. You want to put the gangbangers behind bars so you can make a name for yourself and become a senator. You're not a criminal, Ken—just a politician."

LaRussa laughed again, a grunt. "Thanks for that much, anyway."

"Hey, criminal, politician. It's a fine line."

And this time when Caine left LaRussa's office, the state's attorney did not offer to shake hands.

Little Haiti had encompassed some of the older Miami areas—Little River, Lemon City, Buena Vista East, and Edison Center—to become a thriving part of the south Florida metro area.

Home to nearly 34,000 residents, the area teemed with the verve, music, and bright colors of its Caribbean namesake. Though centered around Northeast Fifty-fourth Street, roughly between North Miami Avenue and Biscayne Boulevard, Little Haiti ran further north up around Northeast Third Avenue and 80th Terrace—a neighborhood with a different rhythm, more muted colors, and the sweaty desperation that came from fighting a war twenty-four-seven.

This was the territory of the Faucones, the fiefdom of Andrew Chevalier, and Speedle and Tripp had been driving around that fiefdom most of the afternoon with no success. Little Haiti was little in name only, and they weren't having any luck finding the Faucone leader.

Plus, their unmarked police car couldn't have yelled "Cop" any louder if it had been a blue and white; and no one in this part of the city liked or wanted to talk to the police.

They were getting ready to hang it up for the day when Speed's cell phone chirped. He jerked it off his belt and punched a button. "Speedle."

"Horatio."

"Sorry, H—we're not having any luck finding Chevalier. We checked out three of his supposed cribs, and nada."

"That's because he's not in Little Haiti."

"Where is he, then?"

"Apartment house near the airport. Says he wants to meet."

Speedle's forehead frowned and his mouth smiled. "Turning himself in, is he?"

"Not sure. I didn't get the call, dispatcher did. Meet him, will you? You're closer than I am. . . . And Speed? Gun in hand."

Caine gave him the address, and before long Tripp was parking the unmarked car in front of a low-slung two-story stucco building painted the color of orange sherbet. Hands on hips, Speedle appraised the place, estimating eight apartments total.

Speedle pointed. "H said Chevalier's in number eight, second floor, back left."

"Well," Tripp said, removing his sidearm from its hip holster, "let's go see what this fine concerned citizen wants to talk about."

"Let's," Speed said with a smirk, getting his own weapon out.

They entered through a flimsy door, walked up stairs whose carpeting was so frayed that one could easily hook a toe and trip. On the second floor, the ratty carpet continued as they went down the hall past the muffled sounds of crying kids and soap operas and game shows, stopping at the last door on the left—apartment eight.

The hallway smelled of fried food, but Speed couldn't tell if the aroma came from number eight or the apartment across the way. Neither of them stood directly in front of the door. Instead, guns in hand, they each took a side. Tripp gave Speedle a look, then he knocked on the door.

A moment later, the door cracked open and an African-American woman showed them half her face, a sullenly attractive half a face at that.

"Miami-Dade police," Tripp said, his free hand indicating the badge on his sportcoat pocket. "I'm Detective Tripp, this is CSI Speedle. We understand Mr. Chevalier wants to talk."

"You won't need the guns."

Tripp and Speedle exchanged glances and holstered their guns. But both kept their hands on the holstered butts.

She said, "Better," in her thick Carribean accent,

then closed the door. They could hear the chain lock being taken off.

The woman opened the door again, and Speedle saw that the half face he'd seen through the open door did not lie. The woman was really something—tall and thin, Tyra Banks with a short, choppy Afro, wearing a Cabrerra University Hurricanes T-shirt and very short denim shorts, with a slow way of moving that made him think that every single action was a bother to her.

They entered a living room decorated in what Speed thought of as Early Trailer Park—a TV on a stand in a corner surrounded by a garage sale sofa and two heavy armchairs, possibly salvaged from an out-of-business beachfront hotel. The dining alcove to their right featured an aluminum card table and four folding chairs.

"Where's Andrew Chevalier?" Tripp asked.

The woman curled a finger and led them down the hall.

Tripp went first, his hand still on the holstered weapon. Speed watched as Tripp glanced into the bathroom without fully moving in front of the door, then turned and did the same thing with a bedroom on the left; Speedle noted the clean but minuscule bathroom and a tiny empty bedroom.

Their hostess stopped at a door on the right at the end of the hall. She knocked lightly, then went in, closing the door on them, leaving them in the hall.

They'd caught a glimpse of a darkened room, but more significantly, a stench rolled out and caused Tripp to turn away, toward Speedle, gagging.

"What the hell is that smell?" he asked.

Speedle said, "Chicken blood."

The detective gave Speedle a *Say-what?* look.

"Voodoo healing spell."

"Voodoo? Like in sticking pins in dolls?"

"Voodoo," Speedle said, "like in Haiti. Chevalier's birthplace. A lot of people believe Haiti is also the birthplace of voodoo in this hemisphere."

"Do tell."

"It was, in fact, recognized as a legal religion there this past spring."

"Yeah, well, remind me to subscribe to the Discovery Channel."

Speedle shrugged. "You might like it."

The woman opened the door and nodded for them to enter.

They gave each other *what-the-hell* expressions and followed her into the darkness. This time, Speedle took the lead, careful to step over the trail of chicken blood just inside the door.

The walls were a dusky gray, the only light filtering in through partially closed venetian blinds. The room was dominated by a huge king-size bed that barely left room to walk around. Speedle noticed that the trail of chicken blood circumnavigated the room and that dead chickens, their necks wrung, their feathers wilting toward the floor, were hung in each of the corners and in front of the room's only window.

In the bed, naked, a sheet haphazardly thrown over his loins, lay a large black man with flowing dreadlocks: Andrew Chevalier.

The drug dealer was easily recognizable to Speedle, even though the massive man's face was masked by blood-soaked bandages. Other bandages covered wounds to both arms, one leg, and a spot about even with his pelvic bone on the left side.

The CSI had seen enough gunshot injuries, in his time on the job to know that the numerous and serious wounds that Andrew Chevalier had suffered were unlikely to be overcome by voodoo magic.

8

Murder Suite

THE MOODILY ATTRACTIVE African-American woman slipped onto the bed beside the wounded Chevalier, his facial bandages like a bizarre blood-spotted blindfold. She used a wet cloth she'd taken from a tiny nightstand to wipe his fevered brow.

"Call nine-one-one *now*," Speedle said to Tripp.

But Tripp already had his cell phone out.

A raspy breath racked the drug dealer, his massive torso shuddering. Then a very small, hoarse whisper for so big a man found its way out. "Who are you? Who's there?"

"I'm Tim Speedle, CSI. With me's Detective Frank Tripp."

"Homicide," Tripp said.

The faintest smile appeared on the sweat-beaded, bandaged mahogany face. "You're just . . . a bit . . . early."

Tripp said nothing; he had 911 on the line. He stepped back into the hall to finish the call, while Speedle maintained vigil and the lovely nurse in denim short shorts soothed the big blind man's brow.

"Help's on the way," Speedle said.

Another ragged breath preceded, "You . . . you sound like a boy. I called for . . . Horatio Caine."

"I'm a big boy," Speedle said. "I work for Caine. He's kind of tied up trying to stop this gang war."

"So . . . so was I . . ."

Speedle sat on the edge of the bed and leaned closer. "Is that what you were doing at the Archer?"

"It . . . was. And look . . . look what happened to me."

"It's not the Nobel Peace Prize," Speedle admitted.

The woman frowned at Speedle. "You strainin' him. Easy, now."

Speedle said to her, "We'll get him to a hospital."

But it was Chevalier who answered, with something that was half laugh, half death rattle. "Too late for that . . . we both know that. Tim, is it?"

"It's Tim. Look, man, we're gonna try. You're talking to me. You're still alive. You hold on."

Chevalier made a movement, probably intended to be a shrug, though it was more like another shudder. "If I die here . . . I die in the safety . . . the arms . . . of my people. You understand? Why that . . . appeals?"

"Sure," Speedle said.

"If you . . . you get me to the hospital . . . and they patch me up? Well enough for, what . . . another twenty-four hours?" He grabbed a wheezing breath. Then he went on. "Don't you think . . . they come back, and finish the job?"

Tripp stepped back into the room and nodded to Speedle as he took out his notebook.

Time was not on their side, and as much as Speed didn't like to push a dying man, he had an interview that needed doing . . . which was in the dying man's interests, after all, since helping find who killed him was about all Chevalier had left.

"Mister Chevalier—who did this to you?"

The big man didn't miss a beat. "Don't know, damnit. Don't know. Mendoza maybe . . . Wallace's people, could be . . . somebody who found out about our plan."

"What plan?"

Chevalier made a slight gesture with his head, looking blindly toward his pretty nurse, who understood and lifted a glass of water from the nightstand, held it out with one hand, and steadied a straw with the other as the big man sipped.

Swallowing appeared to be painful, and it took the Faucones leader a moment before he was ready to speak again. Speed didn't feel like rushing the dying man, though every second now meant so much.

"Sir," Speed said.

"It . . . it was my plan, really. I think, if I can get the Faucones, Mitus, Trenches, and Culebras together . . . to sit down . . . we could stop this war. Governor declares martial law, all of us lose."

"But somebody turned the peace talk into a hit."

The ganglord managed a brief nod; his wheezing breath grew ever louder.

Speed asked, "Where's your friend Jean-Claude? His fingerprints were at the Archer too."

Chevalier turned his head slightly toward the woman. *"Ou le Jean-Claude est?"*

"Dans le Hummer."

The hooded, bleary eyes trained themselves on Speedle again. "There's a row of four garages . . . behind the building. . . . My Hummer, it will be inside one. Jean-Claude will be inside it."

"Is your friend dead?" Speedle asked.

"Very. . . . I was blinded . . . but Jean-Claude, he got me out of there . . . back to the car. We escaped, but I could tell . . . by his breathing? He was wounded, too . . . could not talk. I ask him to take me here. . . . Sareena is a friend. I knew she would help."

The woman, whose sullenness Speedle now read as sorrow, patted her patient's forehead with the cloth again.

The CSI asked, "Are you up to telling how it went down?"

After another signal from Chevalier, the woman gave him a drink again. Sipping, then swallowing hard, he coughed, in that death-rattle way, and Speedle wondered if the big man had crossed the finish line.

But a moment later, the drug dealer's breathing calmed to a wheeze.

"I negotiate all day, with the other three—we agree to meet at the Archer. Place was closed, didn't think nobody would think we'd go there."

"Somebody did," Speedle pointed out.

"Somebody. . . . Jean-Claude and me, we get there first. It was, after all, my idea for all of us to meet. Jean-Claude checked the main floor, the bar, the lobby, found no one. No sign anybody broke in and got there before us."

"What about upstairs? The empty hotel rooms?"

"We . . . we all agreed we'd each bring only one . . . one aide. I didn't feel comfortable, having Jean-Claude upstairs while I was on the first floor alone."

"Why didn't you go up with him?"

"I . . . I'm a big man. . . . Elevators were down . . . I don't like the stairs. Trouble breathing."

Not like the trouble breathing Chevalier would have any second now, Speedle thought, then asked, "Who was next to arrive?"

"Shakespeare . . . him and his man, they come in next. While the Trench and me, we stay downstairs, Jean-Claude and Shakespeare's guy do the quick sweep, upstairs. I know they did the second floor . . . don't know if they made it to the third."

"So Manny Calisto was the last to arrive?"

"*Oui.* He come in, sit down, and before one damn word gets spoken . . . the shit hit the fan."

"Then Mendoza never made it to the party?"

"No. He . . . miss the fun."

"Or started it," Speedle said.

"He could have. He set the time, the place."

"Why?"

"Different parts of the arrangements, these we split up . . . for . . ." His laugh hurt him. ". . . safety sake."

Chevalier's breathing became more labored, and it was obvious that the end wasn't that far away.

"What about Wallace's group?"

"They weren't invited. They're in too much . . . what's the word?"

"Flux?"

"Yes. Flux. But his men, too. *Oui*, they could have done this thing. 'Specially if they think Calisto is behind the shooting of their boss."

"So, they came in blazing. How many of them were there?"

Chevalier held up two fingers.

"Two?"

"*Oui*."

Speedle and Tripp exchanged glances.

"There were six of you," Tripp said. "They musta been good."

With a feeble nod, the big man agreed. He accepted another sip from his nurse, coughed once, then said, "They jump into the bar from the back."

Speedle knew this meant the hit squad could've come through the back door, the kitchen way, or down the rear stairway from the upper floors of hotel rooms.

Chevalier was saying, "One went to the right, one the left, and before you know it, Calisto and his man—dead. I don't think they even knew the assassins were there. Too fast. Too fast."

"But you saw them?"

"Yes. . . . Jean-Claude, he try to leap in front of me, but we are both hit, and go down."

"Did you see Shakespeare get it?"

"*Oui*, but at least his man got his gun out and fired one round before he was killed."

"Did he hit either of the shooters?" Speedle asked.

"I don't think so . . . but I couldn't see. Jean-Claude's body was on top of me by then, and . . . the bullets, one cuts across my face, blinds me."

"Did you see either of their faces before you were hit?"

"They were in black, faces covered, ski masks. Gloves too."

"Pros, you'd say?"

"Very. Very pro."

"How did you and Jean-Claude avoid these two finishing you off, right there and then?"

"They think we were dead. They check the bodies, Jean-Claude said . . . the other two first. Then sirens start—somebody on the street must have called it in, and you people must've been close by. Anyway, they left, way they came . . . leaving us for dead."

"Did they ever speak to you? Or each other?"

"Nothing at first . . . then, when they thought we were all dead, were checking the bodies, Jean-Claude told me they communicate with hand signals."

"Did you have anyone stationed outside?"

"No one. We each brought one person. To do otherwise was bad faith. . . . Anyway, who knew we were there but ourselves?"

"There's a good question."

"Mendoza! He's probably behind this, but I suppose someone else could've found out, somehow. My people I trust . . . but the others . . ."

His voice trailed off in a delirious fit of coughing.

The woman tried to wipe the big man's forehead, but he batted her hand away as if she'd suddenly become an adversary. In the distance, the siren of an approaching ambulance told Speedle the big guy's chances had just improved.

"Easy, buddy. Your ride's here."

And it was—before the ambulance even arrived.

Chevalier's response to Speed's comment was to abruptly stop coughing, quit thrashing, and lay quiet.

Speedle checked the man's pulse, then looked back at Tripp and shook his head.

The lovely, somber woman keened quietly next to Chevalier.

"You're Sareena?" Speedle asked her.

She nodded once.

"Is this your place?"

She shook her head.

"No more questions," she said in a melodic alto, "Now I mourn this man." She slipped her arm around Chevalier and drew him close.

"We can find the car without her," Tripp said quietly.

"I know," Speedle said, "but H'll give me H if I don't do this."

The CSI moved nearer the woman and said, "Ma'am, I'm going to have to ask you to move out into the other room."

She glared at him, eyes and nostrils flaring, like a horse that was about to kick.

"We need to solve your friend's murder," Speedle said. "He's evidence—everything he's wearing, and his . . . remains, as well. This is a secondary crime scene, and I'm going to have to ask you to vacate."

She withdrew her arm from around the big dead man. She kissed Chevalier on the forehead. She got off the bed and walked up to Speedle.

Then she said, "Go to hell."

And, with great dignity, she left.

Tripp was smiling just a little. "I think she likes you, Speedle."

Speedle smirked humorlessly at the detective, and they exited, too.

They met the EMTs at the door, two skinny guys whose name tags said JOE and BOB respectively, both wearing black-frame glasses and looking like conjoined twins who'd been separated. Sort of.

"He was shot at least half a dozen times nearly twelve hours ago," Speedle told the Joe/Bob twins. "It's a miracle he lasted as long as he did. And keep the woman out of there, okay?"

She was seated at the kitchen table, smoking a cigarette.

"What do we look like?" Joe said, grinning.

"Idiots?" Bob said, grinning.

Speedle felt no response was necessary.

As the EMTs headed down the hall, Speedle said, "We're gonna check out back—we think we've got another d.b."

Tripp led Speedle downstairs at the rear of the building, coming out into a tiny parking lot. Near the building were five parking places; opposite was a four-car garage, each door likely representing a different tenant. All four doors were down, and the building had no windows. Moving across the lot, they both tried two of the doors and found them all to be locked.

"Should we call a locksmith?" Tripp asked.

Speedle shook his head. "Let me try something."

As Tripp looked on, the CSI withdrew a small leather pouch from his back pocket and flipped it open.

"Lock picks?"

"I'm a man of many talents," Speedle said dryly.

Then, choosing two picks, he returned the pouch to his pocket and got to work on the first door.

Six minutes later, Tripp, who was not known for his patience, asked, "Sure you don't want me to call you a locksmith?"

"Go ahead," Speedle said. "Call me a locksmith."

And the CSI flipped the handle, then lifted the door. The garage was empty.

Tripp looked around inside. "They don't connect."

"Who says you're not a great detective?"

While Tripp looked on, eyes narrowed, trying to decide if he'd just been insulted, Speedle pulled the door down, twisted the lock, and moved on to the next one.

The second garage was home to a car—a VW, hardly Chevalier's Hummer.

That vehicle lurked behind door number three.

And the obviously very late Jean-Claude was slumped over the console, apparently shoved out of the way for someone else . . . somebody alive . . . to drive the car.

Or to park it, anyway. Speedle's guess was Sareena had put the Hummer and its occupant in the garage after she had somehow guided Chevalier up to the apartment. Chevalier was large, to say the least, blind from his wounds, and had lost a great deal of blood; slender Sareena would have had a difficult time getting him up the stairs.

How had she managed that? Speedle wondered—voodoo, maybe?

Turning to Tripp, Speedle said, "I better start working the scene."

Tripp nodded and headed off. "I'll have a chat with Sareena."

Speedle called to him, "Find out how she got him up the stairs! My guess is she had help."

Tripp gave Speedle a long look. "Who says you're not a great detective?"

Then the two exchanged grins and got to their respective jobs.

Speedle began by flipping open his cell phone to call his boss.

"Horatio," the cell phone said.

"H, we found Chevalier and Jean-Claude Navarre. Both dead. Chevalier died on us, but Jean-Claude's getting ripe."

"Let's hear the whole story."

Speedle told Caine everything.

"All right, Speed, you work the scene there—I'm going back to the Archer and see what we missed."

"Who says we missed anything, H?"

"Have we solved it?"

"Well, no."

"Then we missed something. Did any of our unit go higher than the first floor?"

"No. There wasn't any real reason to, since the killings went down in the bar. These guys blew in through the back, and just started shooting, right?"

"Do we know that? Couldn't they have already been there, waiting?"

"That stairway off the kitchen, you mean."

"Yeah—holed up in a hotel room."

"That's not bad, H."

"Thanks, Tim. Stay in touch."

Horatio Caine, seated behind his desk in his office, cut off the call with Speed. He was about to go find Delko to recruit him for the Archer trek when he looked up to see Ken LaRussa standing in his open doorway.

The U.S. attorney's gray suite looked typically crisp; the U.S. attorney did not.

The haggard LaRussa said, almost pitifully, "Can we talk?"

Caine nodded and waved the lawyer in. His shirt collar unbuttoned and his tie a loose noose, LaRussa shuffled over and dropped into a chair across from Caine. Red-eyed, face drawn, he said, "I did the inventory, like you requested."

"How many guns are you missing?"

The attorney stared into nothing. Then he quietly said, "Half a dozen."

Caine nodded. "One's an H&K HK53, one's an Ingram. . . . What are the others?"

LaRussa's mouth dropped open. "How the hell—"

"You heard about the hit at the Archer last night? Calisto, Shakespeare, Chevalier, and company?"

"Of course."

Caine twitched a non-smile. "Those were two of the guns that were most likely used in that attack."

His head fell back. "Oh, shit."

"That about sums it up."

LaRussa sat forward, clasping his hands like a beggar. "I brought everything you asked for—security video, lists of guards *and* the shifts they worked the last month—the whole nine yards. And I personally brought it over in my car. One of your guys—Delko, is it? He's unloading it now."

What did the guy want? A gold star? Pat on the back?

But Caine said merely, "Thanks, Ken. Hopefully, there's something there we can use."

LaRussa let out a massive sigh. "What I haven't figured out, Horatio, is how you're going to get through all of it."

"We'll just take as much time as we have to take."

"Even with the clock ticking like it is?"

"We strive to be quick, without hurrying it."

The attorney swallowed thickly. "Uh . . ."

"Yes, Ken?"

"Am I . . . under arrest?"

"No. But I wouldn't start organizing that senatorial campaign committee just yet."

He laughed hollowly. "Funny, isn't it?"

"What is, Ken?"

He shambled to his feet. "How your priorities can change overnight?"

"You didn't have a loved one killed, Ken. Maybe you should count your blessings."

"Horatio—about now, I can do that on the fingers of one hand. . . . Let me know what else you need."

"I will, Ken."

And the attorney trailed out of Caine's office like a lost child looking for a path in the forest.

Caine felt a stab of sympathy for the man, but he reminded himself that LaRussa, however cooperative, was still a strong suspect.

Cutting through the lab, Caine found Calleigh hard at work, happily lost in the tedium of trying to match bullets from the latest crime scene. Further along, he found Delko camped in front of a monitor, already watching tapes of the evidence room at the James Lawrence King Federal Office Building. Not wanting to take them away from these potentially productive tasks, Caine decided to go back to the Archer by himself.

Soon Caine was parking the Hummer in the yellow in front of the Archer Hotel. He fetched his crime scene kit, showed his badge to the officer out front, crossed the fresh crime-scene tape, and headed for the back of the building. As he came around the corner, a uniformed officer approached him, and Caine held up his badge again.

The cop opened the rear door for Caine, who slipped into the darkened hallway. He gave his eyes a moment to adjust: the power was still out in the hotel. From his sportjacket pocket, he withdrew his mini Maglite and hit the power switch. Then he laid the light on a nearby counter, set down his case and pulled on a pair of latex gloves.

After picking up his gear, he played the beam of the flash around the corridor and didn't see anything he hadn't seen before. This wasn't the floor he was worried about, however—he and his detail had gone over the first floor thoroughly.

Once again he moved past the stainless steel cupboards and cabinets of the kitchen, but he did not go through the swinging door into the bar; rather, he turned right, heading up the back stairs toward the second floor.

The steps were narrow, the carpeting new. He bounced the beam back and forth, particularly on the floor, as he scanned slowly for trace evidence. The electrostatic print lifter would be of little use on this carpeting, and if—as Speedle had reported Chevalier as saying—the killers had worn gloves, the chances of getting fingerprints off the banisters were poor.

Just the same, Caine didn't touch either side as he climbed to the second floor.

At the top, he emerged into a tiny alcove that met the corridor that took a right toward the front of the building. He followed the hall, his flashlight helping him search for any trace evidence. Testing doors as he went, Caine found them all locked—eight rooms on this floor, four on each side, none open. In the front, he found a cramped check-in desk and a display full of brochures touting the sights in the south Florida area.

The Archer was one of those Ocean Drive hotels that made as much, if not more, off their bars and restaurants as renting out their limited number of rooms. For that reason, the check-in desk was moved off the first floor to provide more space for restaurant and bar seating.

In this cobbled-together check-in area squeezed onto the second floor, the front desk consisted of dark, cheap wood topped with a Formica counter, arrayed with mini-stands of more brochures and a short stack of complimentary Miami *Herald*s. Behind the counter could be spied the top of a computer monitor and printer; beyond that the traditional wall of cubbyhole mailboxes.

Caine shone his light around behind the desk;

without power, he couldn't turn on the computer, but maybe he could find something else to help him.

And in a drawer to the right of the computer, he found exactly what he was looking for—a short piece of plastic, about the size of a credit card. Caine examined the Ving key under the light: in gold letters, on one side, were printed the words *Property of Archer Hotel—Pass Key*.

Key in latex-gloved hand, Caine returned to the far end of the hall. If the gang watchdogs had come up, as a security measure before the aborted peace powwow, to do the same thing he'd just done, they'd probably assumed that, since the doors were locked, no one was in the rooms.

Sloppy thinking, guys, Caine thought. *Got you killed.*

Because if the killers had hidden on the second floor, chances were they'd lurked behind one of these locked doors; and it made sense that, since they'd entered from the bar from the rear, the hit squad had probably stayed in a room toward the back.

His personal choice—had he been planning the hit downstairs—would be to pick the room that right now was on his right. Should anything go wrong, the hitters would have a firing line from there to the back stairs. Because of the angle, it wouldn't be a great line of fire, but it would be better than having no shot into the alcove at all, which was what the room across the hall would provide.

Shining his light on the lock with one hand, he used the other to slip the pass key into the slot, then pulled it out. Normally, a little green light would come on and you could open the door. Without power, he didn't know for sure if the key would work. . . .

But the light flickered, and Caine heard a faint click. He pushed down on the handle, throwing his shoulder against the door as he went. The door opened, and he was inside.

Holding the door open with his foot, he lifted his crime scene case from where he'd set it down out in the hall.

Alone in the dark room now, Caine drew the curtains. Even with the sun going down soon, light from the city at night would supplement his flashlight.

First, he swivelled around the room, getting the layout: a queen-size bed jutting out from the wall at left, a nightstand on either side; across the room, a small round table with two chairs beside it, a long dresser, with a TV atop, running along the wall immediately to his right. He took half a step back and shone the flashlight into the bathroom.

Bingo—a tile floor . . .

Now he had a chance of getting a footprint. His beam found the toilet—the seat was up. *Well, at least one man had been in here. . . .*

For the first time in this case, Horatio thought they might finally have caught a break. One chance to collect this evidence; that was it. He started with the electrostatic print lifter. He pressed the Mylar sheets out on the floor one at a time, hit them with the charge, then picked up the sheet and cataloged it. When he was finished, he had half a dozen sheets of Mylar, each the size of a folded-in-half newspaper.

Next, he went into the bathroom on his hands and knees and picked up any hair or piece of fuzz, or anything else he might find. Each tiny sample went into an evidence envelope and was cataloged.

Finally came the toilet. A dirty job, but somebody had to do it, and the CSI supervisor was elected; so much for executive privilege. But this could prove a key job—after all, it might identify the killer. Of course, it could also identify some innocent tourist with a bad aim. . . .

Still on hands and knees, Caine carefully went over the rim of the toilet with his flashlight . . . and then, near the front edge, he saw it—the glistening yellow liquid pearl. Using a cotton swab, he picked up the sample from the porcelain surface. With that cataloged and everything loaded into his crime scene case, he was ready to start on the big room.

He began with the bed. Using a RUVIS (Reflective Ultraviolet Imaging System), Caine went over the bed seeking bodily fluids. The RUVIS would illuminate any human by-products—sweat, urine, semen, feces—and, as Caine well knew, most hotel rooms were literal hotbeds of DNA samples. Finding a couple of hairs on a pillow, he bagged them, too, and slipped the envelope in his pocket.

As he dusted the table and chairs for prints, the scenario played out in his mind. . . .

There are two of them in the hotel room; the hit team may or may not have a third and or fourth member waiting in a car on the street for a quick getaway.

They've been watching out the window, waiting for their guests to arrive: Chevalier, Calisto, Shakespeare.

The three gang leaders and their goons are here now, just one flight of stairs down. These two know Mendoza isn't coming . . . doing his bidding perhaps, or otherwise aligned with him. . . .

One of them is in the bathroom. He takes a leak, drips once, zips up, and joins his confederate in the room.

They're ready now.

Each has an automatic weapon—one an HK53, the other an Ingram. They lock and load and silently move to the door. Using hand signals, one warns the other that two underlings are scouting the hallway.

The killers wait, their guns aimed at the door just in case.

They're ready if the fight breaks out up here instead of downstairs. This is not their first time at the rodeo. . . .

The knob moves, turning slightly, one of the scouts trying the door of this room. Fingers tighten on triggers and the killers tense . . .

. . . but the knob holds, the door's locked, the scouts are satisfied.

Idiots.

The killers listen carefully, hear the scouts go to the end of the hall, trying every door, then doubling back and going down the rear stairs . . . the very path the killers will be taking momentarily.

They wait for a short time, allowing themselves to relax and calm from the adrenaline rush. Very soon, the adrenaline will be flowing again; but until that moment, they must be calm, relaxed . . . and most of all, silent.

One signals that it's clear and they're going ahead. The other unlocks the door and slowly opens it. They slip into the hallway, in sync, two people moving as one.

They creep down the stairs, careful to keep to the edges so the steps won't creak beneath their weight. In the distance they can hear the faint voices of their prey as they chatter nervously, wondering where Mendoza is, no doubt.

The killers get to the bottom of the stairs. The kitchen is pitch black, the only light coming from a small lantern Chevalier brought and has sat on top of the bar.

Signaling again, the killers make their move. They explode through the doorway, one cutting to the left, the other going right, toward the bar. The guns spit fire, the bullets buzzing like homicidal insects, stinging fatally, casings ejecting, each clinking as it hits the floor, the smell of cordite flooding the room.

One hitter takes out Calisto and the Mitu guard with him. Neither man knows what hit him—they're dead before they touch the floor.

The second hitter is only a millisecond behind his confederate, but it's enough: the Faucone bodyguard jumps in front of Chevalier. The killer nonetheless manages to drop them both, the bodyguard hit in the chest, Chevalier hit at least once in the face, taking several more as he lumbers down.

The first hitter shoots Shakespeare, but the Trench's guard has pulled out his gun and fires wildly as this killer takes his time, swivelling toward the shot and letting off a quick burst that opens the Trench's chest to send up a misty pink cloud as the man falls to the floor, dying. The first hitter signals to the other, they begin to check the dead, but soon sirens in the distance encourage haste.

What the hell? None of the victims are moving; then another hand signal, and they're out the door.

Caine smiled grimly. Probably took them about half a minute to pull off the slaughter. . . .

Fingerprinting done, Caine loaded up his kit. He took a moment and sat in a chair at the little round table and broodingly tried to put the pieces together. But he remained somewhat out of his element, with these gangbangers.

Impulsively, he called Burnett on the cell phone.

"You in the middle of anything?" Caine asked.

"No. Just got back from making arrangements for Joanna. Listen, would you be one of the pallbearers, Horatio?"

"Jeremy, I'd be honored."

"No. The honor's ours. . . . But this is your call, Horatio—what is it you wanted?"

"Some more consulting."

"No problem. You making any progress on last night's hit?"

"Yes."

"Excellent."

"For one thing, we found Andrew Chevalier alive. He's gone now, but he talked before he went."

"Oh, that's a break."

Caine filled Burnett in, broad strokes.

Then Burnett said, "Sounds like you're thinking Mendoza."

"Well, he's the one who didn't show for the meeting. That sure pins the prime-suspect ribbon on him. Of course, it could be someone inside one of the organizations."

"An internal power play?"

"Yeah. Like you said, Jeremy—it's banana republic politics. You got any ideas along those lines?"

"Hmmm. Chevalier's people were all loyal, at least as far as we knew. They all felt like family. A lot of them have ties back to Haiti."

"What about Shakespeare's crew?"

"Well, that guy didn't trust anybody and probably with good reason. The Trenches were just as apt to kill each other as one of their rivals."

"So they're a possibility."

"Sure, only I doubt Shakespeare would've told anyone in his organization what he was up to and where he was going. Shakespeare was so paranoid, he probably didn't even tell the lieutenant he brought along the *real* reason."

"That leaves Calisto's crew."

"With the Mitus, it's all about the green. They go with the flow—the cash flow. Calisto's inner circle was trustworthy, far as it goes . . . again, according to the intelligence we had. And the ones outside the circle would never hear about a meeting like this."

"Which brings us back to—"

"Mendoza. He did set the time and place."

"He did indeed."

"Hell, Horatio, he might've booked his guys into that hotel as soon as he got the call."

Caine grunted a non-laugh. "It's got to be him."

"Why?"

" 'Cause we haven't figured out a way for anyone else to have found out about the meeting."

"It is starting to sound like Mendoza. Any idea where to find him?"

"Not," Caine said, "the slightest."

Burnett laughed, once. "I been there. . . . Give me a couple of days. Maybe I can scare him up for you."

"Is Matthers cool with this?"

"I wasn't planning on asking permission."

"Don't like putting you out on that limb," Caine said. "But I'll take any help I can get."

"Horatio, I been there, too."

Caine and Burnett exchanged good-byes, and the CSI supervisor gathered his kit—and his evidence—and checked out of the Archer.

9

Boots Made for Walking

EVERYONE CAME IN BRIGHT and early on Saturday—well, early anyway.

With the death toll over sixty and counting, that meant overtime for everybody. The extra pay, as well as the chance to close cases, made up for the tough hours. But Horatio Caine's crew had taken on a zombielike air, and the CSI supervisor worried that even these dedicated pros might compromise their work.

Nothing to do but bite the bullet (or, in Calleigh's case, process it).

The chief of the MDPD, after all, had passed the word down the line—verbal, not a memo—that this war had to be stopped by weekend's end or first thing Monday morning, the National Guard would come marching into Miami to occupy the city and declare martial law.

Nobody wanted that—not the police, the mayor, or the businesses who depended on tourists for so much of their income. Martial law sent the unmistakable message that the MDPD had failed in its mission to protect and serve.

Like the chief, Caine saw that as something that could not be allowed.

Miami had been battling a fluctuating reputation for at least two decades, with its drug-wars image; much of that had been overcome in recent years, in large part due to the excellence of a police department of which Caine's CSI Unit was no small factor.

Once tourists decided that Miami wasn't safe to visit, wooing them back was an iffy and difficult procedure. And who could blame them? If the city couldn't protect its own citizens, it wouldn't be able to protect tourists, either. The economic impact of this sort of war could be extremely damaging in the long run, and catastrophic in the short run.

Much as he abhorred politics and concerns driven by commerce, Caine prided himself on his role in keeping this volatile city safe for its citizens and its visitors. Sometimes working the aftermath of violent crime could wear on CSIs, drive them to depression and even despair over the human condition.

Caine continually told his people, "Our goal is justice *for* victims, by the apprehension of perpetrators, which prevents *more* victims."

A crisis like the gang war had a bad side effect: Other crimes, non-gang-related murders in particular, were in danger of receiving short shrift.

Right now Caine sat at his desk, sifting through the piles of information relating to such cases generated by his team over the last five days. The problem with murders was that one never knew what piece of evidence would be the key one; so the CSIs indulged in a kind of evidence overkill, collecting every possibility, each fiber, fingerprint, anything that might conceivably provide a lead.

The team had been diligent with these cases, too, but the reality was the system was being choked by the sheer abundance of evidence collected in three-score homicides.

Lab technicians worked around the clock; still, it seemed like victims were piling up faster than the lab results. Priorities were supposed to be in place, but sometimes the evidence chain hit a road bump and you got the sort of thing that Caine was looking at now.

According to the report generated from the fingerprint lab overnight, they had gotten prints off the Valor pistol Delko had found in the sewer outside the Archer.

It had already been established that the gun appeared not to be related to the gang shooting, that it had been the murder weapon in the killing of a Jane Doe.

Of two sets of fingerprints on the gun, one belonged to a young man named Jimmy Hamilton, who'd been printed when he'd gotten a job at the Palace jai alai fronton. The other set was unidentified. Gang war or not, this was too good a lead to let pass by. . . .

The detective of record was Yelina Salas. The robbery/homicide detective was one of the best in Miami, but she was also Caine's sister-in-law . . . or, anyway, former sister-in-law. She was his brother Raymond's widow.

They worked together frequently and clicked well,

but an awkwardness remained. Actually, even when
Ray was alive, there'd been an awkwardness, as Caine
and Yelina had dated prior to her involvement with
his brother. Even now, three years later, both of them
were trying to deal with their sorrow over Ray's death
and an attraction that Caine sensed was mutual,
but . . . well, awkward was the word.

He gave Yelina a quick call, and she agreed an interview with the Hamilton kid was called for.

"You should probably come along," Yelina said. "If
you can tear yourself away from this gang war."

"Do you really think I'd figure our murdered Jane
Doe should have to wait in line?"

"No."

"Pick me up?"

"Sure."

Soon, she drove up out front, and he hopped in. He
was wearing the shades he was never without out-
doors, and a sportcoat and tie. They exchanged smiles
and greetings.

"So much for my day off," Yelina said. Her original intention this Saturday was reflected in her at-
tire: jeans and a sleeveless black top with a scoop
neck.

He always glanced away when he first saw her, like
his eyes were a child's fingers and the detective's
beauty a hot stove. Yelina managed to look both slender and voluptuous, a tall, commanding woman with
a huge mane of dark hair; her wide blue eyes, long,
straight nose, and full lips, all set in an olive complexion, lent her an exotic quality.

"You ready for this?" she asked.

"Yeah. I've been over the evidence."

She smiled faintly; sometimes he suspected she found his stiffness around her a little amusing.

The drive to the Hamilton family home was thankfully short and easily filled with small talk about Caine's nephew, Ray Jr.

Just off Galloway and Southwest Fourth, the middle-class stucco home painted a very light pink was typical of the neighborhood, a low-slung one-story structure with a tile roof and an attached two-car garage. The doors were closed, but a white Vibe was parked in the driveway.

They went up to the front door, Yelina in the lead; Caine, as a cop himself, did not always defer to the detectives on cases, as CSIs in some jurisdictions were required to. But out of respect, he usually gave Yelina that courtesy.

The detective rang the doorbell, and a young man barely twenty-one—which he'd have to be, to work at the Palace Fronton—opened the door. He wasn't a bad-looking kid, with his short dark hair, bushy eyebrows, and cleft chin. Harmless looking, in a Palace T-shirt, jeans, and socks.

At first, seeing a beautiful woman in a scoop-neck top, the kid grinned, but it was more embarrassed than flirtatious. "Whoa. Hello."

"Hello." Yelina held up her badge. "Are you Jimmy Hamilton?"

The color drained from the kid's face; he nodded.

"We're from Miami PD. I'm Detective Salas, this is Lieutenant Caine. May we come in?"

"Do you . . . need a warrant or anything?"

Hands on his hips, Caine smiled tightly at the boy. "Why, son? Have you done something wrong?"

He swallowed and said, "I just . . . I mean . . . Come on in."

The kid opened the screen door for them and led his guests into the living room. The house seemed neat and orderly, nothing too cheap, nothing too expensive, everything very middle of the road and in good shape—rent-to-buy furniture that had been paid off.

The young man was sweating now, though it wasn't terribly warm in the house, and his brown eyes were darting, looking at anything in the room but the two cops.

Caine and Yelina exchanged glances, acknowledging how sadly easy this was going to be. Her expression asked Caine if he'd mind carrying the ball here.

So it was Caine who asked, "Why don't you sit down, son—mind if we do?"

"No. Please."

The boy sat on the edge of an armchair and his guests took the couch. Caine leaned forward, and his smile was of the tough-love variety.

"Jimmy, we're really busy right now. Maybe you've seen the papers. Bit of a crisis."

The boy swallowed, nodding. "These gangs, shooting everything up."

"That's right. So we don't have any time to waste right now. We're not going to beat around the bush here, Jimmy." Eyes narrowed, Caine met the young man's eyes and held them, then he spoke in a very measured, meaningful fashion. "We've got . . . your fingerprints . . . on a gun we found."

The boy's hands came to his face, and he began to weep.

Yelina and Caine exchanged another glance; both were compassionate by nature, but it was too early in the game to offer support.

"The gun," Caine said, "was used to kill a woman in Bayfront Park."

Swallowing, Hamilton looked up, face streaked with tears. "I . . . I know."

"Did you kill that woman?"

Hamilton wiped his eyes on his T-shirt, pulling it up and exposing his pale belly. "No! No . . . God, no."

Again Caine glanced at Salas, who looked as confused as he felt. *Why the tears, then?* Caine wondered.

But what he said was, "Jimmy . . . if you didn't shoot this woman, how did your prints get on the gun?"

The kid let out a long, shuddering breath; his lower lip quivered, but he managed to hold back further tears. For now.

He said, "I knew you'd be coming here someday."

"Is that right."

"I . . . I don't know how I knew . . . but I knew. And I promised myself that, no matter what, I'd tell you the truth."

"That's good, Jimmy."

"I wasn't . . . wasn't strong enough to come forward. Too afraid."

Again, the detectives traded glances.

"But when you came," the boy was saying, "I swore to myself, I'd tell you what happened."

"Then, Jimmy, why don't you?"

"Well, first off, like I said . . . I didn't kill that woman."

"But you know who did?"

"Yes. Mike Garner."

Another shared glance, then Caine said, "Jimmy, that name doesn't mean anything to us. You're gonna have to bring us up to speed."

The kid began to cry again.

Yelina rose and handed him a tissue from her purse; she put a hand on his shoulder. The boy looked up at her with a trembling smile and thanked her. Then he blew his nose, and she sat back down.

"Garner is this . . . this bully who's always kicking my ass. He's like my, my . . . nemesis." He swallowed snot and straightened up. "Well, finally, I got sick and tired of it . . . and . . . I decided I was going to kill him."

Caine raised a hand. "Jimmy—we're going to have to take a second now, and give you your rights."

He nodded. "Like on TV."

"Like on TV," Caine said. "Detective?"

Yelina read the boy his rights, which he said he understood.

Then, carefully, Caine said, "Would you like to go on, Jimmy?"

"I . . . I would. Or should I get an attorney or something?"

"That's your choice. But if you didn't kill this woman, maybe you should just get it off your chest."

"That's what I want to, Lieutenant."

"So this Mike Garner was a bully. Wasn't deciding to kill him a little . . . extreme?"

"Not when you been getting humiliated and beat up by the same person for five or six years."

"Tell us about that."

Hamilton nodded, touched the tissue to his nose, gathered his thoughts, and then said his piece.

"Mike Garner had been kicking my ass since high school. We were in shop class together, and he'd make fun of me and it spilled out on the sidewalk, after school. Anyway, I thought it would stop after high school, but it didn't. I enrolled at Dade County Community College and, wouldn't you know it, there was Mike Garner again. Two more years of his bullying me, taking money from me, vandalizing my car, scaring off any girls that might have been interested in me—"

"Jimmy," Yelina said gently. "Why didn't you call the police?"

"Garner said he'd kill me if I ever told anybody anything."

Caine said, "Did you believe he would do that?"

"I saw him kill a dog once—with a hammer."

With a raised eyebrow, Caine said, "So you kept quiet."

"Yeah . . . and then when I got the job at the Palace, I figured I was finally rid of him for good."

"But," Caine said, "you weren't."

"No. He started coming in as a customer. After that, he began staking out my car, and I'd find him waiting for me when I got off work. He seemed to really get off on making my life miserable. I was some kinda . . . sick hobby for him. Finally, I got so scared, I got a gun."

"The Valor," Caine said.

Hamilton swallowed, nodded. "My uncle had given it to my dad for protection—you know, in case anybody ever broke in. But my dad wouldn't touch it. He doesn't like guns, so it's been in his dresser ever since. There it was, just waiting for me to take it. So I did."

"Where are your parents now?"

"Missionary work in Mexico. You know, trying to save people? Through the Lord. They'll be gone another month or so."

Caine wondered if these parents considered their son worth such attention.

Then he said, "So you're here alone?"

"Yeah."

Yelina asked, "Did you think he might come here and try something?"

"Anything was possible. He's sick in his head."

"So," Caine said, seeking forward movement, "you were afraid of Garner, and carrying the gun—"

"Yeah, and finally I turned the tables on Mike. I followed him one night—from the American Airlines Arena, on foot. Heat pre-season game that night? I caught up with him at Bayfront Park. My plan was to go up to him, call his name, and when he turned around, I'd . . . I'd shoot him."

"But your plan didn't work?"

He made a self-deprecating face. "Not hardly. When I called his name, he whirled on me, saw who it was and started to laugh, he was kinda drunk from drinking beer at the game, and I . . . I just choked. I couldn't do it. I was afraid. It was just a few seconds, but it was enough for him to take the gun from me."

He covered his face with a hand. Not weeping now, though.

"Jimmy," Caine prompted.

He looked up, red eyes unblinking. "Then . . . then he slapped me. He slapped me till I fell on my knees. He said he was going to punish me. This woman came walking by . . . she was homeless, I think, she had a bag of pop cans. Only she wasn't dirty or in rags like most homeless people—she even had a kind of beat-up purse over her shoulder. And he said, 'Hey Jimbo, watch this!' And he shot her!"

He began to cry again.

Yelina went to him, offered him another tissue, and put a hand on his shoulder.

He dried his eyes and went on, occasionally looking up at Yelina, and then over at Caine.

"He . . . he shot her. Right there, right in front of me. It was Mike Garner that killed that poor woman. But I gotta say, he seemed . . . seemed kinda surprised he'd actually done it. He almost was, like, scared, when he told me that if I ever told what he'd done, if I ever tried to cross him again in any way, he'd kill someone who really meant something to me—not . . . not just my dog, this time. He meant my parents."

"Jimmy," Yelina said, "can you prove any of this?"

The kid shook his head. "I didn't see anybody else around that part of the park."

"There was," Caine said, "a second set of finger-prints on the gun."

For the first time, hope sparked in the boy's eyes. "See! That proves it. They gotta be Mike's prints."

"Even so," Caine said, "what that proves is that you both touched the gun. Did anyone see the two of you together anywhere that night?"

"No. I knew he was going to the game. I didn't sit with him or anything—we weren't exactly pals. And after he shot the woman? I took off running . . . but he caught me and made those threats."

Caine asked, "That purse you mentioned—the dead woman didn't have that on her, Jimmy."

"Oh, that's 'cause Mike took it off her, after he shot her. I guess he wanted to make it look like a robbery. But I thought all it did was make her look even more homeless."

"Jimmy," Caine said, "you're going to have to come with us."

His expression turned hurt. "But . . . I told you the truth."

"I believe you did."

Alarmed, the boy said, "It's not for murder, is it?"

"If what you've said is confirmed by our investigation, no. But you did help conceal a murder."

"I know. And I . . . I hate myself for that."

Yelina said, "The intimidation, the terror Garner has committed against you . . . if we can confirm that, Jimmy, that'll be mitigating circumstances."

"So I may not get in too much trouble?"

Caine said, "Just keep cooperating, son."

Yelina cuffed him, and they led the young man out to the car. When the kid was locked in the back, Caine looked over the roof of the vehicle at the detective. "Afraid I have to get back to my gang war."

"I know. I'll get a search warrant for Garner's house, and serve it with a uniform."

He nodded. "Good. I'll send a CSI with you. I'll also be getting a court order for Garner's finger-prints."

"Just let me know when the paperwork's ready."

"Will do," Caine said.

He knew he could trust her to deal with this situation. The young man sat in the backseat, no longer crying; he seemed relieved, more than anything. Maybe they'd done some good here, today.

On the way back to the lab, Caine phoned DEA agent Jeremy Burnett.

"Any line on Mendoza?" Caine asked.

"Very damn little, Horatio. Problem is, he's got to have figured out we're looking for him, and he's gone way underground. We'll keep at it—we've got our ways."

Back at the lab, the news wasn't much more en-couraging.

"Anything?" the CSI supervisor asked Speedle, who was seated at a lab counter.

Speed made a disgusted half-smirk. "Chevalier's Hummer didn't tell us anything we didn't already know. He and Jean-Claude were both shot to death—which it didn't take a CSI to figure."

"How did he make it to that apartment?"

"He was a big guy. Hard to kill."

Caine lifted his eyebrows. "But not impossible."

Speed nodded. "Good point."

In the morgue, Alexx agreed with Speedle about the cause of death.

"Nothing much for you, Horatio," she said. "We're still in the wonderful world of gunshot fatality."

Delko was working on evidence from the second Archer hit.

"No one had used that hotel room for the whole week before the Wallace hit," he said. "Business must've been slow at the Archer."

"But it picked up, didn't it?"

"Sure did. Good news is, if we can find your hitter, we can match his DNA with what you got out of the room. That little dribble was a big help."

Small progress at least.

Caine asked, "Did the DNA lab give you any idea how long?"

"They put a rush on it, but you know how far behind they are. We'll be lucky to see it by this time next week."

One step forward, two steps back.

"Keep at it, Eric."

Calleigh was smiling when he finally tracked her down, finding her not in the firearms lab but seated before the AFIS computer, working fingerprints.

The Automated Fingerprint Identification System gave them a massive database of prints to check against, and judging by her smile, Calleigh had just hit one.

Hands on his hips, Caine said, "You've found something."

"Yes I have. I just identified Pablo Santoya."

"Good for you—who is he?"

Pointing out a picture on the monitor, she said,

"Small-time freelancer. He's done a little bit of everything over the years, but he's avoided hard prison time."

Caine studied the picture of a Hispanic male who could be anywhere from twenty-five to thirty-five. Santoya had coal black curly hair and a droopy black mustache. To Caine, this seemed a possible match to the hitter seen at the first Archer hit and the Burnett attack.

Calleigh was saying, "Mr. Santoya didn't wear gloves for the last twenty rounds or so that he loaded into the drum magazine."

"Why would that be?"

"Hard to say. Possibly he was loading the drum with gloves on, like a good boy . . . then got distracted and had to deal with something that required taking his gloves off."

Caine nodded. "And when he went back to finish loading the drum, he absentmindedly did so without putting the gloves back on."

"Good a theory as any. Even so, we only got about three useful prints off those twenty casings, and nothing off the ones ahead of them."

On his cell phone, Caine punched in Burnett's number again. The DEA agent answered on the first ring.

"Horatio. Jeremy, what do you know about a freelancer named Pablo Santoya?"

"Never had the honor of meeting the man, but I know his work. He's a real scumbag. Why? How does he figure?"

Caine hesitated. Santoya might well be the man who killed Burnett's wife, and Caine had no desire to send the DEA agent off on a vengeance tear.

The CSI said casually, "His name just came up as someone we should interview."

"Well, watch it, Horatio—the guy is bad news."

"Appreciate the advice, Jeremy."

He ended the call, then returned his attention to Calleigh. "Do we have any idea where Santoya is?"

She handed him a slip of paper. "This is his last known address."

"These guys often have multiple cribs—"

"Well, that one's all we've got."

"Then I'll check it out."

"Horatio—this isn't a nice man."

He smiled. "I appreciate the concern."

Lightly, she said, "No problem."

The address belonged to an unprepossessing two-story clapboard house just off Calle Ocho in Little Havana. It might have belonged to a family or a little old lady. In fact, it belonged to a suspected murderer, a freelance perpetrator of dirty deeds not necessarily done dirt cheap.

Uniformed officers and the Emergency Response Services team had the structure surrounded before Caine and Tripp went up to knock on the door. As Caine and the detective climbed the four concrete steps, three ERS men in full gear were right on their heels. Everyone, including Caine and his team, had on headsets so they could stay in communication.

Caine could see sweat running down Tripp's face; obviously, the no-nonsense detective was convinced this was the house of the man who had gunned down all those people at the Archer. The bulldog detective's eyes and jaw were firmly set; if a tougher, more street-savvy cop was on the MDPD, Caine didn't know who it could be.

Tripp already had his weapon out, and Caine pulled out his own pistol as they reached the top step. After making sure his backup was in place, Tripp reached out and knocked on the door.

No response.

Large windows on either side of the door were heavily curtained: a gang could be inside, or no one at all. Tripp knocked again.

And still got no response.

The ERS team leader came onto the headset. "We've snaked a camera in under the back door—no sign of movement inside."

"Copy that," Tripp said into his own headset. "Bring up the ram."

"Ten-four," said a voice in Caine's headset.

Delko came on next. "H, there's a garage back here. Silver Lexus inside, with damage to the right front quarter panel."

"Stay put, Eric! Don't get any closer to that car until we know where our suspect is."

"Ten-four."

Two ERS officers hustled up the stairs, hoisting a battering ram with handles on either side. They pulled it back once, then slammed it forward, smashing the knob and lock, splintering the cheap wooden door.

Officers piled into a bachelor-pad living room at odds with the house's exterior, from velvet nude paintings to a huge projection TV, black leather couches, and glass coffee and end tables. The invaders swept their guns around, searching out targets.

Another crash told Caine a team had bashed in the back door and was coming in through the kitchen. The two teams moved swiftly, meeting up in the dining room. The team in back sent two men to the basement, which they reported as clear. The team in front sent two men upstairs.

"He's up here," reported a voice in Caine's headset. "Suspect has been shot twice in the back of the head."

Then another voice came through. "Got another one in the bathtub! Double tap in the back of the head, too."

Caine's stomach lurched.

He had the sudden feeling that they had just caught up with the hit team, but that whoever controlled the shooters had just severed all ties. . . .

Slipping his gun into his holster, Caine said, "All right—everybody out, and step careful! You're in the middle of my crime scene."

Slowly, the ERS team made their way out the front door.

Caine followed them onto the porch. "Guys!"

Faces turned his way.

"Those of you who were on the second floor, and those who were in the kitchen, leave your boots with me."

One of the ERS guys, apparently new, turned to him. "Why, Lieutenant?"

"Because," Caine said, in an easy lecture style, "your footprints are in that crime scene. And I have to have your shoes so I can eliminate those as the shoes of the perp."

The guy frowned and was about to say something else when the team leader came over and put a hand on his shoulder.

"Just let him have the damn boots and he'll get them back to you as soon as he can."

"But, Sarge, it's the only pair I've got!"

"That's why God made socks. Live and learn, kid, live and learn."

Amused by this, Speedle jumped in and gathered the boots, allowing the CSI supervisor to get back in the house and start working. While Delko and Calleigh processed the car, Speedle came in with his footwear collection and worked the house with Caine. So many feet had trampled through the first floor and up and down the stairs that searching for footprints would be a less than wonderful task.

On the second floor were two bedrooms and the bathroom. Caine stopped in the doorway of the latter and looked into the tub, against the far wall. The body in there was that of a shirtless Hispanic.

Not a lot of blood, unlike what one saw in some movies. The vic had been hit with a small-caliber round, probably a .22, and the bullets had pinballed around inside his skull. Twenty-twos didn't make a big mess, but they did provide a large death.

Moving on to the bedroom across the hall, Caine looked through the door to see a body laying on its stomach on the floor. This vic's hands were tied behind him with a plastic electrical tie; as advertised, he too had been double tapped in back of the head.

On this one, however, Caine could see a bushy mustache, leading him to believe he was looking at

Santoya, the Wallace and Burnett shooter; the guy in the bathtub, then, had been the wheelman. The corpse wore an unbuttoned shirt, chinos and was barefoot.

"All right," Caine said to Speedle. "You take the bathroom, I'll take the bedroom. Footprints first, just in case."

Speedle nodded, took the few steps to the room he'd been assigned, and got started. Pulling on latex gloves, Caine hoped for a small miracle. He needed something to tie Antonio Mendoza to these two men, or he'd face an uphill battle connecting Mendoza to the attacks on Wallace and the Burnetts, let alone all the other attacks that had happened over the last week.

Conveniently, these two being dead would allow him to try to tie them to DNA from the hair and/or the urine from the Archer. Plus, if he checked their closets, he figured he would find boots that'd match the prints he lifted from that hotel room's bathroom floor.

In that case, he could close the deal for murder on these two without much trouble. But tying them to Mendoza (or one of the other gang leaders) would be a challenge.

The floor was neglected hardwood, which gave him a chance of usable footprints. He started by using the electrostatic print lifter on the high-traffic areas. As he thought, he lifted a ton of overlapping prints, which would take the computer a good deal of time to sort out.

After finishing the floor, he went over the body to make sure he'd gotten all the trace evidence. Then he carefully cut off the electrical tie; not that he expected to find fingerprints on the narrow surface—these people had been professional up till now—but he took care anyway. One slipup was one too many, right now.

He went over everything else in the room without finding anything of apparent significance. It bothered him that he hadn't found any boots in the closet, or under the bed, though he did find a pair of sneakers and a pair of sandals . . . but no boots anywhere.

Some of the other things he'd picked up might bear fruit in the lab, but he'd have to wait and see. Science did not give a damn about timetables or crises.

Meanwhile, Speedle had dealt with the bathroom and the second bedroom without finding anything of significance, either.

Speed frowned thoughtfully, his natural skepticism sketched in his deceptively soft face. "These guys didn't seem to put up much of a fight."

Caine nodded. "Nothing under their fingernails, no guns in the house . . . and they don't strike me as complacent victims, do they, Tim?"

"Not really."

"Did you find any boots in the other bedroom?"

"No. Assorted footware, but no."

"The bathtub guy have shoes on?"

"He was a barefoot boy."

Caine grunted. "If these guys killed the three leaders in the Archer the other night, where . . . are . . . their . . . *boots?*"

Speedle shrugged. "If it's elves, we could check back in the morning."

Caine smiled in spite of himself. "Not really helpful, Tim."

"Hey, how do we know those shoe prints didn't belong to another guest at the Archer?"

"Without the boots of these vics to compare, we don't."

They gathered with Calleigh and Delko in back near the open dilapidated garage where the Lexus was parked. Calleigh held up a plastic bag with three shell casings.

"From an AK-47," she said proudly.

Delko displayed another bag. "Paint chips that I'm betting will match the parked car they scraped."

Caine frowned. "Either of you find any boots in the car or the garage?"

"No," Calleigh said, exchanging glances with Delko.

"No," Delko said, "why?"

Caine said, "Something's . . . not . . . right."

Calleigh asked, "What isn't?"

"I don't know yet. Our vics definitely killed Wallace and Joanna Burnett, but the peace-talk powwow at the Archer . . . I'm still not sure."

"Why not?" Delko asked.

Caine twitched half a smile. "You two find any guns?"

"No."

"No."

"Then," their supervisor said, "tell me . . . how did our two late lowlifes get guns out of that federal building, and *then* get 'em back in?"

His team looked at him, and each other, with wide eyes. Nobody seemed to have an answer.

"And where," Caine said measuredly, "are the guns that killed Chevalier, Calisto, and Shakespeare?"

Again the CSIs had no answers.

"Also, I might point out that Santoya and his companion did not exactly die of natural causes."

Nods all around; raised eyebrows, too.

"So," their boss said. "Let's get back to the lab and start going over this stuff. Calleigh, you IDd Santoya, so after you work the shells, he's all yours."

"My pleasure," she said.

"Get me any background material on him and find out who the other dead man is. Maybe that'll lead us to Mendoza and whoever's supplying them with guns."

Glancing at the parked Lexus, Caine happened to notice the vehicle's license plate—name of the state at the top and an orange that resembled a peach in the center; number P14 398. Something about that nagged him, but he filed it away and joined in with his crew, packing up their gear.

Back at the lab, Delko was the first to come up with anything.

"AFIS came through on the guy in the bathtub," Delko said. "His name was Santoya, too—Manola."

"Brothers?"

"Cousins. Both originally from Colombia."

"Then how did they get hooked up with Mendoza?"

"They were from Bogota. They weren't affiliated with the Mitus, so they started freelancing. Though DEA could never prove it, they think the cousins worked for the Mitus, the Trenches, the Faucones, and even Las Culebras. One report even had them doing out-of-town stuff for Peter Venici before he got whacked."

"So we can probably connect them to Mendoza, but—"

"We can also connect 'em to everybody else, probably including the Boy Scouts."

Caine sighed. "All-around, all-purpose bad boys."

Delko nodded. "But I think they'll behave themselves from now on, H."

"I would say. Good work, Eric."

Calleigh showed up soon after.

"The casings we found in Santoya's car match the ones fired at the Archer Hotel *and* at Burnett's house. These are our guys, all right."

Caine nodded, once. "Good. But again that brings the question: How did they get the guns in and out of LaRussa's house?"

"Not by themselves," she said, flicking a raise of eyebrows.

Caine thought for a moment, then asked her, "Has anybody started doing background checks on those King Building guards?"

"Not yet—should I?"

"Yeah. Please. We're still missing something."

Coming in, Speedle almost bumped into Calleigh going out.

"CODIS was no help on the two guys," Speedle told his boss.

"That's all right, Tim," Caine said. "We've identified both of them with fingerprints."

He filled Speedle in on the Santoyas and what they'd done over the years.

"Well," Speed said with a shrug, "at least we know who they are. Were."

Caine frowned in thought. "Tim, start working on the videotape from the King Building. See if you can figure out how those guns got out."

"I'm all over it."

"Calleigh's going to start doing background checks on the guards. Let me know as soon as you've got something."

After Speed went out, Caine's cell phone rang. He answered with his usual "Horatio."

"Hi, it's Yelina."

"What did you find out about Mr. Garner?" he asked.

"Thanks for providing that second-shift CSI, Horatio. We served the warrant on young Mr. Garner."

"And?"

"Regular Eddie Haskell—sweet as he could be to me, doesn't know what his old 'high school bud' Jimmy could be talking about."

"Do tell."

"Only, while I talked to him outside, the CSI searched the house. Guess what? Mike kept the purse as a souvenir."

Caine smiled; now and then, the bad guys were stupid, and that was as helpful as good police work.

Yelina was saying, "Garner changed his tune, copped to being there, but he said he just happened to be with Hamilton when it went down. Claimed he never touched the gun and that Hamilton made him take the purse."

"Well, he's got a problem. His prints are likely the other ones on the gun."

"That's how I see it, too . . . and we'll have him in a sweet inconsistency."

Caine allowed himself a small sigh of relief. Jimmy Hamilton was in trouble, no doubt about that, but Jimmy's testimony and the mitigating circumstances would help see to it that the young man wouldn't be bullied by Mike Garner again.

"Good work, Yelina."

"How are you doing on your case?"

He filled her in on what had happened today. "But," he concluded, "finding whoever hired these guys isn't going to be a slam dunk."

"You'll figure it, Horatio," she said warmly. "I have faith in you."

"Thanks."

Her belief in him felt good.

Alone in his office again, his team back to work, Caine would start by feeding the footprints from the Santoya house into the computer. Once that was done, he could separate them and maybe find a clue among all the smudges and dust.

He hoped so.

The clock was running, and their chance to solve this thing would be gone in twenty-four hours. Once the governor got involved, Caine knew the investigation would likely leave his hands. . . .

He forced himself not to think about that. They still had one day, and that could be a lifetime.

Just ask the Santoyas.

His cell phone rang, and he answered it to find a tightly irritated Len Matthers on the line.

"What the hell is the idea of getting Jeremy involved in this investigation?" the DEA honcho demanded.

"It's strictly on a consulting basis, Len."

"Do I have to tell you how many conflicts of interest are involved?"

"That's why—"

"I'm telling you right now, Caine—drop it."

"Drop what?"

"Involving Jeremy! His wife was one of the victims—how will it look if a DEA agent is out playing Dirty Harry, looking for his wife's killer? He's already technically a suspect in the Calisto slaying!"

"I'm well aware, Len. But I don't have to tell you this is a citywide crisis and that I need to tap into the expertise of the town's top gang expert."

"Well, end it now. Or I'll take steps to take over this entire investigation on the federal level."

"I'll give your request consideration, Len."

"It's not a request! You promised cooperation, Horatio."

"Hasn't Detective Tripp been updating you?"

"He has . . . but it's been damn vague, and he failed to mention you involving Jeremy."

"A question, Len—"

"What?"

"Any weapons your agents confiscate as evidence . . . where are they kept?"

"Well—in the evidence lock-up at the King Building. Same's true of the FBI and the ATF, and . . . why?"

"Just wondering," Caine said. "Thanks for the input, Len."

And clicked off.

10

Internal Affairs

THE TEAM WAS running on fumes now.

They'd all caught short naps here and there throughout the night while they'd waited for a program to run or a lab result to come in, but as the Sunday morning sun slanted in through window blinds, the interminable nature of the shift from hell made itself clear.

Horatio Caine tried to make up for the unjust effort he was demanding of his people by pushing himself the hardest. But even the normally effervescent Calleigh was fraying around the edges.

When Caine stopped by to check Calleigh's progress with the background checks on the guards at the King Federal Building, he found her bent over a pile of papers, her eyes home to a filigree of red, her silver-yellow hair (usually so carefully coifed) haphazardly pinned up out of her way.

"Any luck?" he asked.

At least her smile hadn't dimmed. "Morning, Horatio. I consider it 'luck' I haven't passed out yet."

He forced a smile. "Staying conscious is a plus, in this work."

"Really? And when did you last catch some sleep?"

"If we don't crack this in the next twenty-four, we'll all have plenty of time to nap."

"When they bust us all back to traffic," she asked innocently, "will you still be in charge?"

He did a rare thing for Horatio Caine, particularly at work: He laughed out loud.

"Thanks, Calleigh. I needed that."

"I'm glad. But I'm afraid that's about all the help I have for you right now—these guards are squeaky clean."

He sighed. "Not surprising. A federal facility has clearances of the highest order."

A half-smirk dimpled the lovely face. "Not high enough to keep its gun lockup from turning into a lending library."

"I hear you." He thought for a moment. Then he said, "It's time to take a hard look at a couple of federal higher-ups."

"Ken LaRussa?"

"Yeah. And after you finish with him, try Leonard Matthers, at the DEA."

"We're fishing, aren't we?" she said, still smiling but glum.

"Afraid so. But the waters around Miami are perfect for that. Start with LaRussa."

"He's been awfully cooperative."

"What choice did he have?" Caine tilted his head. "It's his evidence lockup that's our lending library."

"Yes, it is," she said, and got back to work.

Caine found Speedle in an office, seated with his back to the door, a still from a videotape on the TV in front of him. Studying the picture for a moment, Caine tried to figure out why Speed seemed so fixated on this one frame.

Then a sound emerged from the young CSI— snoring.

Caine, smiling, was debating waking Speed when the CSI suddenly sat up, as if in fright, a sheaf of papers on his lap spilling onto the floor. Apparently, even asleep, Speed had sensed his boss's presence.

"Rise and shine, Tim," Caine said, moving next to him.

"Just resting my eyes, H," Speedle said.

Caine put a hand on the young CSI's shoulder. "Hey—we've all been working long hours. A nap here and there won't hurt."

Speedle was already picking up the papers he'd pitched. "I was watching the tape and started taking some detailed notes, and making some comparisons with records. . . ."

"And?"

Speed swivelled to the side to face his supervisor. "And there's something outta whack here. I started going through LaRussa's inventory list, and something doesn't add up."

"Are we talking the AK-47?"

"Not the guns—*other* evidence kept in that lockup."

"What kind?"

"The controlled-substance kind, H—drugs."

Caine pulled up a chair and sat next to Speedle, who explained, "They confiscate drugs on the street and bring them into the evidence room; then someone checks out some to take to the lab for testing. All standard operating procedure. But"—he pointed with one hand to a sign-out sheet he held up with the other—"they're checking out way more weight than's necessary. And then it's impossible to tell, on the video, whether they're bringing back the same amount, or even the same stuff."

"Just how much is being removed—for 'testing'?"

The normally unflappable Speed definitely looked flapped. "How about, three and four keys at a time? We'd *never* send that much to the lab all at once."

"And you think they're bringing back less than they checked out."

"Yeah, or making a switch."

"So who signed the stuff back in?"

Speedle held out the sheet for Caine to read. The signature and quantity lines were unreadable.

With a half-smirk, Speed said, "Looks like a drunken dyslexic guy . . . or any doctor writing a prescription."

"So they were signing in just for cosmetic purposes."

"For the video camera, right."

"These dates—they always returned the drugs over the weekend, when there was no guard on duty."

Nodding, Speedle said, "When there was no one watching but the camera. No one ever seemed to notice that."

"Speed . . . this a good catch. A really good catch."

"Thanks, H," Speedle said. But he wasn't smiling. "How does it tie in with our gang war?"

"Hard to say, exactly." Caine shrugged. "Certainly our gangs all deal dope, so this might indicate whichever gang had entry to check out a gun was also helping itself to contraband."

"But what gang would have access to the evidence lockup?"

"Quite a list, Speed—gangs called the FBI, the ATF, and the DEA, among others."

"The whole federal alphabet soup," Speed said, looking sick.

"Troubled waters, my friend. Watch where you swim."

"And look out for fins."

Caine's attention turned toward the monitor. "What have you found on the videotapes? About the feds checking out the dope, I mean?"

With a frustrated shrug, Speedle said, "Not a hell of a lot—these guys are very careful. You never see their faces on camera. They know where it is and they look away or duck around it."

"But they look like agents, or at least federal employees."

Speed shrugged. "They're wearing suits."

"Do we see anything? Enough of the back of a head to identify ears? Or hair, or lack of it? Find *something*, Speed."

Speedle swivelled back toward the monitor. "That's why you pay me the medium-size bucks, H."

Caine was on his feet now. "And Speed? Soon would be good."

As he passed the morgue, Caine paused, wondering if he should disturb Alexx; more than anyone on Caine's beleaguered team, the coroner had seen her workload expand in the gang-war crisis. He was about to step away when the door swung open and an exhausted Alexx slipped into the hall.

"Well, Horatio," she said. "Dropping by to see me? Somebody with a pulse makes a pleasant change of pace."

He gave her a small, embarrassed smile. "I was going to give you a pass. I figured another body, even one *with* a pulse, was not what you needed right now."

She waved that off. "Which of us isn't too busy? I should be in church . . . and *not* my cathedral of the dead, in there." Shaking her head, displaying an atypical weariness, Alexx added, "My friend, this week has been like nothing I've ever seen before."

"We've worked hurricanes."

"That comes closest. But hurricane victims haven't been shot up by automatic weapons. . . . I have the preliminary lab results on Joanna Burnett's autopsy, by the way."

"Anything interesting?" Caine asked.

"Possibly. Would you be surprised to hear she had sex the day she died?"

"Not really."

"What if the DNA of the male didn't belong to her husband?"

Caine took the question like the sucker punch it was. After a moment, he managed, "Is that what you're telling me?"

Gravely, Alexx nodded.

"Why would you check that?" he asked.

"It was a murder, Horatio. With a female victim, I always run that down. Shouldn't I have?"

Chagrined, Caine said, "Of course you should. I

didn't mean that to sound—where did you get Jeremy's DNA to cross-check?"

"From his blood on her clothing, night of the shooting at their home. I ran it twice."

Caine's hands settled on his hips. "Joanna Burnett was having an affair."

"Or at least a one-night stand. Or an afternoon delight."

People kept secrets—as a CSI he knew that better than most—but the Burnetts had always seemed to have a happy marriage, the proverbial perfect couple.

"Good job," he said.

But she had a mournful expression. "I'm sorry. She was your friend. But she was human, Horatio. We all are."

"I know," he said and found a semblance of a smile. "That's what keeps CSI in business, right?"

She laughed in her worldly-wise way. "Right."

"Alexx, you get something, let me know. Don't wait for me to come knocking."

"I will," Alexx said. She took a deep breath, let it out, and reentered her cathedral of the dead.

Still processing this troubling news, Caine found Delko in the break room nursing a donut and an iced tea.

Sitting next to the CSI, Caine asked, "Morning, Eric—and what have you been up to?"

"Working on footprints."

Caine frowned. "I hope we haven't duplicated efforts."

"I don't think so, H. I was looking for the boots that the Santoyas wore in the hotel room."

"If," Caine reminded him, "it was them at the Archer."

"If it was them."

"And?"

Delko smirked humorlessly. "Nothing. I took an electrostatic lift from both the brake and gas pedal of the car, garage floor, basement floor in the house. . . . *Anywhere* they might have been that wasn't all tromped over."

"And you didn't find anything that matched."

"Not a thing. How about you, H?"

"I used the computer to separate the prints." Caine shook his head. "Things were stacked eight and nine deep. It was like the whole ERS team marched through that house."

"Sort anything out?"

"I did: Two sets of boots that didn't match any of the others."

Delko sat forward. "Either of 'em the ones from the Archer?"

"One is."

"Cool!"

"The other we haven't seen before."

Delko thought about it. "So . . . the Santoyas both had boots and they got rid of them."

"Maybe so, but the Santoyas were both barefoot when we found them, remember. *These* bootprints were on top of their barefoot prints."

"If that's true . . . what happened to the boots?"

"Maybe they walked out. After walking in."

"What are you getting at, H?"

"Try this on," Caine said, not liking what he was about to say, not liking the way it felt in his stomach, or the way the words tasted in his mouth. "Suppose the boots didn't belong to the Santoyas."

Delko's face creased with frown lines. It was clear he saw what Caine meant, and he didn't like it either. But he said nothing, which spoke volumes.

"Excuse me, Eric. I've got a judge to call."

Delko's eyes flared. "On a Sunday morning?"

"Yes, on a Sunday. I don't care if he's in church or on the golf course. Stay close, I'm going to want you to pick something up for me in a while."

"I'm here, H."

"Oh, and Eric—one more thing . . ."

"Yeah?"

Caine raised a lecturing finger. "Don't tell anyone, I mean anyone, what we talked about."

"Except for Calleigh and Speed, you mean."

"I mean them, too . . . for now. They've both got plenty to do, anyway."

Caine made his call, and, an hour later, the fax machine spit out the document he'd been waiting for. He returned to Delko, doing lab work now, and said, "Come along."

"I thought you were sending me, H."

With a sneer, Caine said, "Eric, the more I thought about it, the more pissed off I got."

Delko's eyes widened. His boss rarely swore.

"We're both going," Caine said. "Tripp, too."

As they walked out the door, Caine got on his cell phone and called U.S. attorney Ken LaRussa at home. His wife answered, and after some dancing around, Caine convinced her to fetch her husband.

When LaRussa's voice came on the line, the words

were friendly, but the tone was wary. "Horatio, what can I do for you?"

"Meet me at the King Building in half an hour."

"What?"

"I don't really need to repeat that, do I, Ken?"

"Horatio, be serious. Can't this wait till tomorrow? This is Sunday, goddamnit—we just got back from services!"

"Well, that's good, Ken."

"What do you mean?"

"You've already said your prayers." The edge in Caine's voice sharpened. "We're coming now and we're bringing a court order. You're going to want to be there."

Caine punched the End button before LaRussa could respond.

In little more than half an hour, Caine, Delko, and Detective Frank Tripp were at the King Federal Building and had gone through security into the lobby, where a jumpy LaRussa was waiting. The lawyer wore jeans, a blue chambray shirt, and a look that said he was seriously torked about being dragged down here on a Sunday morning—but Caine sensed it was a pose, in part, anyway.

LaRussa was scared.

And he should be.

Not that Caine could care less about the attorney's mood, and when LaRussa started toward them, nearly yelling his outrage, Caine simply handed him the judge's order and kept walking toward the elevator. The lawyer, reading the document as he followed the invading trio, caught up just as the door opened.

Getting on the elevator with them, LaRussa had a wide-eyed, horrified look, acknowledging the new level the investigation had risen . . . or perhaps sunk . . . to.

"Drugs?" the U.S. attorney blurted. "You're taking drug evidence?"

"Specific lots," Caine said, pointing to the court order in the attorney's trembling hands. "For testing."

"Testing?"

Tripp said, "Is there an echo in here?"

Caine said, "We have firm evidence that agents are taking suspiciously large quantities of drugs to be tested, and we'd just like to make sure they're bringing back the same amount they took out."

Delko put in, "Or the same substance."

Looking from the CSI supervisor to the younger man, LaRussa said, "What are you two talking about?"

Caine glanced at Delko, handing him the ball.

Delko said, "We're talking about taking out coke and bringing back baking soda."

"Oh!" LaRussa said, throwing his hands. "No *way*, no frickin' way! This isn't possible."

LaRussa fumed, placing his hands defiantly on his hips, the search warrant hanging like a flag football towel near his waist.

Caine gave the attorney a mock-pleasant look. "I hope you're right, Ken." And Caine's eyes narrowed, the pleasantness turning into something hard and unforgiving. "Because if I was wrong to trust you? And you are behind all this? I'll cuff your ass and drag you to the death house, personally."

This prompted LaRussa into silence.

Which was helpful, because the trio of officers had

a job to do. In the end, they left with several different bags of drugs: cocaine, marijuana, meth, heroin, their own little pharmaceutical buffet in the back of the Hummer.

All the time they worked, the U.S. attorney stood watch, seething but saying nothing. Whether LaRussa simply didn't know what to say, or merely sought to protect his constitutional rights, Caine couldn't say.

Prompted by a call from Caine, Speedle and Calleigh met them at the door as Delko backed the Hummer into the garage. The mood awaiting them was celebratory as they climbed out.

"The U.S. attorney's office!" Speedle whooped.

Calleigh gave Delko's arm a squeeze. "You little fed-buster, you," and Delko grinned, eating it up.

Coming around the back of the Hummer, Caine was not grinning; his grim expression froze his crew into embarrassed silence.

"Inappropriate," he said crisply, hands on hips.

Looking for bad guys in a federal building was not the turn he had wanted this case to take, and he surely didn't want his people celebrating it.

"I know we've bumped heads with Agent Sackheim and the FBI from time to time, and other federal agencies," he said, "but if this turns out the way it appears to be heading, it'll mean a black eye for all law enforcement in Miami."

"Aren't you pleased that we're getting somewhere?" Calleigh asked, mildly defensive.

Caine frowned at her. "Pleased about maybe busting other cops? No. And I doubt any of you are, either, if you think about it."

Speed and Calleigh nodded, looking deflated.

Caine immediately felt bad about berating them—after all these long hours, his people could have used a little team spirit, even if misguided.

"Guys," he said gently, "if LaRussa's behind all of this . . . if he's the head librarian dispensing guns and drugs . . . we'll bust him and any other federal employee. We just won't gloat."

Delko said to his coworkers, "Think about how we feel about Internal Affairs."

That made the point, with genuine nods all around, and Caine said, "Another thing—make sure we do chapter and verse on this stuff, when it comes to logging it. I don't want anyone accusing us of making a switch on this end. This is the feds' batch of fleas."

"Fleas?" Calleigh asked.

"You lie down with dogs, you get up with fleas," Caine said, eyebrows raised. "I don't want us to need a flea bath too."

Calleigh smiled at him. "You're so eloquent, Horatio."

He laughed once. "Get to work, you guys."

They unloaded the Hummer in silence, stacking the contraband pouches on carts, then steering the carts into the lab. Delko would supervise the testing while the others worked the rest of the evidence.

As he handed bags out to Speedle, Caine asked, "How's it going with the videotape?"

"Quality of these tapes ain't exactly HDTV, H. You couldn't tell Halle Berry from Pee Wee Herman."

"Were the cameras themselves tampered with?"

"I'm thinking as much. I figure our bad guys knew that nobody paid any attention to these things and they futzed around with the focus."

Nodding, Caine said, "Let's take it to Tyler and let him work his magic."

"Tyler's not in, H. For some people, today is Sunday."

Caine bestowed Speed a tiny smile. "Call and tell him Monday's come early."

Forty-five minutes later, a very disheveled-looking Tyler Jenson came into the lab. The lanky, long-necked, young AV tech had a wide, easygoing, engaging smile and tousled blond hair.

He also had a good attitude, saying, "What can I do to help?" when Caine and Speed approached.

The CSI supervisor laid out the problem.

"Hey, let's see if I can turn VHS into DVD for ya."

Jenson led Caine and Speed into the tiny room that housed the tech's AV equipment. He flipped some switches, turned some knobs, then flopped into his captain's chair in front of his computer monitor, while the equipment buzzed and warmed up like a 757 preparing for takeoff.

Soon they were looking at a black-and-white image twisted out of focus. To Caine's displeasure, Speed's dour definition of the security tape's picture was proving correct.

"Well, doesn't this suck," Jenson said rhetorically. "Someone's definitely tampered with the equipment. But give me a couple hours, and maybe I can turn this mud into some kinda landscape."

"That would be good," Caine said. "Clock's ticking."

Jenson grinned. "Isn't it always?"

"Yes, but this time it's a bomb."

"Got ya," Jenson said and shooed them out.

They walked down the hall toward Caine's office.

"H," Speed said, "what do you want me to do while we're waiting?"

Good question. Calleigh was running background on LaRussa and Matthers, Delko was testing the drugs, and now Jenson was working the tape.

Then his conversation with Alexx came back to him, and he said, "Find out what you can about the victims."

"Gee—I may have that report ready for ya right now, H. They were dirty, low-life drug dealers."

"Not Joanna Burnett," Caine reminded him.

Speed frowned. "No. Not her, but she was collateral damage—"

"Pretend it's any other murder. Look for a motive."

"What, I should talk to her husband?"

"No. A good place to start is with friends. Find out who her best friend was, and do an interview. Keep it low key. Stay off the radar."

Speed looked confused. "If that's what you want, H, I'm on it. But it doesn't make sense to me."

"Does to me. Go."

Speed went.

Back in his office now, Caine was just settling in behind his desk when his cell phone chirped.

"Horatio," Caine said.

"It's Sackheim, Horatio." The FBI agent's voice was tightly angry. "What the hell's going on over at the Federal Building?"

"It's a part of my investigation, Bob."

"What happened to keeping me 'constantly' in the loop?"

"Detective Tripp's been keeping you apprised, right?"

"Selectively, it would appear. If you suspected a security breach in the King evidence lockup, why the hell didn't you tell me?"

"It might have been premature. I had no desire to blacken Ken LaRussa's reputation unnecessarily. I mean, we're all on the same team, right, Bob?"

"Jesus! Do you have any goddamn idea how many cases, for how many agencies, could be compromised by this thing?"

"That's why we've taken it slow, Bob."

"As far as I'm concerned, this is a breach of good faith. How would you like to be facing obstruction of justice charges, Caine?"

A *click-click* told Caine a call was waiting.

"I have a call on the other line, Bob. We'll have to take this up at a later date."

"Caine, don't fuh—"

And Caine took the other call.

"It's Jeremy, Horatio. I can't believe you busted Ken LaRussa!"

"Good news sure travels fast in this town. Only, Jeremy—I didn't bust him. We just served a search warrant on the Federal Building."

"Really. Why?"

"Some things we wanted to check out."

A short chuckle preceded, "Little late to be playing this close-to-the-vest with me, isn't it, Horatio?"

"Maybe I'm just trying to heal up the new orifice your boss cut me."

"Matthers bitched to you?"

"Hasn't he to you?"

"I've frankly been avoiding him and the office. Anything I'm doing for you is on my own time, and calling in markers from friends and informants."

"I do appreciate that." Caine tried to keep his voice light, breezy. "As for the Federal Building, I just wouldn't want to be the source of unfounded rumors. Look what's happened already. How many people think we actually busted LaRussa this afternoon?"

"Well, it's the word on the street," Burnett said. "I have mixed feelings myself—LaRussa's a self-serving weasel, but I never made him for bent."

"That's all I can say right now, Jeremy. But anything you hear about Mendoza's location—"

"Hey, that's the other reason I'm calling. I do have a line on our head Culebra. We may be closing in on Mendoza. What do you want us to do if we get to him?"

"We?"

"Nickerson's working this with me."

Caine shifted in his chair; Matthers's concern about Jeremy turning into Dirty Harry flashed through the CSI's mind. "If you have a lead, Jeremy, turn it over to me or to Frank Tripp—this is an MDPD case, and if you play a lone-wolf hand, I won't be able to protect you."

Burnett's tone was serious but reassuring. "I get you, Horatio. I want Mendoza alive as much as you do. I want him to pay for what he did to Joanna, and not with a bullet. I want this hump to wallow on death row until he finally gets the lethal injection he deserves."

"Jeremy, I repeat: If you have a line on Mendoza, tell me now."

"Let me run it down first. I promise I won't do anything rash."

Caine didn't know whether to believe Burnett or not, but the DEA's answer to Eliot Ness could well be the only person who had a chance of finding Mendoza before the governor sent in the guard.

"All right, Jeremy, run down your lead, and if you find Mendoza, you call me or Tripp, straightaway."

"Of course."

"I mean it, Jeremy. If you're directly involved, you could taint the bust, and this evil bastard will walk."

"He's yours," Burnett said, "after I find him."

And Burnett clicked off.

Calleigh knocked on the jamb of the open door. Caine looked up and waved her in.

She perched on the chair opposite and said, "Do you *really* think Kenneth LaRussa instigated this gang war?"

Caine tented his fingers. "I can see one scenario . . ."

Ken LaRussa puts the gang war in play, making secret alliances with a gang or gangs by sharing contraband and providing weapons. Manipulating the alliances, hiring the Santoyas as hit men, the U.S. attorney wipes out his collaborators under the guise of more gang war fatalities.

He targets the one man who has the knowledge about the gangs to see through his scheme: Jeremy Burnett.

Then LaRussa manipulates the police into a position where LaRussa himself stops the war, catapulting himself into the national spotlight.

"He just didn't count on us catching up with him

first," Caine said, finishing up this one possible take on the facts.

"He also didn't count on Joanna Burnett dying," Calleigh said.

"Or Jeremy surviving."

"I suppose it all makes sense. . . ." She sat on the very edge of the chair, her eyes bright and yet searching. "But, Horatio—he seems so squeaky clean. He's happily married, no financial troubles, doesn't have too much money either, is nice to his cat and dotes on his kids. He even pays his taxes on time, from what I could find out. And his wife is active in the Hispanic-American community, working against everything the gangs stand for."

"Does it ring true to you? Or is this a facade?"

"If so, it's a really, really elaborate one. Mr. LaRussa just doesn't seem like the kind of man who would think the ends justify the means, on this grand a scale, anyway."

Caine shrugged. "Guns and maybe drugs are getting out of the evidence room at the King Building, without anyone getting caught. And who's in charge of that room?"

"LaRussa is, of course; but that makes him a bad administrator, not a bad guy."

"A valid point," Caine said. "But even if he's only guilty of negligence, how many are dead because of it?"

She had no reply to that.

"Now start in on Matthers," Caine said. "The DEA chief."

"You have a scenario that fits him?"

"You can pretty much plug him into LaRussa's, only public office wouldn't be Matthers's goal—climbing in the DEA nationally would."

Delko joined them and dropped onto the green sofa against the wall. "The cocaine and heroin we tested in the gas chromatograph and mass spec both came back as pure . . ."

Caine raised an eyebrow.

Delko grinned boyishly. ". . . pure *baking soda*, that is. And the marijuana came up oregano."

Caine threw a look at Calleigh. "The man in charge is the man responsible."

Delko said, "Who's responsible?"

"Ken LaRussa," Calleigh said. "At least that's what Horatio thinks."

Delko shrugged. "Makes sense—he was in charge of the evidence room."

"My point," Caine said, "is that whether he's our would-be mastermind or not, he's negligent, and the buck will stop with him."

From the doorway, Speedle said, "Bye-bye Washington, D.C., then." He sauntered in and flopped onto the sofa next to Delko. "Break time, huh? H, I just got off the phone with Laura Parker."

Calleigh and Delko looked at Speed as if he'd spoken Swahili.

"Joanna Burnett's best friend," Speed explained.

But Calleigh and Delko still had no idea what this was about, and Caine didn't stop to fill them in, asking Speed, "What did she say?"

"She didn't—she wants to talk to you, H. She doesn't trust anybody else."

Delko said to Speed, "Your reputation must precede you."

"Cute," Speed replied, then said to Caine, "So I took the liberty of setting up a meet."

"Where and when?"

"Hutchinson's convenience store, on Galloway—in half an hour."

A knock at the open door drew their attention to DNA tech Toni Escobedo. She said to Caine, "The DNA you got at the Archer, in the hotel bathroom? It does not belong to either of the Santoyas."

The other CSIs were astounded by this news, but Caine himself took it stoically; he would have liked to have been surprised, but not finding a pair of boots for either man in their house, or their car, had made her report likely.

Caine asked, "Any idea who it does belong to?"

"Not yet, Lieutenant. But it's not in CODIS."

The Combined DNA Index System was a repository for DNA, just as VICAP included violent offenders and AFIS gathered fingerprints.

"I'm doing a search of other databases," Escobedo continued, "but that could take quite a while."

"Stay at it," he told her, knowing "quite a while" was a commodity they did not have.

She began to go, then hung back, saying, "Oh, one thing though—the DNA belongs to an African-American."

Caine frowned thoughtfully. "Could that mean someone Cuban?"

"It could—not all Cubans are purely Hispanic; some

are of African ancestry. I suppose the man could be Cuban, yes."

Which counted in Mendoza and Las Culebras.

The group dispersed, and Caine went to meet with Laura Parker.

Hutchinson's convenience store was less than a mile from HQ. Caine got two cups of coffee, paid the cashier, and took one of the booths along the window. Late afternoon on a Sunday, business was spotty, the row of booths all Caine's.

And Laura Parker's.

Not making eye contact with the cashier, the woman came quickly in and made a beeline for Caine's booth; she was seated before he could stand and politely greet her.

Laura Parker was a petite, attractive blond in her late thirties, though her prettiness was given the test by no makeup, reddish-cast eyes, and a red nose—from crying, not drinking. She wore a denim jumpsuit with a red cotton shirt beneath.

"Mr. Caine," she said.

He was on the local news often enough to be used to people he didn't know recognizing him. "Mrs. Parker?"

The woman nodded.

"Thought you might like some coffee."

"Thanks."

But she didn't touch it. In fact, neither of them touched their Styrofoam cups throughout their brief conversation.

"You were Joanna Burnett's best friend?"

She nodded; despite her country club breeding, her

manner was furtive, as if she were an escaped felon. "Since high school."

"I'm sorry for your loss."

"Thank you. Joanna spoke well of you, Mr. Caine."

"Make it Horatio. And may I call you Laura?"

She swallowed. "Sure."

"Why did you insist on meeting here? My office is nearby. If you're nervous, a public place—"

"Is better than somewhere where I might run into Jeremy Burnett or one of his cohorts."

Caine nodded. "I see. And why are you hesitant to run into Jeremy? I presume if you were Joanna's best friend, you were friendly with him, too."

"*Too* friendly . . . once upon a time." She dug cigarettes out of a pocket of her jumpsuit. Lighted up, tremblingly. "You don't mind?"

"No. Just relax. I'm here to listen, and to try to help."

She breathed out smoke, dragon-style. "You have to understand, Mr. Caine . . . Horatio. Joanna and I . . . our friendship. Oh, Christ, I don't even know where to start."

"Beginning usually works."

Looking out the window at the darkening street, she said, "My marriage broke up about three years ago. I was always envious of Joanna and Jeremy. For their perfect marriage. One night, at the club, I found myself alone with Jeremy outside, on the veranda, and I impulsively kissed him. I was a little drunk."

Caine said nothing.

She let out a sigh of smoke. "I called him at work and apologized the next day. Told him how embarrassed I was, and . . . he told me he'd enjoyed it. That he'd always secretly had feelings for me, and . . . do I have to go on?"

"You had an affair with Jeremy."

"Yes. Brief, torrid, tawdry, just what you'd expect. And of course, I lost Joanna, traded that cheap fucking fling for the best friend I ever had. . . . Lost her, anyway, until last month."

"Why last month?"

Gesturing with the cigarette, making smoke trails, the woman said, "She called out of the blue, and I started to cry and apologize, and we ended up meeting for lunch. She told me that she and Jeremy were having trouble, and that the marriage was over. I said . . . was he . . . cheating again? And she said, no—*she* was."

"Now she was having an affair."

"That's right. She'd long fantasized about getting 'even.' She said she did it impulsively . . . probably like I went after Jeremy that first night . . . but that it had developed into something serious. That she intended to tell Jeremy, and there'd be a divorce. They didn't have any children, so it was strictly— But then last week, we had lunch again, and she said she'd had second thoughts. That Jeremy had been especially sweet of late, and she felt she'd fallen in love with him all over again."

"And what about the man she was seeing?"

"I spoke to her the morning she died. She was meeting him at a motel, where they often went . . . but she was going to break it off." She swallowed hard and pressed the heel of a fist to her forehead. "That very afternoon—the afternoon of the day she died!"

"It's all right, Laura . . . stay calm. What else did she say?"

Nervously shrugging, the woman said, "That she was going to spill everything to her husband. She felt that if they could forgive each other . . . they'd both strayed, after all . . . that they could make a clean start."

Caine's mind quickly mounted a scenario: *Could a jealous lover have attacked the Burnetts outside their home? Imitating the gang slaying of the day before to cover his tracks?*

"Who was he, Laura? The man?"

"I don't know. That much she kept from me. An understandable discretion. But I would assume some-one close to Jeremy."

"Why that assumption, Laura?"

"Well, remember, she started out only wanting to 'get even' with her husband. Jeremy had an affair with me . . . her best friend. So I'd say she chose one of his best friends. To settle the score."

Caine thanked Laura Parker for her help and ad-vised her to say nothing of this to anyone.

In the parking lot of the convenience store, Caine was already assembling the pieces. . . .

The DNA of the man Laura had slept with the day she died—putting the "good-bye" in good-bye sex—identified her lover as an African-American.

Gabe Nickerson fit that description, and another: He was Jeremy's best friend.

He was also a former DEA agent who'd been knowledge-able about the evidence lockup at the Federal Building.

He headed the Hummer in the direction of Nickerson's house.

Six months (and a lifetime) ago, Caine had been to Nickerson's house for an interagency celebration after a particularly big drug bust that Burnett and Nickerson had made against the Culebras.

Using his hands-free cell phone, Caine called Judge Javier Ojeda at home; Caine had cleared the judge when a prostitute had died in His Honor's shower. So the judge kept his argument to a minimum when Caine asked for a search warrant for the home of Gabriel Nickerson.

Next, he called Alexx. "How fast can you and Toni get a DNA match if you've already got both samples handy?"

"Fast. Why?"

"I want you to test the DNA from Joanna Burnett's sex partner against the sample from the Archer Hotel bathroom."

"Will do."

"Let me know soon as you know."

His next call went to Speedle.

"Speed, get the crew and join me to execute the search warrant that you'll find in my fax machine."

"What's the address?"

When Speedle found out whose house the warrant was for, he was astounded. "No, H! Gabe's behind all this?"

"Joanna's murder, at least. I think the rest, too."

"Holy. . . . See you there."

Caine hadn't gone far, driving away from the setting sun, the sky a bruised purple and red in his rearview mirror, when a call came in for him.

It was Burnett.

"We've got Mendoza cornered in Little Havana."

Caine's hands tensed on the wheel. "Where?"

Burnett told him.

"Stay put, Jeremy. Gabe with you?"

"He's right beside me."

"Don't do a thing until I get there—promise me!"

"I promise."

"If not for my sake, Jeremy, then Joanna's."

"Horatio, for Pete's sake. I promise!"

And Burnett was gone.

11

Die with Dignity

HORATIO CAINE BARRELED east on Northwest Twenty-fifth, siren howling, lights flashing red and blue against a sky whose darkness was almost complete, dusk finally giving up the ghost.

He tapped the brakes, turned right, and accelerated up the ramp onto the Palmetto Expressway south. Weaving through light Sunday evening traffic on SR826, Caine prayed he got to his destination before Burnett and Nickerson attacked Mendoza's hideout; as a CSI, he was used to getting to the scene when the shooting was over, but this time his fervent hope was that it hadn't started yet.

His call for black and whites to beat him to the scene was complicated by news of a running gun battle between the Faucones and the Mitus in Little Haiti, which appeared to have drawn every spare patrol car in the city.

"There's a gang war going on, Lieutenant," the dispatcher was good enough to remind him.

For just a second, he wished the National Guard were already here.

He radioed the crew to inform them where he was going and what he wanted them to do at Nickerson's. Speedle told Caine that Detective Frank Tripp was already on his way to meet the CSI Unit at Nickerson's.

"But I'll get back ahold of him, H," Speed said, "and reroute him to Little Havana. Sounds like you could use the backup."

"Good."

"H, Alexx is right here—wants to talk to you."

Speed put her on.

"Horatio, I don't know how you knew this . . . but the DNA from the Archer and Joanna's lover are a match."

"Tell Speed to get you something at Nickerson's to run a further comparison."

"You really want a bow tied on Gabe Nickerson."

"More like cuffs—in the back."

He thanked Alexx for the info, ended the call, then swore to himself, knowing that it would be only a matter of a very short time before Nickerson and Burnett acted—if they hadn't already done so before they called him. Easy enough to ring Caine after the fact and pretend a shoot-out was imminent when it really was over. . . .

He flew down the ramp off the expressway, ran the red at the bottom, and cranked the wheel hard left onto Tamiami Trail. Once he'd made the turn east, he cut the siren, leaving on the flashers. He wanted to get there fast, but he also didn't wish to announce his arrival any sooner than necessary. Without backup, the element of surprise might be a nice thing to have on his side.

The traffic on Tamiami Trail was heavier than on the expressway, with four lanes of traffic crawling along. Some were families on their way to dinner, or churchgoers going to or from evening services, while others were just couples out cruising because the weather was finally nice, after several unseasonably hot, rainless days.

Moving at a snail's pace that had him wondering why he even bothered with the flashers, Caine made his way eastward. Tamiami Trail gave way to Southwest Eighth Street, the same street but going under an alias, just as most of the streets in Miami did: seemed like every thoroughfare had at least two, if not three, names. SW 8th, Tamiami, became Calle Ocho in the heart of Little Havana.

As Caine passed Southwest Twenty-seventh Avenue, the tenor of the surrounding neighborhood changed. More and more signs were in Spanish, the stereos of cars blared salsa, not rap, the majority of passersby on the sidewalk were decidedly Hispanic. A hardworking neighborhood, this was—a place where people had fled oppression for the American dream. Caine liked the music and the food of Little Havana, but most of all, he liked the people. Every day they strove to get ahead, to make life better for themselves and their children.

They also spent every night battling the negative influence of Las Culebras and the drug culture brought in first by Johnny "The Slouch" Padillo, and then built upon by his successor, Antonio Mendoza.

Although Las Culebras had gained a significant foothold in the area, they hadn't been able to completely take it over. Unlike in Little Haiti, where the late Andrew Chevalier had run everything with a velvet-gloved iron fist, Mendoza had met resistance from proactive groups in the Hispanic community— like the one Mrs. Ken LaRussa was involved in.

The address Burnett had given Caine was south of Calle Ocho, and when he finally got the chance, Caine turned right. Traffic was all but nonexistent now, as he filtered back into the residential neighborhoods that rested a few blocks from the bustle of the main drags. Where Calle Ocho was constantly under siege from traffic, only the people who lived in these quiet neighborhoods ventured back into the twisting trails of side streets.

A left, a right, then straight, and eventually another left had Caine travelling east again, this time near Shenandoah Park. He killed the flashers and, after half a block, as he neared his target, the lights too. As he eased down the street, he couldn't help but wonder if Burnett had given him a bum address.

How easy for Burnett to send Caine on a wild-goose chase while the vengeance-seeking DEA agent did away with Mendoza. The terrible irony was: Burnett would be doing the bidding of his disloyal former partner, Nickerson, the man who—unbeknownst to Jeremy—had bedded and then murdered Burnett's beloved Joanna.

A scenario had formed more or less instantly in Caine's mind after hearing Laura Parker's convenience-store confession.

Nickerson is secretly in league with Mendoza, feeding the ganglord confiscated dope from federal busts and weapons from the lockup in a gang-war takeover. Staying close to his ex-partner Jeremy—who is still an active DEA agent, and an obvious threat—Nickerson's emotions get the best of him, and he finds himself embroiled in an extramarital affair with the still lovely Joanna.

When Joanna breaks it off, threatening to confess the affair to her husband, Nickerson uses the gang war as an excuse to stage a hit on Jeremy; both Jeremy and Joanna had been targets, but the Code Orange Kevlar had saved Nickerson's partner.

If this was true, it put Jeremy in impending danger of Nickerson staging the DEA agent's murder in the context of the Mendoza raid.

And—in perhaps the most ironic turn—the other person in danger right now was Antonio Mendoza himself: Nickerson could kill the Culebras leader or manipulate the grief-wracked Jeremy into doing it. Either way would cover Nickerson's tracks and, at the same time, execute a perfect double cross of the gang leader.

Then, in the wake of the various gangs facing leaderless chaos, Nickerson would take over the illegal drug trade in Miami himself. Who better to set up a network of criminals to carry out his ambitious business plan than a man who'd been in Miami law enforcement for twenty years?

And as Alexx's DNA news indicated, Nickerson himself had been in on the slaughter at the Archer, possibly with one or both of the now (late) Santoyas . . . whom Nickerson had later executed.

A complicating factor, however, was Jeremy's phone call: Nickerson knew Caine was coming. Which meant the CSI was likely walking into a trap, an ambush in which both he and Jeremy would be made to look like victims of the gangbangers whose hideout had been raided.

He could wait for backup—Tripp would be there soon. But if he did, Jeremy might die. . . .

He got to the correct block and saw Burnett's car parked about halfway down on the left. Caine slid the Hummer in behind the vehicle. He slipped out and closed the door as quietly as possible; looking in Burnett's car, he saw nothing or no one.

All seemed quiet. In fact, the neighborhood itself seemed gripped in an unearthly quiet—no sound of TVs or radios or even a squalling child. It was, as the old movie cliché went, *Quiet . . . too quiet. . . .*

The house Burnett had given him the address for was two more doors up, on the other side of the street. Moving as silently as possible, he crept forward, nine-millimeter in hand, badge on a necklace (he was, after all, prowling a neighborhood with a gun at night), his eyes constantly searching for something out of place or a telltale movement.

Clouds covered the moon now, and the few stars had no sparkle. The weather, which just scant minutes ago had been fine, seemed to have shifted to suit the eerie calm; now the air was warm and moist, and Caine, as he edged ahead, felt like he was trying to breathe underwater.

The house was an old two-story clapboard. Most of those in this neighborhood had long since been torn down in favor of one-story stuccos that not only were easier to take care of but were also better for weathering the south Florida coastal storms.

No lights were on in the house, and few were on in the homes of neighbors. For so early in the evening, the neighborhood had seemingly gone to bed. Glancing all around as he approached, Caine saw no sign of Burnett or Nickerson. He feared they might already be inside the house.

No sign of Frank Tripp yet, either.

The yard, like those of its neighbors, was small, orderly, and without clutter. The houses on Caine's side of the street were quiet, mostly dark stucco affairs, and Caine wondered if the DEA agent and/or his ex-partner might have set up shop in one of them. A few cars were scattered along the street, but Caine could make out no figures seated within, either in the front or (an old surveillance trick) backseats.

He was staring at the house—a nondescript dwelling that would make a perfect safe house for a druglord gone underground—wondering what to do next, when a window on the upper floor flashed white, and the crack of a gunshot split the silence.

Then another window strobed similarly, and two more shots rang out, slightly muffled, coming from within the house.

Now he understood the neighborhood's ominous calm—*fear.* These were probably not the first gunshots of the evening.

Nine-mil in hand, Caine ran to the front porch, where he could see that the door stood ajar. Squatting, making a low, small target of himself, Caine nudged the door open wide. . . .

The room was dark, no lights on in the house. With

his handgun in his right, he used a small flashlight with his left. . . .

Caine had a view on the living room, at left, and a stairway opposite him. The living room was reminiscent of the Santoya pad—black leather sofa and easy chair, glass end table and coffee tables, a big projection TV.

On parquet floors of the old home—the interior had been restored—two Culebras were sprawled, one at left, near the couch, the other more or less right in Caine's path; they were on their backs, and the shots they'd taken to the head said they were dead.

Slipping inside, gun at the ready, putting his back to the wall, Caine used the flash to examine the carnage, and, even without moving deeper into the room, he could read the scene easily: The man nearer Caine had answered the door and been gunned down for his trouble, and the other one had risen from the couch to receive his fatal shot. Guns—likely their own—were near the dead men's hands.

Caine listened carefully.

He could hear muffled conversation upstairs. The entryway to the kitchen revealed what seemed to be a small, vacant room, though someone could be cowering in there. To his near left, against the wall, was the staircase, a partially open affair—three steps to a landing, then half a flight leading up to another landing, beyond which the stairs presumably took a jog left.

On that half flight lay another dead Culebra, his eyes wide and unseeing, much of the inside of his head splashed and spattered on the wall behind him, an abstract painting awaiting a frame. The gun in the dead man's hand might have been part of a different kind of frame, though it could well have flown to his fingers in self-defense.

Caine started up the stairs, careful not to make noise and—CSI to the end—doing his best not to disturb any evidence near the sprawled stairway corpse around which he climbed.

Half a flight up, at the landing, the stairway took its expected jog. Another doorway awaited, and—as he cautiously climbed the remaining half-flight—conversation could be heard. Clearly now.

Jeremy Burnett's voice said, "He's dead, all right."

"Good riddance," Gabe Nickerson's said. "Mine have gone to see Jesus, too. . . . Horatio oughta be here any time now."

"And I am," Caine said.

Emerging at the top of the stairs now, the CSI entered the wide, square central hallway off of which various doors fed, including an open door to a bathroom with the light on, making it much easier to see.

Nickerson stood in a doorway at right, and Burnett crouched over the corpse of Antonio Mendoza—a .45 automatic in the dead man's hand—just outside a doorway at left.

Both men wore Ninja black, though no masks, and each had a Desert Eagle automatic in hand.

"You missed it," Nickerson said, grinning. "Hell of a firefight."

Caine said, "Gabe, I want you to toss that gun . . . nice and easy . . . on the floor. I don't want it going off. Jeremy, until I know exactly what's going on, you do the same."

Blinking, Nickerson said, "Horatio, you can't—"

"I can. Do it."

Nickerson and Jeremy exchanged glances, and shrugs, and they sent their weapons skidding across the bare floor, where they spun harmlessly to a stop on the polished wood.

Still in the doorway to Caine's right, Nickerson stood with his hands up, though kind of at half-mast. At left, Burnett remained crouched over Mendoza's body; he did not, however, put up his hands. Of course, Caine hadn't asked him to. . . .

"Firefight, huh, Gabe?" Caine said. "Like the St. Valentine's Day Massacre was a 'firefight'? Like the way you killed your hirelings, the Santoyas . . . and like the 'peace conference' at the Archer was a firefight?"

Nickerson grinned again. "You really want me to say anything, Horatio? You haven't even read me my rights yet."

Caine said, "Once a cop . . . thanks for the advice."

And he read the man his rights; but all of their positions—Caine with the stairs to his back, Burnett crouched over the corpse, Nickerson with hands up—remained the same throughout.

Burnett asked, "What's this about, Horatio?"

"Well, I'll let the evidence speak to that, when the time comes."

"Come on, man! What the hell is this?"

With a small shrug, Caine said, "I will share one piece of evidence with you, Jeremy. Your friend Gabe here left behind a little drop of himself at the Archer Hotel, a tiny urine sample that puts him at the Archer when the slaughter went down."

Not all of the evidence on that point was really in—

the Archer Hotel hitter was Joanna's lover and DNA-identified as an African-American, but Caine felt confident in making the jump to Nickerson and running a bluff that might elicit some voluntary confirmation.

"I don't believe it," Jeremy said.

Caine went on. "That same DNA sample was compared to semen in Joanna's body. She and Gabe had sex just hours before he sent the Santoyas to kill you both. . . ."

Burnett shook his head. "That's crazy. Gabe and Joanna?"

"Don't listen to him, buddy," Nickerson said.

"They were having an affair," Caine said. "She wanted to get even with you for your fling with Laura Parker, her best friend . . . so she and your best friend . . . get the picture?"

Glaring at the man across from him, Burnett said, "Gabe . . . you *lied* to me . . ."

Nickerson, obviously alarmed, said, "He's playing you, Jeremy!"

Burnett's gaze flicked to Caine. "You are playing me, Horatio. . . . Joanna loved me. I *know* she loved me."

"She did," Caine said. "That's why she broke it off . . . and planned to tell you about it. And that's why Nickerson wanted her dead."

And at that moment Caine knew: knew the mistake he'd made. Jeremy had not *been a target, had never been a target—only Joanna.*

The thought had barely flashed through the CSI's mind when the still crouching Burnett snatched the .45 from Mendoza's limp fingers and lurched to his feet and blasted away at Nickerson, who didn't even have time to lower his hands, the man's head exploding in a burst of blood, bone, and brain, his body dropping back into the room behind him like a bag of grain flung from a truck.

"Drop it, Jeremy!"

Caine and Burnett now faced each other—a mere eight feet apart, at most—with their respective handguns trained.

Burnett's features were as tight as a clenched fist, veins popping out on his forehead under the dark Caesar bangs. "He lied to me. The son of a bitch . . ."

"Lower your weapon, Jeremy—you're not going anywhere."

As if to underscore Caine's point, sirens split the night. Distant, muted; but coming. . . .

Still, Burnett did not lower the weapon. "He . . . he told me Joanna had found out . . . had found out that—"

"That you and Nickerson were in business together. The drug business. With another partner in the late Mendoza, here . . . who probably fed you drug busts over the years, minor stuff of his own, major stuff of his competitors."

"You're . . . you're guessing, Horatio. Stick to evidence."

"Not guesses—assumptions based on evidence." Caine's eyes narrowed. "Gabe told you Joanna had discovered the business you and he and Mendoza were in, together. That she knew you were expanding, planning to take over the whole city's drug trade for yourselves and frame Mendoza for the gang war that had set the stage for your secret takeover."

The sirens grew closer.

Burnett, his eyes bleary now, but the gun still

trained on Caine, said, "Yes . . . yes. He told me that she . . . she knew. And Joanna was straight as could be . . . you know how idealistic she was . . . her causes. And . . . Gabe said . . . said that she had to go."

"And you went along with it, Jeremy. You even put yourself on the firing line, knowing your vest would protect you. Code Orange, right? You even jumped in front of her—whether to protect her, at the last minute, or to make it look better . . . what's the difference? You helped murder the woman who loved you."

Burnett swallowed. "Who . . . who I loved."

The sirens continued to swell.

The CSI said, "Emotions are funny—look at how I let our friendship blind me. I should have known, almost from the start—you were way off on that license plate . . . a trained observer like you? When I saw the real Lexus plate, at the Santoyas, I could see how far 'wrong' you've been. You were trying to frame Calisto—it's obvious. But I was blinded. By friendship."

Burnett shook his head. "I know you'll never understand, Horatio . . . but after so many years in the DEA, working to take guys down but really just . . . running in place . . . battling a problem that could never be erased. Gabe and I . . . at first, it was just a retirement plan, then . . ."

"Then you got greedy. You wanted to be Scarface—just like the gangbangers. And that's why Gabe felt Joanna had to die—if she told you about her and Gabe, who knew what you might do? Why, you might even kill him over it. . . ."

Burnett raised the gun a trifle higher—and suddenly his arm seemed steadier. And his gaze. A decision had been made.

"Shoot me, Horatio."

"What?"

"Shoot me, or I *will* shoot you. . . ."

"Just put the gun down, Jeremy."

The man's smile was only technically a smile. "Am I asking so much? *Shoot me*—put your gun in Mendoza's hand, and tell any story you want. You have a houseful of dead gangbangers and two dead DEA agents. . . . You can save the law enforcement community a lot of embarrassment."

Caine's laugh was short and hollow. "And let you go out a hero? Gabe, too? Not gonna happen."

The sirens were out front now . . . and then cut off abruptly.

"Give me this much, Horatio. . . . We were friends once. Don't make me pull this trigger . . . I don't want to shoot you, Horatio. But I swear I will if you won't put me out of my damn misery."

"*No.*"

Burnett's chin tightened. "Can't you let me die with a little goddamn dignity?"

And Burnett's arm stiffened, his finger tightening on the trigger . . .

. . . and Caine fired once, twice, three times.

The bullets hit Burnett in the chest, as if three spikes had been pounded into him, and sent him toppling back through the doorway.

Caine stepped over Mendoza and into the bedroom, where Jeremy Burnett lay, staring up unblinkingly at the ceiling. The CSI holstered his weapon and put on his latex gloves, then bent to retrieve the .45 Burnett had dropped when he'd fallen.

Burnett's face turned toward Caine and said, "You . . . you bastard."

Caine gave his old friend a tight smile. "I knew you'd have your Kevlar on—that's why you shot Gabe in the head. Wonder how many ribs you broke this time?"

"You son of a . . . you couldn't do it, could you? Couldn't let me die with honor."

Caine got to his feet and looked down at Burnett. "Jeremy, it doesn't work that way—you can't die with honor . . . unless you live with honor."

Burnett said nothing more.

The CSI met a startled-looking Detective Tripp at the head of the stairs, where the detective emerged, gun in hand.

"What in the hell . . . ?"

Caine said, "We can start with my witnessing Jeremy Burnett murdering Gabe Nickerson. Burnett's in there. This house has *not* been cleared. Read Burnett his rights, would you? And then get his ass out of here. I don't want that garbage contaminating my crime scene any further."

And Horatio Caine went downstairs, allowing Tripp and the uniformed cops to do their work. He got on his cell phone and called Speed, summoning the crew from Nickerson's home to the Mendoza safe house.

As he'd said to Tripp, they had a new crime scene to process.

* * *

Just as Caine had refused to lie to protect Jeremy Burnett's reputation, so too did the evidence insist on telling the truth.

DNA tech Toni Escobedo matched a sample from Gabe Nickerson's house (taken from the late former DEA agent's toothbrush) with the urine droplet DNA Caine had gathered at the hotel, to conclusively prove Nickerson had dribbled on the toilet in the Archer Hotel before he and Burnett had gone downstairs and massacred three drug dealers and their lieutenants.

Electrostatic prints lifted from the Archer's bathroom matched Nickerson's boots, and the prints from the Santoyas' house matched Burnett's—the very boots the duo had worn to their latest slaughter at the Mendoza safe house.

The videotape from the evidence room at the James Lawrence King Federal Office Building had been enhanced by AV tech Tyler Jenson enough to show both Burnett and Nickerson as they left bogus drugs in place of the good drugs they had lifted, and as they removed weapons from lockers.

While Ken LaRussa was innocent, he was also finished as a potential political candidate and might likely lose his U.S. attorney's position, having allowed all of this to occur on his watch . . . and under his nose.

Some, Caine knew, would call the late Burnett and Nickerson heroes for gunning down dope dealers, no matter what the circumstances. Tabloid theories would be offered that the two late DEA agents had been vigilantes, not would-be interloping druglords themselves.

That much "dignity," such shredded "honor," Caine would gladly allow them.

Caine did hold himself responsible for the murder of the Santoyas. They were killers, but he had been the one to tell Burnett that the CSI team was looking for the cousins, giving the DEA agents a chance to clean up their mess before the police and the ERS team could make the scene.

He'd also been too late to save Mendoza and his bodyguards. This he regretted, however much the death of a ruthless gang leader might be seen by many as beneficial to the community.

A week ago, Miami had been reluctant home to five major gangs. Now all of the gang leaders were dead, and dozens of bangers had been killed in a violent spree that had ended when the media had promptly been given the Burnett/Nickerson takeover story.

No National Guard would invade Miami, at least not until the next hurricane. . . .

Still, the drug problem would not go away, and these same gangs—once they had regrouped and new leadership had come to the fore—would no doubt thrive again. The realities of Miami's location and population made that inevitable.

And Horatio Caine did not relish the black eye local law enforcement was indeed receiving, now that celebrated DEA agent Jeremy Burnett had been exposed as a greedy rogue cop who'd put money in his own pocket, thanks to the sad needs of poor souls addicted to sticking needles filled with dope into their arms.

Of course, a certain gratification might be found just knowing that one day soon, Jeremy Burnett would be facing his own needle—specifically, a lethal injection.

The Sunday night they processed the Mendoza

house (or actually the early morning hours of Monday), the CSIs wound up back at HQ, where Caine gathered his crew in the layout room to give them a collective "Good job."

Tired as they were, their curiosity got the best of them; they'd just spent six hours processing evidence at the crime scene, and now they wanted to understand what had really happened, which Caine explained, and how two presumably good cops like Burnett and Nickerson could turn so bad—on which Caine, at first, declined to comment.

Speed said, "I don't know, H—in a way, it's easy to see how men like Jeremy Burnett and Gabe Nickerson could be so frustrated in their work that . . . you know . . ."

"That disillusionment finally turned to cynicism?" Alexx said.

"Yeah," Speed said, nodding.

"And then to greed," Delko offered.

"I think it was a power trip," Calleigh said. "Look at them, finally on top of the drug lords . . . boldly going around executing the very perps that had slipped out of their grasp over the years."

"Then hijacking their business," Delko said with a humorless smirk.

Nodding, Speed said, "Yeah, I can see it."

And Horatio Caine said, "You know what?"

All of them looked at him.

"I can't."

With that—the last word going to their boss—the CSI Crime Unit went home. They had tomorrow (or today, which was already Monday, after all) off.

Presumably.

Author's Note

My assistant Matthew Clemens helped me develop the plot of *Heat Wave*, and worked up a lengthy story treatment (which included all of his considerable forensic research) from which I could work. Matthew—an accomplished true-crime writer who has collaborated with me on numerous published short stories—has taken several research trips to Miami, returning with extensive photographs and notes on locations. This has added considerably to any sense of place this novel may have. Matt and I would once again like to acknowledge criminalist Lieutenant Chris Kauffman CLPE—the Gil Grissom of the Bettendorf Iowa Police Department—who provided comments, insights, and information that were invaluable to this project. Thank you also Lieutenant Paul Van Steenhuyse, Scott County Sheriff's Office; and Denise O'Connell, R.N., Newburg, Oregon.

Books consulted include two works by Vernon J. Gerberth: *Practical Homicide Investigation Checklist and Field Guide* (1997) and *Practical Homicide Investigation: Tactics, Procedures and Forensic Investigation* (1996). Also helpful were *Crime Scene: The Ultimate Guide to Forensic Science*, Richard Platt; *Jane's Gun Recognition Guide*, Ian Hogg; *Scene of the Crime: A Writer's Guide to Crime-Scene Investigations* (1992), Anne Wingate, Ph.D; *Three Month Fever*, Gary Indiana; and *The Visual Dictionary of Human Anatomy*, text by Richard Walker. Any inaccuracies, however, are my own.

Jessica McGivney and Ed Schlesinger at Pocket Books provided support, suggestions, and guidance. The producers of *CSI: Miami* were gracious in providing scripts, background material (including show bibles), and episode tapes, without which this novel would have been impossible. In particular, I'd like to thank Corinne Marrinan.

Anthony E. Zuiker, Ann Donahue, and Carol Mendelsohn are gratefully acknowledged as the creators of this concept and these characters; and the cast of the show must be applauded for bringing the characters to life and making it easy to write for them in the theater of the mind. Our thanks, too, to various writers for *CSI: Miami*, whose inventive and well-documented scripts inspired this novel and have done much toward making *CSI: Miami* the rare spin-off worthy of its predecessor.

MAX ALLAN COLLINS, a Mystery Writers of America "Edgar" nominee in both fiction and nonfiction categories, has been hailed as "the Renaissance man of mystery fiction." He has earned an unprecedented twelve Private Eye Writers of America "Shamus" nominations for his historical thrillers, winning twice for his Nathan Heller novels, *True Detective* (1983) and *Stolen Away* (1991). His other credits include film criticism, short fiction, songwriting, trading-card sets, video games, and movie/TV tie-in novels, including the *New York Times*–bestselling *Saving Private Ryan*.

His graphic novel *Road to Perdition* is the basis of the Academy Award–winning DreamWorks 2002 feature film starring Tom Hanks, Paul Newman, and Jude Law, directed by Sam Mendes. His many comics credits include the *Dick Tracy* syndicated strip (1977–1993); his own *Ms. Tree*; *Batman*; and *CSI: Crime Scene Investigation*, based on the hit TV series.

An independent filmmaker in his native Iowa, he wrote and directed *Mommy*, premiering on Lifetime in

1996, and a 1997 sequel, *Mommy's Day*. The screenwriter of *The Expert*, a 1995 HBO World Premiere, he wrote and directed the award-winning documentary *Mike Hammer's Mickey Spillane* (1999) and the innovative feature, *Real Time: Siege at Lucas Street Market* (2000).

Collins lives in Muscatine, Iowa, with his wife, writer Barbara Collins; their son Nathan is majoring in computer science and Japanese at the University of Iowa.

There's more mystery and drama
awaiting you in

CSI: Miami™

FLORIDA GETAWAY

by
Max Allan Collins

Turn the page for an electrifying
preview . . .

Just this one last fare, Felipe Ortega thought as he wheeled the limo through the light late evening traffic, heading west on the Dolphin Expressway toward Miami International. Then he could go to see Carolina Hernandez, his latest girlfriend. Salsa music pulsed through the limo's powerful sound system—tuned to 95.7 El Sol, *"Salsa y Merengue, todo el tiempo,"* as their ad promised.

The vehicle's monster sound system was a perk Felipe relished . . . although he figured his pickup, "Thomas Lessor," would probably prefer easy listening, or maybe that baby boomer "classic rock." But in between clients, Felipe could give the stereo a real workout, playing real music.

The pleasant evening inspired Felipe to put the front windows down—why breathe recycled air when the outside world was cooperating so nicely? But the loudness of the music did get him an occasional dirty look, particularly at stoplights, before he got on the expressway. He would ignore these looks-to-kill and just focus on the straight-and-narrow, the heel of his hand keeping rhythm on the steering wheel.

Twenty-four, and slight of build for his six feet one, Felipe gave off an easygoing vibe that assured the world—and his clients—that he was harmless, even sensitive. Although this gentleness had been often misread growing up just off the famous Calle Ocho in Little Havana, Felipe had learned early in his young manhood that women appreciated his vulnerability.

As one who'd been bullied as a boy, Felipe surprisingly now found himself the subject of envy among other men. Hombres much bigger, some better-looking, most with more money, tried their luck with the same ladies; but in the end, Felipe was usually the one that won those feminine hearts.

For a decade now he had traveled the path of a Don Juan, but this new girl, Carolina, she had Felipe thinking about settling down, about retiring his Lothario lifestyle and being with just one woman forever. She was smart, she was funny, and would make as wonderful a wife as she did a lover, as wonderful a mother as a wife. Never before had thoughts of settling down stayed with him like this . . . it had been weeks.

Checking his watch, Felipe knew Carolina would already be home from her hostess job at the Leslie, one of the Art Deco hotels on Miami Beach. Carolina had worked there for the last year and made pretty decent money. The tall beauty, her straight raven hair flowing to the middle of her back, was to lure tourists off the Ocean Drive sidewalk and into the sidewalk café of the hotel. With her looks, it wouldn't have mattered if she had the personality of a potted plant; but she was in fact a charismatic, friendly, flirty girl blessed with a smile that could light up all of South Beach.

Thinking about her, he let the limo drift across two lanes and drew an angry honk and an obscene gesture from the pissed-off driver of a passing Geo Storm. Out of respect for the elderly, Felipe declined to return the gesture. Just then he caught sight of an overhead sign and jerked the wheel to the right, gliding the limo across two lanes just in time to catch his exit.

Following the ramp around, spiraling down through the pools of yellow spilled by mercury vapor lights, Felipe cruised through a stop sign, crossed a street, and rolled into the parking garage of Miami International Airport, the salsa music still blasting as it reverberated off the parking ramp's concrete walls.

He braked to take the printed ticket from the machine, then moved ahead. As the car rolled slowly onto the second level, Felipe reached over and shut off the radio. He made sure to turn the volume down and change the setting to some dull-as-dishwater station before even thinking about parking the car.

But even with the radio off, Felipe's fingers tapped out a rhythm on the steering wheel as he eased through the concrete maze toward the livery spots. Though much of the airport traffic evaporated at night, the limos still moved in and out at a fairly regular clip. Many of the celebrities and VIPs landed their private jets here late at night to avoid the paparazzi.

Pulling into a space, Felipe saw that tonight was a slack traffic evening. Mondays usually were, the jet set who came in for the weekend mostly long gone or on their way home by now.

Two spaces over, puffing casually on a cigarette, a white-bearded old man wearing a chauffeur's uniform leaned against a black Cadillac; Felipe didn't recognize him—a sub, maybe—but nonetheless bestowed the man a brotherly nod, and the codger waved with his smoke. Even older than Felipe's Tio Acelino, the driver looked sixty if he was a minute, and Felipe wondered idly if he'd still be renting out his car to pay the bills when he was this viejo's age.

Driving for the rich and famous was generally a young man's job, but Felipe was well acquainted with the idea that you had to do what you had to do to keep the wolf from the door. Even as lucky as he'd been in his life—and Felipe knew he had been lucky— he had to wrestle that wolf from time to time himself. Despite his natural attractiveness to women, he still had to spend some money to impress, sometimes more than he would have liked.

Married life would change all that. He and the beautiful Carolina would be partners. Who could say what wonderful vistas lay ahead, what opportunities for both of them. The excitement of such prospects, the new life ahead of him, put Felipe in a particularly up-tempo mood.

He plucked the microphone from the dashboard and keyed the button. "Dispatch—you there, Carmon?"

"What do you want, Felipe?" came a crackling voice from the speaker.

"I'm at the airport. Tell Tío Acelino."

"This your last trip for the night?"

Felipe glanced at the clock on the dash and thought about Carolina waiting. "Sí. This last drop-off, and then I head home."

"Fine. Just let me know when you get him where he's going."

"Will do."

Grabbing the handwritten placard bearing the client's name—LESSOR—Felipe locked up the limo, easily made his way across the lanes of light traffic, and strolled into the airport.

Between eighty-five and a hundred thousand souls passed through Miami International every day, depending on which day of the week it was, but most of those were long gone by the time Felipe entered, only a skeleton crew of the thirty-three thousand MIA employees still here at this hour. He passed a businessman towing a carry-on, a pair of women in floral dresses, and a drunk couple that looked like they'd hooked up in the airport bar and were off to a motel to do something about it. *Ah, romance*, he thought. Holding up his placard, the chauffeur stood just outside the baggage claim area and waited.

Barely five minutes later, a tall, good-looking *yuma* with girlish blond hair and a sharp suit pointed at the placard, then curled his finger as if scratching the air, in a condescending "come here" gesture.

Patronizing or not, the possibility of a good tip from

the client caused Felipe to jump forward. A redcap was coming their way, pulling a cart with Lessor's luggage. As the businessman tipped the redcap—a ten!—Felipe took over pulling the cart and gestured to his fare, heading for the car. Lessor quickly caught up, then established a faster pace.

"Hablas ingles?" Lessor asked, striding briskly for the exit.

Practically running as he dragged the cart and willing himself not to sound annoyed, Felipe said, "Yes, sir—I'm a Miami native."

"I would have said Cubano," the man said, nothing positive or negative in his voice, just a fact.

"My grandparents on both sides fled from Castro," Felipe said conversationally, still managing to keep up as he hauled the cart. "My parents were just kids. We've been here ever since."

"Really," Lessor said, his voice cold, a signal that their chat was over.

Lessor went out the automatic doors and then Felipe finally got out in front, leading the man across to the parking ramp and then the limo. They went down the passenger side of the sleek black vehicle, Felipe knowing the man would want to sit inside, maybe pour himself a drink while the chauffeur loaded bags in the trunk. He beeped the alarm and heard the locks pop, then deposited the cart at the rear of the car, leaving Lessor by the back door.

Returning to the client, he opened the door for him and Lessor climbed in; but before Felipe could do anything else, the older chauffeur from before appeared again out of nowhere.

"Got a light, kid?" the old man asked.

Felipe shook his head. "Sorry, Viejo, I don't smoke."

The old man shook his head. "Nasty habit," he said, and a gun materialized in his hand.

The weapon was small and shiny and, for just a moment, Felipe thought it was one of those trick lighters—pull the trigger and a flame pops up. Then he looked closer and realized the viejo's beard was fake, which somehow said the gun was real, and a chill coursed through him.

"Driver!" Lessor called, sounding a little pissed. "What is the holdup?"

Holdup was right. . . .

Two more men, both wearing rubber masks, came around on either side of the car, from wherever they'd been hiding. One, on the driver's side, wore a rubber Bill Clinton mask and the other, who'd come up behind Felipe, was in a Richard Nixon mask.

Nixon eased the chauffeur out of the way and swung into the car with Lessor, a small silver pistol in his right hand as well. Felipe had been carjacked one other time and knew enough to keep his mouth shut and not look any of the men in the eye for too long. These things scared the shit out of you, but if a guy kept his head, he could survive.

Felipe heard Lessor say, "What the hell . . . ?"

Then silence. Lessor had probably seen the pistol in Nixon's hand. His client's arrogant attitude would be held in check now. But the silence spoke volumes, about Lessor's fear, and the lack of any commands from the intruder—no sounds of a robbery. Maybe all they wanted was the car. . . .

On the driver's side, Clinton kept a watch on the parking garage, his gun-in-hand out of sight, but not out of Felipe's mind.

The fake-bearded viejo—was he really an old man, or was that just more makeup?—waved Felipe toward the back of the car.

"You just relax, Fidel," the old man said. "Ain't nothin' goin' to happen to you, you behave. *Comprendo?*"

The old man dragged out the last word, making it sound like *comb-pren-doe.*

"Comprendo," Felipe said, putting the syllables back together, and nodding.

Felipe made the short walk around back, to the trunk, the old man's lack of menace somehow reassuring.

Clinton joined them in back of the car. His voice muffled through the mask, he pointed to the trunk and said, "Open it."

Felipe used his remote and did as he was told, but doubt crept into his fear now. If these pendejos wanted the car, why take him and Lessor along? That made it kidnapping, even if they dumped the pair alive and well along a roadside. . . .

"Give me your hands," Clinton said.

A bad, sick feeling began to crawl through his belly, but Felipe stuck out his hands.

"Behind you," Clinton growled.

Turning his back to Clinton, Felipe put his hands behind him, and then could feel the man removing the remote from his grasp, and duct-taping his wrists. For the first time, Felipe wondered if he and the client were going to get through this night alive.

"I'll do what you want," Felipe said. "You don't have to tie me up."

Finished binding Felipe's hands, Clinton spun the driver around and slapped a piece of duct tape over his mouth.

"Get in the trunk," Clinton said.

Felipe froze.

"We want the passenger, kid—not you," the viejo said reassuringly. "Let somebody else do the drivin' for a change."

Clinton added: "Just shut the fuck up and don't raise a fuss, and you'll live through this shit no problem."

Then they helped him into the trunk and shut the lid on him. He heard the beep of his own remote click the lock.

The inside was blacker than anything Felipe could imagine, and stuffy. He could see nothing and he couldn't move much. He wasn't afraid of the dark—he never had been, not even as a child—but he certainly was scared now.

He heard them dump Lessor's bags into the backseat with their owner, or so he hoped. Next, he heard the driver's door close and a moment later the engine throbbed to life. His stomach churning, Felipe did his best to remain calm . . .

. . . but it wasn't easy. From up front, he could hear the yuma businessman's strained voice, as the man begged for his life. Though the words were garbled through the padding of the seat, that the man was pitifully pleading was unmistakable.

Occasional words could be made out. "Please,"

Felipe heard, the voice high-pitched, whiny. Then there would be a whole sentence where he couldn't understand a syllable, then suddenly that mournful "Please," at the end again, like an urgent "Amen" at the close of a prayer.

Then the radio came on—loud—and the audio blur of scanning for channels provided an unnerving if brief soundtrack to Felipe's discomfort. A station was settled upon and, caught in midsong, suddenly Frank Sinatra was singing, "It Was a Very Good Year."

The car stopped for a few seconds—they were paying the parking attendant, so the masks would be off. But that meant Lessor was in the backseat with a gun pressed into him, seeing their real faces. Men like this didn't leave witnesses, did they?

On the other hand, the man in the trunk told himself, that was bad for Lessor, but not for Felipe—he had seen only those rubbery presidents' faces and that fake beard. They had no reason to kill him. None. He felt panic rising in his throat.

Stay calm, he told himself, *stay calm.*

The call had come in early in the morning, a limo illegally parked across three spaces in the metered public parking lot just north of the Eden Roc.

The uniforms were about to have the car towed when one of them noticed the smell. The cop with the twitchy nose made the tow truck wait while he called in the Crime Scene team.

And now, with the sun rising and the heat of the day building, Lieutenant Horatio Caine stepped down from his silver Miami-Dade Hummer and closed the door with a snick that might have been a round fired from a silenced automatic.

Horatio Caine never seemed to tan, no matter how much time he spent in the Florida sun. The upside was he never got white circles around his eyes or little lines on his temples from his ever present shades, either. His red hair and freckles and that fairer-than-fair flesh bespoke an Irish heritage, and what appeared to be a constant scowl gave him the appearance of a man forever pissed off. But Caine's CSI team knew the serious expression only bespoke a natural intensity—he wasn't irritated, just focused on the work.

His vehicle sat only a few feet behind its twin, which had arrived earlier. Caine walked to the back of the Hummer and opened the rear doors.

Coming around the passenger side of the vehicle, Tim Speedle and Eric Delko strode into view. Caine started toward the limo. It sat horizontally across three spaces, rather than being pulled in nose-first. Whoever left it here wanted it to be found, this much he knew. His gut told him that the reason the perp wanted it found was not going to be a pleasant one.

"What have we got?" he asked.

Speedle pulled a UV alternate light source case from the floor of the Hummer. "Well, H—we've got a mess."

Not a good omen when a criminalist described a crime scene as a "mess."

"Chauffeur, Felipe Ortega, according to his license," Speedle explained. "Dead in the trunk of his limo, trussed up with duct tape."

"Dead how?"

"Looks like he asphyxiated on his own vomit." Speedle shrugged, made a face. "It's a little rank, H. He made a number three."

By which Speed meant the victim had evacuated both his bowels and his bladder upon dying, a common occurrence.

Delko trailed along behind the pair as they moved toward the car; a perimeter had been established by draping and tying crime scene tape around parking meters. Several uniforms stood fifteen to twenty feet away, respecting the crime scene—and avoiding the stench.

Ducking under the tape, Caine entered the perimeter and glanced down into the trunk. The sickly sweet smell of death mixed with vomit forced Caine to breathe more shallowly and through his mouth in order to keep his own breakfast down.

The body lay on its right side in an S-shape, the knees bent, the man's hands bound just as Speedle had said. Bits of vomit that had run out the man's nose clung to the duct tape gag and the man's cheek, and a small sample had puddled on the floor of the trunk. The victim appeared young, mid-twenties and Hispanic.

"Somebody really had it in for this guy," Delko said. "Bad way to go."

Caine looked up at the younger man, his expression sharp but his tone soft. "Evidence tell you that?"

Delko winced, shook his head.

Caine twitched a smile. "Work the evidence, Eric. Not your feelings?"

"Right, H."

The cell phone in Caine's pocket chirped and he withdrew it and tapped a button. "Horatio Caine."

The voice was sultry and pleasant. "You're a hard man to track down, Lieutenant Caine."

He allowed a tiny smile to find its away across his face. "Well, Catherine—you're a detective. I wouldn't expect less of you."

"Horatio—you recognize my voice . . . I'm flattered."

"You do make an impression." Caine wasted no time. "I'm assuming this isn't a social call. What can I do for you?"

The voice on the cell phone explained the case in question, quickly and efficiently, ending with the new DNA evidence recently uncovered. Caine had heard of Lessor, and the Boyle family into which he'd married, but had never encountered Lessor or any of the Boyles, professionally or otherwise. He knew of the case vaguely because it had been covered in the local media, due to the family's connection to Miami.

"So," Caine said, "you'd like me to arrange a pickup on Thomas Lessor for you?"

"If you could handle it yourself, that would be reassuring."

He turned and surveyed the limo; this crime scene could be processed without his supervision easily enough. "Do you know where Mr. Lessor will be staying?"

"Most likely he's at his wife's hotel—the Conquistador. There's a family home, but he apparently prefers to stay at a suite there. To be near the business office."

Caine glanced north on Collins Avenue, his gaze moving toward the Westin and, just before that, the Conquistador. "I think I can manage that," he said, finally.

"Thanks, Lieutenant."

"Now, Catherine—it's Horatio."

"I'll owe you, Horatio."

He smiled half a smile. "I'll call when we've got him. What's your number?"

She told him, and he entered it into his cell phone's speed dial.

"And I'll fax the paperwork to you straightaway," Catherine said.

"Good. I'll collect Mr. Lessor and get back to you."

Caine pressed END, slipped the phone away, and turned back to his two CSIs. "You two work the scene. I've got to do a favor for a friend."

The two younger men exchanged a look of surprise.

Caine ignored them. "Who was the driver's last client?"

Delko shrugged. "Driver's sheet is gone. The limo's listed to a"—he checked his notebook—"Acelino's All-American Livery. They've got an office on Flagler in Little Havana."

"And what did they have to say?"

Another shrug. "Can't get ahold of them—they must hit the office about the crack of noon."

"But you left a message."

"I did."

"And you'll keep trying."

"I will."

"Good." Caine motioned toward the limo. "Work the scene. Call me if you get anything."

"Anything," Delko said, "or anything interesting?"

For an endless several seconds, Caine looked at Delko with his sunglasses-obscured eyes. Then he said, "Eric, I think I'm gonna leave that judgment call up to you."

And Horatio Caine went to do his favor for Catherine Willows, never imagining that the man he was planning to arrest had been Felipe Ortega's last pickup.

As many as 1 in 3 Americans
have HIV and don't know it.

**TAKE CONTROL.
KNOW YOUR STATUS.
GET TESTED.**

To learn more about HIV testing,
or get a free guide to HIV and
other sexually transmitted diseases.

**www.knowhivaids.org
1-866-344-KNOW**

09620